TRIPPING THE
MULTIVERSE

JADE AND ANTIGONE
BOOK ONE

ALISON LYKE

Black Rose Writing | Texas

ISBN: 978-1-68433-626-5
PUBLISHED BY BLACK ROSE WRITING
www.blackrosewriting.com

Printed in the United States of America
Suggested Retail Price (SRP) $18.95

Tripping the Multiverse is printed in Traditional Arabic

*As a planet-friendly publisher, Black Rose Writing does its best to eliminate unnecessary waste to reduce paper usage and energy costs, while never compromising the reading experience. As a result, the final word count vs. page count may not meet common expectations.

TRIPPING THE MULTIVERSE

CHAPTER 1
THE ORION CENTER'S FAILED EXPERIMENT

Jade heard Antigone talking before she stepped into the Orion Center's makeshift pressroom. Antigone's voice grated Jade's ears almost as much as the smell of burned coffee, a staple of under-attended press conferences, assaulted her nose. Jade, who disliked anything that required speaking aloud to other humans, already expected a tough afternoon, and now Antigone assured her one.

When she entered, she saw, with relief, that Antigone had already cornered someone else. He was a tall, lean, clean-shaven young man whom Jade didn't recognize. The press pass on his lapel labeled him Abraham Wize, but Antigone called him Christian.

"My dad named all the kids in my family after figures in Greek literature," Antigone told Abraham. Jade knew this already because everyone who met Antigone for over five minutes knew about her family's naming policy.

The pressroom, which on most days was a break room, contained half a dozen journalists, far fewer than the nearly one hundred to whom the Orion Center had extended an invitation. A man in a white lab coat mingled with the reporters, and a woman in a pantsuit fussed around a table, laying out deflated doughnuts to go with the scorched coffee. Jade surmised that the woman must be Harriet Fletcher, the Orion Center's research director, and the laboratory's spokeswoman. Harriet's wild, upswept hair undid the professionalism of her smart pantsuit. Her hair was enormous enough that it might be mistaken as part of a 1960's Halloween costume, if it were not January 4th. Jade moved behind Harriet, hoping the hair would hide her from Antigone.

"Homer is my brother. I have twin sisters Daphne and Chloe, which stretches it because you're supposed to spell Daphnis with an 'i' and an 's,' and he's a man. Then there's Andromeda; she's got the best name, I think. My dad named me after the play by Sophocles, you know."

Abraham shook his head because he did not know.

"Oh, Christian," Antigone lamented, "no one reads anything anymore." Without pausing, Antigone turned and pointed at Jade. Harriet had exposed her by moving to greet an important newcomer. Jade ignored Antigone and pretend to be unduly interested in a jelly-filled doughnut.

"That's Jade. She hates me," Antigone said, loud enough that a few other attendees took notice.

Jade looked up at Abraham and Antigone, slowly and reluctantly. Dressed smartly, as usual, Antigone looked put together in a way Jade only dreamed of. Through an inexplicable force, Jade felt herself walking over to them like she was a paperclip, and Antigone was a horrible electrified magnet that had just turned on. When she made it over to their corner, she stood and waited for whatever awful thing Antigone would say next.

"Jade, meet Christian," Antigone introduced him, and he reached out to shake Jade's hand.

"My name is Abraham Wize, actually," he said as he shook Jade's hand. Now that she was closer, Jade read his *American Christian Journal of Science* issued press pass.

"Christian, this is Jade. She sent an op-ed to my journal complaining that I'm reckless and dangerous because I wrote an article about menstrual stem cells. Do you know what menstrual stem cells are, Christian?"

Abraham turned purple and had a sudden coughing fit that propelled him several steps away from the two women.

"Doctors use a special cup to harvest menstrual blood!" Antigone shouted over Abraham's coughs. "Stem cells from menstrual blood may be more scientifically viable than the ones collected from bone marrow!"

Abraham looked as if he might die if Antigone continued her explanation of menstrual blood stem cells.

Antigone pulled her phone out of a small purse slung over her shoulder. "I took pictures for the article if you want to look at the harvesting cups."

When he caught his breath, Abraham said, "I have to go." He ran towards Harriet's table of sad, old doughnuts. It seemed to be an afternoon where all present must choose between dry pastries and Antigone's company.

"Let him take *that* back to the *American Christian Journal of Science*," Antigone chuckled.

"As usual, Antigone, you are only partially correct in your characterization of my story," Jade said stiffly. "I was careful not to name you in my article condemning menstrual stem cell theory. I offered a thoughtful, detailed rebuttal to the practice, citing the research of three top obstetricians."

"I never said menstrual cell reclamation was a wonderful thing to do, Jade. It's trendy in Europe," Antigone defended herself.

Jade exhaled and steeled herself. "Our job is to report accurate science, not what's popular."

"It can be both. Nobody knows what's healthy for you, anyway. Drink coffee, don't drink coffee, you know. Our turn, Jade." Antigone nodded as the gentleman in the lab coat who had been circulating around the room approached them. He was dark with tight, black curls framing his face, and he was beaming with excitement. He didn't match the stifled tone of the rest of the room.

"Greetings, Jade Hill from the *Journal of American Sciences* and Antigone Pagonis from the *American Science Journal*." He shook each of their hands. "I'm Ra Adronis, and I'm a research technician here at the Orion Center."

Antigone studied the name tag clipped to his pocket. "Ra, like the Egyptian sun god?"

"It's short for Radical." He was flustered.

"Why not 'Rad?'" As Antigone pressed the issue, Jade felt secondhand embarrassment.

"Would you want to have the name Rad?" His fluster turned to irritation.

"Better than Antigone," she muttered apologetically.

"Do you have questions for me?" Ra asked, ready to move past his name.

Antigone asked, "How safe is this?"

And, Jade asked, "What are the safety precautions?" at the same time.

Then Antigone said, "Samesies."

"Well," Ra said, "the electromagnetic collider creates a minor collision of quarks, which constructs a miniature black hole. A second machine, known as a parallel collider, replicates the black hole in the other side of the room. The two black holes then make an Einstein–Rosen Bridge. When you place an item in the first black hole, the bridge transports it to the second black hole. You are safe as long as you don't touch the black holes."

Jade opened her mouth to ask another question. Still, Ra spoke over her, "But, as an added precaution, you will be behind radiation shielding glass in an observation room raised above the event laboratory."

"Okay," Antigone said. "Do we get safety goggles?"

"Again," Ra said with patience, "you won't need them; you will be behind glass."

"You always see people in safety goggles when they're observing these things," Antigone said to Jade as Ra headed toward the door leading into the maze of laboratories. Harriet stood in the doorway and beckoned for everyone to follow her.

As they walked out of the room, Antigone narrowed her eyes at Abraham and waved her phone at him. "Menstrual blood harvest cups," she half-whispered.

Abraham turned his head sharply to show that he had heard her, then quickened his pace.

The Orion Center buried their electron collider underground, and the trip to the laboratory required a long elevator ride deep into the belly of the building. The elevator only held six people at a time. Jade attempted to get on a different lift than Antigone, but she somehow ended up next to her, anyway.

"Do you think the teleportation machine here is for real?" Antigone asked Jade.

"No," Jade said. "I think it's a likely hoax, or they're unsure of what is causing the phenomenon, so Orion is labeling it as black holes."

"Yeah. I think it's fake too. Like the clones in China."

As promised, the Orion observation room was high above the collider. Onlookers peered down and into the mouth of a massive machine in the shape of a tube. Most of the tunnel was walled off, so it looked like a giant, blind worm bursting into the laboratory. A smaller, though still tubular machine, sat opposite the larger one.

"Okay," Ra said to Jade and Antigone, "you ladies stand here." He positioned them right in front of the glass, almost touching it, so the women saw their reflections. Both women studied the ghostly versions of themselves that floated above the laboratory.

Jade was taller with light brown skin and thick hair that rested on her shoulders. She was thin, aside from her thighs, which were muscular from a lifetime of running. She wore an oversized cardigan that made her look even more delicate, wrapped around her like a blanket.

Antigone was curvy, with long, dark auburn hair, and skin she tanned at a salon, made to appear more bronzed by the bright white blouse she wore tucked into a navy striped pencil skirt.

Antigone looked around the observation deck. "Ra didn't tell anyone else where to stand, just us," she said. "He put us in the front row."

"Maybe he likes us," Jade suggested.

"I think you made a joke, Jade," Antigone laughed. "We can be friends, you know. You can call me Anti, that's what my friends call me." She pronounced it like "Auntie."

Jade said, "No, thank you."

"I forgot you hate me." Anti was lying anyway. Her family called her Anti, and that was only sometimes. She didn't have any friends.

"I don't hate you," Jade said reflexively.

"Good afternoon." A female voice sounded over an intercom. Jade turned and saw Harriet holding down the listen button of an old, white intercom system. Three researchers had populated the previously empty lab below. The person speaking seemed to be the head researcher. She wore a black lab coat, while the other two researchers, a man, and a woman, were wearing the traditional white.

"My name is Elizabeth Margaret Marina, and I'm the senior lab director here at the Orion Center."

"She's wearing safety goggles," Anti whispered and nudged Jade, who hushed her.

"What you are about to witness today, you may call a miracle. But we are rational minds, so I prefer to call it a happy accident," the research director went on. "We discovered the Einstein–Rosen Bridge you are about to witness by mistake, as many of our greatest breakthroughs have been. After the experiment, I will explain at length how it works, but I think it is best if you witness it beforehand."

Elizabeth held up a battered copy of King Lear, opened it, and signed the inside cover. "You will soon witness this copy of King Lear disappear and reappear on the other side of this room after passing through our laboratory-created Einstein–Rosen Bridge. My signature will prove it the same book."

"She might have signed two books," Jade noted.

"King Lear is my favorite Shakespeare. It's pretty much the story of my family," Anti said.

Jade shushed her again.

"I'm Cordelia," Anti blurted.

In the room below, one of the white-clad lab technicians pulled a large switch, and the machine hummed. The area in front of the mouth of the collider took on a shimmery, shifty quality. Elizabeth held up King Lear one more time and placed it on a table set in the collider opening. As she stepped back, the mouth of the collider turned very dark black. Black wasn't the best way to describe it; it was more of a lack of space or a blot in existence.

The second technician turned on the smaller machine, and there was a blinding flash of light that rocked the people in the observation room back a pace. The laboratory below turned dark. There were a series of slight pops, and then the hum of the machines halted. Harriet released the intercom button.

"What happened?" Anti asked.

The lights in the lab flickered back on, and the copy of King Lear was in the second machine's base.

"That was the worst magic trick I've ever seen," Anti scoffed. "We don't need David Blaine to explain this one."

"Where's Elizabeth?" Jade asked. "What happened to the lab director?"

"I'm sure she ran away when she realized we would expose her as a fraud," Anti said.

"I'm sorry," Ra announced. "We will have to evacuate the observation deck."

Anti looked around while Harriet hustled them toward the elevators in small groups. "Where's Christian?" Anti asked Ra.

Ra shrugged his shoulders. "Who?"

The elevator doors were closing before Anti could explain, and, just as quickly, she rose through the floors, moving farther and farther away from the failed experiment. When Anti reached ground level, the elevator doors slid open to reveal Harriet, standing uncomfortably close.

"No need to worry," Harriet smiled aggressively as the group of reporters pushed past her, attempting to flee the disappointing presentation. "We can reset it and try again this afternoon."

A member of the press grunted something coarse and uncharitable. Anti offered an ambiguous nod before she moved on to collect her coat from a pop-up rack someone had placed outside of the pressroom. Her jacket was red, one shade darker than her hair, with oversized buttons and a fabric belt that wrapped around her waist. As she tied her belt knot, she scanned the area for the missing journalist. Seeing neither him nor Jade, whom she was hoping to grill on the strange incidents of the day, Anti left the warmth of the Orion Center for the steely cold of a Mid-Atlantic January.

Anti took a bus home. She had a car, but she preferred someone else in charge of the vehicle. She seldom drove in winter, when the streets were often icy, and squalls could make the roads hard to navigate without warning. It took much longer to travel via bus, but Anti had the time.

The bus stopped downtown, long enough to let an entire extended family on. A father, a mother, a slim, teenage boy, two children bundled in so much outdoor gear they resembled colorful potatoes, and their grandfather trundled aboard. While they boarded, Anti looked out of the window and noticed something odd. There was a smudge on the sidewalk in front of a cellphone repair shop. It was light yellow, stretched from the ground to the shop's awning, and looked as if someone had smeared petroleum jelly on the world—or perhaps on her eye.

Anti rubbed her eyes and then tried to clean the bus window, but the smudge stayed. She watched a woman walk through it. The woman didn't seem to see the stain at all. She headed right for it, blurred while she was inside of it, and came out the other side unharmed. Before Anti investigated any further, the family all found seats, and the bus sped away.

Anti thought little about the blob, and she went home that evening without much of a story to report due to the failure of the Orion Center's experiment. She ordered in for dinner and ate her Stromboli and cannoli uninterrupted. Her solitude may have been the reason she noticed nothing unusual. Jade, however, returned to a full house and experienced strange happenings soon after that.

CHAPTER 2
BLUEBIRD

Jade returned from work to find her sister, Amber, experiencing a crisis—as indicated by an abundance of howling followed by the soothing voice of their mother. Jade hoped to stay in her room until the storm subsided, so she scuttled past the ruckus, confident her family hadn't noticed she had returned home from work. Jade was back much earlier than she had said she'd be, because of the Orion Center's snafu.

Jade had the smallest of her home's three bedrooms, despite her being the older sister. Amber needed more space because she required more of everything. Jade's room, like the rest of the house, had a bare wood floor that her mother insisted Jade clean with oil soap twice a month. Thus, the smell of oil soap was never far from her nostrils and signified home to her. Aside from the odor of oil soap, Jade's room also held a queen-sized bed with a homemade quilt, a woven rag rug—also handmade—a corner computer desk, and two small, overloaded bookshelves placed on either side of her only window. Since there wasn't room for anything else, her vanity was in her closet.

She sat down at the computer desk and attempted to piece together her notes concerning the day's experiment, endeavoring to create a story to sell to the science journal. As she was not a salaried employee, the magazine would not pay her for her time unless she came up with an article. Her mother dashed Jade's hopes of being ignored by her family for long enough to produce a report by bursting through her door, carrying a forest green dress made of an infinitesimal amount of fabric.

"Amber has to wear this in an hour to advertise the White Canvas Boutique at that turtle party, but it's too big. No one at the Boutique is answering the phone. Do you have time to take it in?" Jade's mother asked.

The family matriarch was a short, round woman, who looked regal when she stepped out of the house but like a caricature of a ragged housewife almost every other time. Since she had not yet gone to work or to the store that day, her mother wore an old sari, no makeup, and wiry hair that stuck out in odd places.

"It's not a turtle party," Amber raged in the hallway behind her mother. "It's a gala benefitting the flattened musk turtle."

"I don't have time to take it in," Jade's mother said, ignoring Amber. "I'm working all night in the E.R. I have to get ready for my shift, then I need to go."

"Did the dress fit her last week when White Canvas gave it to her to wear?" Jade asked with false innocence.

"Don't be cruel," Jade's mother hissed.

"Have Daddy do it." Jade turned back to her computer screen to end the conversation.

"Your father couldn't sew his way out of a paper bag."

"That makes no sense. You wouldn't sew your way out of a paper bag; you'd sew your way into a paper bag," Jade pointed out.

"It's a figure of speech, smarty-pants. 'Sew your way into a paper bag' doesn't sound right."

"But, it's technically accurate."

Jade had accomplished her goal of changing the subject. In the hallway, Amber cried hard in a way that would make most women look hideous but somehow made her look even more beautiful.

When they stood side by side, it was easy to tell Amber and Jade were sisters. They were both tall and thin with the same light brown, freckled skin and the same upturned eyes and elfin features. Still, by some trick of genetics, Jade looked ordinary, and Amber was stunning. With no inclination to gain any viable skills, Amber had parlayed her beauty into a lucrative career as an actress for local television advertisements. This made her into a minor celebrity whom charities invited to musk turtle galas, and boutiques offered free clothing to wear. Jade did not approve of Amber's career path.

"I'll fix the dress," Jade said with resignation. "Put it on so I can pin it."

Amber paused her hysterics long enough to thank her sister.

"I'm not doing it for you," Jade grumbled. "I'm doing it for the flattened musk turtles. Their numbers have dropped because of the loss of wetlands all over the country."

"Why do you know so much about musk turtles?" Amber asked.

"I read a lot. Anyway, I could ask why you don't know more about musk turtles. It's your gala."

Fifteen minutes later, Jade had finished fitting her sister. Amber lost an inch from her waist and bust in the two weeks since the boutique gave her the dress.

"Can you try to finish it by four-thirty?" Amber asked. "I want to do my make-up after I put it on."

"I'll finish it when I finish it," Jade muttered. After Jade fit her, Amber left the room in a cloud of hubris and overpriced perfume.

While she sewed, Jade contemplated Amber's recent weight loss with a mix of worry and anger. In anger, Jade tried to recall a time when Amber was asked to do something kind for someone else and had followed through. She could not. In fact, Jade struggled to remember a time Amber was asked to do something for herself and followed through. It seemed Amber was stuck in perpetual babyhood, and her entire family was cast as her doting mothers.

Jade was hemming the dress while deep in these self-pitying ruminations when she felt odd. First, she seemed lighter and thinner, as if her weight was barely sinking her body into her soft mattress. Then, Jade felt like there was something alive, moving around inside of her face, trying to burst out. Jade jumped up from her bed, ran over to her closet, and flung open the closet door so she could study the mirror on the closet vanity.

When Jade peered into the mirror, she saw her sister's face reflected in place of her own. Jade reached toward her sister's face and watched as her sister's hand reached forward, all framed by the mirror's fading, pink roses. She pulled her hand back and touched her face. The mirror Amber touched her own face. Jade tapped the mirror again, and her reflection reached out toward the surface in unison.

After a few more moments of introspection, Jade closed the closet and reached for her smartphone. She had never used the "selfie" function before, so it took some finagling before the front-facing camera turned on. Jade saw her sister's face on the phone, just like she had in the vanity.

I've turned into Amber, she thought, then assumed she was dreaming, since turning into her sister was not possible. Jade slapped her own arm, which had turned into Amber's silky, hairless arm. She hit herself softly at first, then harder. She slapped her face, even harder, and watched as a red hand mark stained her sister's beautiful face in the phone's camera.

This isn't a dream; this is a nightmare. When Jade was little, and she had nightmares, she would wake herself up by jumping from something high off the ground. She might climb a bookshelf or ladder, then jump off and wake up. If there was nothing nearby to climb, or if jumping from a mundane object didn't work, Jade would wake herself up by jumping out of a window.

Dreams can read your mind, she knew, so she had to work quickly and with little thought. If she gave the nightmare too much time, it might figure out what she was up to, and try to stop her. Jade raced across her room, flung open her window and climbed onto the windowsill. Then she jumped. A nanosecond too late, she realized that she was not dreaming.

As she fell, a sudden instinct overtook her. She felt movement under her skin again, and she sensed she was lighter and smaller than before. *I am a bird*, she thought, *I can fly; I am a bright bluebird.* She pictured a bluebird in her head. Not an actual bluebird, because she'd never seen one, but the drawing of one she'd seen in an ornithology book. She repeated the idea of a bird and its image over and over in her mind.

Blue feathers burst from her arms, her face elongated, and she was no longer falling—she was flying. As a bluebird, Jade landed on her windowsill. She perched there, thinking in a mix of Jade thoughts and bird thoughts. Jade investigated her bedroom, her bluebird eyes resting on Amber's dress, which was now an abandoned lump of green cloth on the floor.

She heard someone approaching her door, so she flew inside, transforming back into Jade as she landed on the floor. This transformation was quicker and smoother than the shape-shift to a bird.

"What was that?" her mother asked through the door.

"I dropped a book," Jade lied.

"Are you done with the dress, then?" Her mother opened the door a crack, and Jade blocked it from opening further as she scooped the dress from the floor.

Breathless, Jade said, "No," and straightened her glasses.

"Are you okay?" her mother asked, concern wrinkling her smooth brow. She pushed past Jade, looked for the fallen book, and found none.

She had begun transforming from "Mom" to Haidee Hall, the night shift emergency room ultrasound technician. She smoothed her hair back into a slick ponytail, and she lined and shadowed her eyes. Haidee was still in her old, stained sari, her metamorphosis not yet complete.

"I'm okay," Jade said and nodded. "Great, fine, wonderful." Jade hoped her exuberant affirmation would hurry her mother out of her room. It did, but her mother gave an odd glance before leaving. As soon as her door closed, Jade collapsed onto her bed. She laid there for a minute, then sat, hunched over her computer, and searched, "What happens when you go crazy?"

After ten minutes of fruitless and contradictory internet searches involving brain tumors and accidental ingestion of psychedelics, Jade realized that, crazy or not, she still had to fix her sister's dress. So, she sat on the edge of her bed and took in her sister's waistline.

Jade worked mechanically, dropping more than a few stitches, but Amber didn't notice when she put it on, and she flitted out the door to her musk turtle gala without so much as a "thank you." Jade's mother had left for the evening too, and her father was somewhere in the depths of the house, tinkering, reading, napping, or finding some other way to make himself scarce. Jade was virtually alone and going mad at the possibility of suddenly changing into a bird again.

The thought that the Orion Center exposed her to radiation during her time there had crossed her mind. Still, by that time, the Center was closed, and she figured she should see a doctor before accusing the Center of mismanaging radiation. She had Antigone's email address, but Jade declined to contact her. The idea she might damn Antigone by refusing to warn her of a potential disease nagged at Jade's mind, but not enough to force her to contact the woman.

Jade was still awake at four in the morning when her sister shuffled in, banged around in their shared hallway, and then retired to her bedroom. She considered poking her head out into the hall and asking if Amber had eaten dinner. If she needed a sandwich, Jade would make her one. But Amber locked herself in her room by the time Jade opened her own door. Jade managed to fall asleep, though, so she didn't hear her mother come in around six.

•　　•　　•

Jade planned to call her primary care physician early the next morning, hoping to find a physical explanation for the previous evening's events. Phone calls with near-strangers were an arduous task for her, however, and she had to spend half an hour rehearsing her conversation with the receptionist. An incoming call interrupted her preparation.

"Am I speaking with Jade Hill?" a sharp, female voice asked after Jade reluctantly answered.

"Yes."

"This is Harriet Fletcher, Research Director for the Orion Center for Applied Quantum Physics."

There was a long, awkward pause while Harriet waited for Jade to acknowledge her, and Jade waited for Harriet to continue.

"Do you remember yesterday's Einstein-Rosen Bridge experiment?" Harriet asked, and then added, "Are you still there, Jade?" in case the silence was technical in nature.

"Yes," Jade answered both questions.

"I know this may sound like an odd inquiry," Harriet started. She seemed like she may try for another pause to allow Jade to speak, but decided against it, "but, have you had any health effects following our electron collider malfunction?"

Jade thought for a moment. "Yes," she said.

"Would you care to go into specifics on your health effects?" Harriet asked. She sounded annoyed.

"No," Jade answered.

"Right." Jade's short answer clearly bothered Harriet. "Would you mind returning to the Orion Center for an interview with our researchers? We are prepared to offer a free physical examination."

Jade weighed over the prospect of explaining her situation to an Orion Center scientist verses describing what happened to her personal doctor. Her consideration took too long because Harriet interrupted her musing.

"Jade? Do you have poor cellular reception?" Harriet asked.

"I'll come to the Center," Jade said, at last.

When she arrived at the Orion Center, Jade was not at all surprised to see Anti there as well in the break room—which doubled as an occasional pressroom and currently appeared to be a medical triage area. The staff pushed tables together and laid sheets on top of them, making everything look like an emergency relief hospital in a disaster film. The only thing missing was the wounded. Everyone seemed fine. Anti was sitting on one table listing complaints to Harriet, who, as usual, had upswept her hair using so much hairspray that it looked lacquered.

Anti was wearing a smart, black jumpsuit, with wide, flowy legs and a cinched waist over a flower-patterned blouse. Jade looked down at her own, well-worn cardigan, long-sleeved tee-shirt, and jeans, and wondered how it was possible for Anti to just walk out of her house looking so put together.

"My left wrist and my right jaw hurts, and my vision is blurry," Anti complained to Harriet. "When I walk, I go wobbly—watch." She jumped down and took a few steps in the manner of a person pretending to be drunk. Harriet smiled sympathetically and patted Anti's arm.

Surveying the room, Jade noticed that she and Anti were the only reporters from the previous day. The other patients were the two assistants who had been in the lab when the collider malfunctioned. One was lying down on a makeshift bed with headphones on. The other sat up on the edge of a table reading a magazine. Neither looked ill.

When she saw her enter the room, Harriet left Anti to her fake wobble and headed toward Jade. She shook Jade's hand, looked concerned, and led her to one of the makeshift beds.

"Where's Ra?" Jade asked Harriet.

"Who?"

"The lab technician who ran the press room at the recent collider experiment," Jade explained. "He said his name was 'Radical.' He made me stand in front of the room."

"I don't know who that is," Harriet said, her anxiety growing. "I thought Hayden was the only one running the pressroom."

Jade sighed. She had to force the words out of her mouth. "He spoke with Antigone as well."

Harriet nodded. "I'll ask her." She smiled and focused on Jade. "But right now we need to concentrate on you. Can you tell me what's been happening to you since the event?"

"I can, but I don't want to. It sounds insane. I feel insane."

"We've seen a lot of strange things around here," Harriet reassured her in a clinically cold voice. "Tell me what's happening, or we can't fix it."

"I turned into my sister, then I turned into a bluebird," Jade said in a rush as if she could make the words run away from her by the sheer force of them exiting from her lips.

Harriet nodded again. "Good, good," she said. "That makes sense."

"It does?"

There was a loud thud as Anti fell from her bed, dragging the sheet with her.

"I'm okay," Anti said, standing up, but making sure she appeared to wobble while remaining upright. "Hey, where's Christian?" she wondered aloud, and everyone ignored her, which Anti was used to.

"Come with me, young ladies," Harriet beckoned to Anti as she steered Jade by the shoulders.

Harriet guided Jade and Anti to the elevators, and once again, they descended into the bowels of the laboratories. Anti had given up her unsteady gait when she realized Harriet believed something might be truly wrong with her. Harriet shut the two women in a windowless, white room, furnished only with a desk and three chairs.

"Please wait here." Harriet turned and locked the white door behind her.

"It's like we're in trouble. It's like we're in the principal's office in high school," Anti said.

"I believe we *are* in trouble, Antigone, but I'm not sure what kind," Jade replied. "I'm sure it's not our fault, though." She looked Anti up and down. "At least it's not *my* fault."

Anti looked into Jade's eyes, trying to scry into her soul. Jade stared back, attempting to communicate her own fear without having to articulate it.

They sat in silence for as long as Anti could handle it, which was not very long at all, and then Anti asked, "Did anything truly happen to you? I'm just messing around in case something pops up down the road, and I need access to their help or meds. Who knows what they exposed us to? If anything is wrong, Orion or *The American Science Journal* better pick up the tab," Anti rambled.

"I turned into my sister, and then I turned into a bluebird," Jade said.

Anti laughed. When Jade didn't crack a smile, she asked, "Are you for real?" Jaded nodded solemnly.

"Damn, Jade," Anti chuckled, "you're crazy. I didn't know you were certifiable. That makes me feel better about the whole menstrual stem cell op-ed."

"I don't think I'm crazy. The collider experiment did something to me." Jade stood up and started pacing the white room.

"How could the collider turn you into a bird? Can you elaborate? I don't get a lot of this science stuff."

"This 'science stuff' is literally your job." Jade stared at Anti with apparent animosity. "You're a science journalist."

"Not on purpose. And I know some of it, just not quantum theory, but from what I understand, a black hole can't just turn you into a sister bird."

Jade was unsure about what part of Anti's statement to address, so she disregarded most of it. "What we encountered yesterday was not a black hole. At least, they didn't mean it to be. It was an Einstein-Rosen Bridge connecting one point in space to another, via a bridge through another dimension."

"You mean a *hole* in space that was *black*, where they put *King Lear* in one hole, and it came out of the other *black hole*?" Anti asked. "Almost like they dropped it… through a *hole*."

"Do you want me to explain this or not?"

Anti gestured for her to continue.

"Either they exposed me to radiation from the experiment at such a high level that it has already liquified my organs, starting with my brain, or the Einstein-Rosen Bridge altered my personal dimensional stability."

"I knew it. I'm calling my lawyer." Anti reached for her phone, dialed, and found out she didn't have a cell phone signal so far underground. "Well, as soon as we get out of here. You should call yours too."

"I don't have a lawyer." Jade came from a world where having a lawyer to call was an unfathomable thing that only happened to characters on television shows.

"That's okay. You can use mine. We'll class action this place."

Harriet opened the door, and Anti repeated her last sentiment, louder, "We will class action all of you." She jabbed her finger at Harriet. But, when she saw the two men in lab coats follow Harriet, her demeanor subdued. They carried handheld devices featuring long handles, screens, and sensors on the ends of branches.

"What's wrong with us?" Anti whined.

"You're likely fine. We believe some electrons in your body may have shifted into a neighboring dimension," Harriet said as the men in white coats ran their gadgets up and down in the space around Jade's body, "slightly."

"What does 'shifting slightly into another dimension' mean?" Anti whined louder. "How is that fine?"

"We're not sure. But you should be glad you are left in this dimension. The experiment transported lab director, Elizabeth, into a different one altogether, and we can't find her at all." Harriet was not soothing.

"Is that what happened to Christian?" Anti panicked. "Is that what will happen to us?"

"She means Abraham the reporter from the *American Christian Science Journal*," Jade interrupted before someone could ask who Christian was. "We didn't see him after the experiment, and he wasn't in your triage today."

"Abraham migrating to another dimension is a possibility." Harriet's calm voice agitated Anti, who was doing a poor job of standing still while the men in lab coats ran their sensors over her. "We will investigate these readings and be back." Harriet left again, followed by the men in lab coats.

"I feel like I'm going to pass out," Anti puffed. "I don't want to be halfway into another dimension."

"I'm the one who is dimensionally unstable," Jade pointed out. "Did anything ever happen to you?"

"I saw a blob on the bus."

Jade looked at Anti as one might look at a street corner preacher shouting about the end of time. Jade refused to engage with Anti further, despite her swings between panic and rage, and instead, she paced the room until Harriet returned.

While they waited, Anti's rambling became more and more cyclical, rounding the topics of lawyers and lawsuits, blobs and multi-dimensional fears, and finishing up with worry about the whereabouts of Christian—before starting again.

When Harriet returned, alone this time, she had the demeanor of a doctor delivering a fatal prognosis. "We have found traces of multi-dimensional electrons in your systems."

"Both of us?" Anti asked. "Because nothing happened to me. I just saw a blob. Jade's the one with the weird stuff going on."

"Yes. However, there are some negatives and some positives," Harriet reported.

"What could make up a positive in this situation?" Jade asked, her brow lined with worry.

"Jade can take on new physical, organic forms through visualization, and Antigone has gained an ability we have decided to call 'extra-dimensional sentience.'"

"You have to explain extra-dimensional sentience to me," Anti demanded.

"It is the ability to detect naturally occurring dimensional bridges and to predict events in your current dimensional environment, among other things."

"Other things?" Anti propped herself up against one of the white walls like a Victorian woman having a case of the vapors.

"We at the Orion Center have a proposition for you ladies," Harriet said. "You seem concerned about Abraham. Would you two want to enter a neighboring dimension and attempt to locate him?"

Anti said, "No," and continued her hysterics.

Jade asked, "How?"

"Antigone can sense the opening to nearby dimensions, and you can replicate the native fauna of the dimension. You two have complementary skills."

"How do I get out of here?" Anti barged out of the white room and said, "I'm calling my lawyer. I'm calling two lawyers," she added on the way out.

Harriet looked at Jade. "Well, you can't do it without her," she said.

CHAPTER 3
THE BUNNY AND THE BLOB

The diagnosis of extra-dimensional sentience shook Antigone, so much so she was afraid to drive, and she ordered a car on her phone app, leaving her own vehicle at the Orion Center. She did not want to take a chance on the bus for fear she'd have to look at a blob again.

Anti had the car drop her right in front of the porch that led to her swanky, two-bedroom apartment. Even in this trendy and safe part of town, Anti wouldn't risk walking a single block. The world outside appeared vengeful and oppressive to her.

She paused on her stoop with her key in her hand. She took a last glance around, which she soon regretted because the park next to her building had taken on a shimmery quality visible in her periphery. Anti looked away, not wanting to see what otherworldly horror might await her.

Anti realized she had a choice. She could run into her apartment, rejecting the mystical happenings in the park, or she could look and face whatever consequences came from her curiosity. Her inquisitiveness overcame her fear, and she turned to look at the park. She saw the same small city park she encountered every day without thinking of it. There was a small, open field, a few benches, a swing set, and a slide, all unoccupied because of the January chill.

There was, to her horror, a blob similar to the one she'd seen from the bus window yesterday. It was in the middle of the field's grassy expanse. This one had a sparkling, metallic sheen to it, and looked as if someone had made a glittery gold, smudgy thumbprint on reality. She looked at it for as long as she could stand before it overtook her and, finally, Anti swung her door open and ran up the steps to her apartment.

Inside, Anti sunk into her puffy, suede sofa. She picked up her phone, and her finger hovered over the "call" button. As usual, Anti wanted to talk to someone but was short of companions. She sifted through a few possibilities: her lawyer, Harriet, or someone else at the Orion Center, the police, a news station. Anti considered calling her parents, but they had a way of placing the blame for every problem squarely on Anti's shoulders, and she didn't want to hear about how her extra-dimensional sentience was her own fault. After much consideration, she spoke to no one and decided to force herself to sleep.

She woke several hours later, at half-past midnight, to her phone buzzing. She groped for it in the dark, sure it was a wrong number. When she read the screen, she saw Jade's name on her caller I.D. *How does she even have my phone number?* she wondered. By the time she finished her waking, groping, and wondering, it was too late. Jade had hung up. Anti found herself a little disappointed.

A minute later, a text popped up: *I want to do it.* Jade's message read.

Anti thought for a second and typed: *The class-action lawsuit?*

No. I want to use our dimensional irregularities to find Abraham.

Anti texted back, *Why?*

We are science journalists, Jade answered. *It is our job to explore where others can't and to report what others won't.*

Anti thought about her response, which was unusual; she rarely thought anything through before saying it. She didn't care much for science journalism. It was just her job, and she was good at it because she knew about science and was a decent writer. However, the park blob loomed in her mind, as did her unfulfilled desire to talk to someone about it. If she was going to go through extra-dimensional sentience, she didn't want to go through it alone.

She typed: *What's the plan?*

• • •

Jade and Anti had texted all night, so they were all frayed nerves and lumps of exhaustion by the time they oozed back into the Orion Center's multi-purpose room, which had been converted from a triage back into its normal, break room state. They pushed the tables back to their usual places, and the hospital sheets were all gone. Harriet had offered them coffee, which Jade had declined, but Anti sipped on a Styrofoam cup, her lips seldom leaving the rim.

"There are thousands, perhaps millions of dimensions adjacent to this one," Harriet said to the women. "That's how the Einstein-Rosen Bridge experiment was supposed to work. The second bridge passed the copy of *King Lear* through a neighboring dimension, then back into ours. But the containment field on the first bridge failed, and it engulfed the laboratory and the surrounding areas with a large spill of multidimensional electrons."

"So it covered us in splooge from a bunch of other dimensions, and that's why I see blobs and Jade's a bird?" Anti asked.

"I wouldn't say 'splooge'… *ever*… but, yes." Harriet looked at Anti with distaste. "The spill caused wild effects for those it encountered. The field destabilized Jade's physical dimensional structure, and it did the same thing to you, Antigone, but to your mind. For others, like Abraham and Elizabeth, the particles acted like a bridge, pulling them into another dimension."

"Are we going in after Elizabeth once we get Abraham?" Anti wondered. "Are they in the same place?"

"No. Unfortunately, we did not locate Elizabeth's dimensional destination. But we know, with ninety-seven percent accuracy, where Abraham is. For you to access Abraham's current dimension, we'll need to create another Einstein-Rosen Bridge using the collider."

"Because that bridge worked *so* well last time." Anti rolled her eyes.

"I thought you said I needed Antigone if I wanted to retrieve Abraham," Jade said. "I can just go into the dimension alone after you open the bridge."

"Thanks for trying to go in without me." It was hard for Jade to tell if Anti was genuine or facetious. "But you'll need me and my extra-dimensional sentience to find the wormhole back into our dimension. There might not be a collider over on the side. I thought you were supposed to be smart."

"Antigone is correct," Harriet said. "The two of you require some training before you are ready to enter another dimension. Jade needs to practice altering her form and controlling the alterations. Antigone must learn how to discover, identify, and distinguish between interdimensional bridges, wormholes, and black holes. However, time is not on our side. We are unsure of the conditions in the dimension that has trapped Abraham. Every hour he is in there, he is in increasing danger."

"Great, can't wait to go in after him," Anti groaned.

After another half hour of discussion, during which Anti complained that it all sounded like too much work, it was decided that the women would complete a day and a half of training before attempting to follow Abraham into the new dimension. The first day they would receive separate instruction, and the second day they would practice together.

Training Day 1: Jade

A researcher named Marshall watched Jade as she sat, staring into the eyes of Lulu, a fuzzy, cute brown rabbit. Jade was supposed to be altering her own, fluctuating electrons until her body matched the rabbit. Instead, she wondered how many researchers the Orion labs had because Marshall was just the latest in a parade of dozens of head scientists, leading researchers and laboratory analysts who watched her change her form to match animals and people.

Jade felt she didn't need the training; she had always been a quick study, and she would rather learn about the science behind the dimensional instability. When Harriet brought her cat Cornelius into the lab, Jade changed into the tabby, replicating almost every inch of the pet. She couldn't get both eyes to turn brown, though; one remained green, like Jade's own. When Cornelius hissed at her facsimile, Jade transformed herself into such a convincing version of Harriet that Cornelius jumped into Jade's arms and purred.

Since the Cornelius trial, Jade's experience had been less instructional and more of an investigation into how many pets she could change into. It seemed like every member of the Orion Center staff had a beloved animal they wanted to see Jade replicate. Once she shifted into the pet, they would laugh or clap with amazed delight. Then, their joy would turn to unsettled silence when Jade would copy the Orion Center employees themselves. The observation would often end afterward, with Jade shifting back to her own form and the lab worker scooping up their pet and hurrying away.

Jade became adept at copying clothing, down to the fabric texture and imperfections. She grew expert at mimicking shocked facial expressions. She could never copy any animal or person absolutely, though. There was always at least one defect.

When Marshall brought in Lulu the bunny, it was the first time Jade had any significant issue imitating an animal. She thought maybe she couldn't focus, or perhaps her body had enough variation for one day, or maybe the effects of the blown Einstein–Rosen Bridge were temporary, and she was returning to normal.

"I knew they were messing with me," Marshall said when Jade couldn't change into Lulu.

Just as he reached for the rabbit, Jade felt skin crawl and then burst. Her face twitched as long rabbit whiskers popped out, and soft brown fur sprouted on her arms while she shrank.

"Holy smokes!" Marshall hooted. He leaned in to examine Jade. "You made the inside of her ears brown, though," he said. "Lulu has white ears. But great job overall."

Jade made a mental note that rabbits may be a sticking point for her.

Training Day 1: Antigone

Anti's first day of training did not go as well as Jade's. To begin with, the researchers were unsure of the range of her powers. Extra-dimensional sentience, or, as the Orion Center staff had called it, EDS, had almost unlimited potential, but Anti's abilities could be restricted to just a few EDS phenomena.

"Most people have legs, and most of them can walk," Harriet explained. "Some people can use their legs to run, and some people can sprint. Others can use their legs to do extraordinary things like acrobatics or ski jumps. Your EDS is your own pair of 'legs.' We're not sure if we're preparing you for a stroll or a high-wire act."

"I feel I might be just limping along," Anti joked. Harriet did not laugh. She did, however, give Anti a checklist of all the possible experiences she might have with her EDS. The list included: visualization of dimensional portals, precognition, telepathy, clairvoyance, and clairsalience.

"What is clairsalience?" Anti asked.

"The ability to smell into another dimension," Harriet explained.

"Oh." Anti waited for Harriet to clarify. When she did not, Anti asked, "What do other dimensions smell like?"

"Dark chocolate," Harriet answered, "or sometimes, burning hair."

Anti told Harriet that the only strange things she'd experienced so far were two shimmery blobs, the one she saw from the bus, and the one in the park across the street from her house.

"I didn't smell anything," Anti added.

"That 'blob,' as you call it, was your visual cortex's rendering of a dimensional bridge. Dimensional bridges may be naturally occurring, or they may be machine-made, like the ones we make at the center. How a bridge appears gives you clues about where it leads. You must be able to identify the bridges, and you must be able to determine which bridge leads back to your home dimension."

Anti threw her head back and said, "Argh. This sounds so hard. Why couldn't I get a simple power like Jade's? She just woosh, turns into any creature." Anti snapped her fingers aggressively.

"Perhaps, your ability is easier to manage than Jade's. You don't have to do anything but pay attention," Harriet told her.

Anti had already crossed the room and was looking at a desk full of supplemental training material, including a training book, a set of augmented reality goggles, and silver and black device that resembled an advanced remote control.

"What were you saying?" Anti asked as she picked up the augmented reality goggles. "What are these for?" She put them on, incorrectly, without waiting for a response from Harriet.

Harriet, at the end of her considerably long rope, said, "Those are for training, to help you identify distinct Einstein-Rosen Bridges."

"How do you turn it on?"

Harriet adjusted it on Anti's head, pressed a button on the side of the goggles, and four different shiny globules appeared in the room in front of Anti. Like the other bridges she'd seen, these looked like jelly smudges on the surface of reality. It seemed like maybe she could just blink them away, but blinking did nothing to clear them from her vision. Anti felt she could almost make out the dimensions on the other side of these translucent blots.

"In front of you are replications of four portals to very different dimensions—" Harriet started, but Anti interrupted her.

"Why do the bridges look like shiny blobs? The ones we saw in the experiment looked like black holes."

"These bridges are naturally occurring, and the ones from the failed experiment were manmade. Our dimension is shaped like a bubble." Harriet drew a circle on a whiteboard that had been placed next to the desk full of training materials. Anti could see the board through the blobs in her augmented reality. "But we are not like floating bubbles that you blow with a bubble wand. We're like soap bubbles in a sink." Harriet added several other bubbles, next to the first one she drew.

"There are places where the bubbles touch each other," Harriet continued. "If the membrane between our world and a connected one is thin, then reality around the thin membrane becomes soft, which is the 'blob' you're describing. Sometimes, the realities are so similar the bubbles combine or absorb each other. The transition between these doesn't even make a bridge; it just happens along the edges of reality. When we create an unnatural bridge, like the ones you saw in the experiment, they look like holes because we have a tear in the membrane."

"Tearing the membrane of reality does not sound safe at all. No wonder there was an accident. I'm surprised there haven't been more incidents."

Harriet looked sad and a little lost, but just for a moment, and then she instructed Anti again, "Your job isn't to catalog the hazards of my work. Your job here is to determine the dimensional destination of the naturally occurring bridge."

"Touchy." Anti sucked in a breath.

"As I was saying, some naturally occurring bridges go to alternate realities that look almost like ours, but only have a few differences, and some go to other dimensions with worlds that differ vastly from ours."

"Which kind is Christian in?" Anti, still wearing the augmented reality goggles, started feeling around in front of her, attempting to touch the dimensional bridges that only appeared on the goggle's screen.

"Abraham is in the latter type of dimension. You will recognize it as different from your home dimension the moment you step into it. Because it is so different, there will be no equivalent to the Orion Center in the other dimension. Therefore, you need to identify the bridge leading you back to your dimension. Observe the facsimile bridges in front of you. Only one of them depicts the bridge that leads to our dimension."

"They all look the same," Anti said.

"They do not all look the same," Harriet countered. "Look closer."

Harriet was right. The first portal, farthest to the left, had sparkles swimming around inside the boundaries of its shimmery perimeter. A soft gray border marked the edges of the next one. The third portal had a surface that rippled like water, and there were black spots in the last one, spots that faded in and out.

"You must train to distinguish dimensional bridges by sight, but eventually, you'll be able to use your extra-dimensional sentience to sense the bridge's destination. You probably won't be able to, but can you sense which one belongs to your dimension?" Harriet asked Anti.

"No, but I can guess. It's the middle one with the gray around the edges."

"It is." Her correct answer surprised Harriet. "How did you know?"

"This world has always been gray around the edges for me," Anti replied. "Where do the other dimensional portals lead? Or, where would they lead if they were real?"

"We don't know," Harriet said. "We only observe them and recreate their appearance, but no one's gone through them. Well, no one has gone through them on purpose."

"Why not? Why do Jade and I have to be the canaries in the coal mines?" Anti groaned.

"Because no one could find their way back before. You're the first."

The rest of Anti's training was slow going. She showed no signs of any other abilities related to her EDS. Harriet held up cards and asked Anti what shape was on the other side. Anti identified the forms with even less accuracy than the average person. Harriet pictured scenes in her mind and asked Anti to describe them. Instead, Anti explained all the things she'd rather be doing than developing her EDS with Harriet, including eating sushi, shopping, reading, and washing her hair. In one frustrating episode, Harriet made Anti sniff the air to smell another dimension.

"I can smell your vanilla lotion, Harriet," Anti said. "I wasn't going to say anything, but it's way too much vanilla."

Harriet was beginning to suspect Anti may not have gained extra-dimensional sentience. Her last-ditch effort was a field trip to the park next to Anti's apartment building, where, Anti claimed, she had seen a real, naturally occurring bridge.

Harriet and Anti made the trip accompanied by yet another laboratory technician named Kaylen. Kaylen carried one of the clinical-looking handheld sensors that had first determined Anti's multidimensional nature.

Harriet, Kaylen, and Anti were all dressed in multiple layers of sweaters, coats, and hats to combat the winter weather. A light coating of snow had covered the ground since the last time Anti had looked at the park. However, Anti saw that the bridge was still in the park, looking as shimmery and blobby as ever, sitting in the usually empty area several yards from a playground. Anti used her new coaching to study the portal and found it had a slight green tint.

"See," Anti approached the bridge and waved her hands up and down. "Right here."

Kaylen brandished her sensor in the area around where Anti indicated while Harriet looked on. An LED on her handheld device blinked red.

"She's right," Kaylen said. Harriet nodded and looked relieved.

"This is in the middle of a busy park," Anti wondered. "How has no one walked through it before?"

"They might not notice walking through some bridges." Harriet took the sensor from Kaylen to confirm the readings. "Some dimensions are so like ours, you would never know the difference, and your counterpart from the other dimension would walk through at the same time, so you'd never go missing. Soon afterward, your consciousness would acclimate to the new dimension, and you'd get used to your alternative world."

"Terrifying."

"This one doesn't lead to a dimension similar to yours, so you'd have to walk through it intentionally. Someone would have to sense it or see it, like you, to be able to walk through it on purpose."

Anti stood and stared at the dimensional bridge, pondering her impending trip to the other side of one. She shivered, and not just from the cold. Anti tried to use her sentience to look through it and see or feel what was on the other side. She could not, although she did catch a faint whiff of dark chocolate.

This concluded Anti's individual instruction, which everyone at the Orion Center agreed was woefully lacking, but no one wanted to continue to work with her.

Jade and Anti's cooperative training began the next day.

CHAPTER 4
TRAINING DAY TWO IN WHICH
HARRIET ORDERS A NEW COFFEE MAKER

"What did you learn during your practice?" Anti asked Jade early the next morning. She and Jade were in the Orion Center's multipurpose room for what they hoped would be the last time. Early the following morning, after their combined training, the two women were supposed to head down to the wormhole section of the laboratories to be sent off to another realm.

"Well, I spent some time studying my dimensional instability, so I can understand what's happening to me on a quantum level. After that, I shape-shifted into about half a dozen unique animals and then different people," Jade told her, then listed the animals and the names of the lab technicians who she had transformed into.

"That's amazing," Anti said. "Do me."

"Absolutely not."

"You're lucky. The only thing I learned was how to spot a portal to our dimension so I can get us back. I also learned that I should be able to smell other dimensions, but I can't. Can you just change into a bird again, or something else quick? I really want to see it."

Jade, perhaps unwisely, took this moment to ask a question she'd wanted to ask Anti for several days, but hadn't found the right time to bring up. She also hoped this would change the subject enough to discourage Anti from pressuring her into shape-shifting by request. "When Harriet first asked us to follow Abraham into another dimension, I said 'we're both science journalists,' and you said, 'not on purpose.' How did you become a journalist by accident?"

"I wanted to be a writer. I was interested in fiction, but my parents wanted me to be a doctor." Anti shrugged.

"Isn't your dad a literature professor?"

"Yes, but my mother is a surgeon. I guess they figured she took the better path. All my brothers and sisters are in the medical or science fields. I loaded my undergraduate degree with scientific courses, and then, when I got to pre-med, I couldn't hack it. My dad pulled some strings with people he knew at the *Journal of American Sciences*, and here I am. I wouldn't say I'm a disappointment to them, but they aren't too happy with me either. I have the worst of both worlds. Yes, I'm writing, but not the topic I'd like to write about, and my parents don't like my choice, anyway."

"Well," Jade tried to sound encouraging, "you have the extra-dimensional perception. That could help with your career."

"Right. So, not only am I terrible at everything else, but I also have the worst superpower, and I can't even use it properly."

Jade, who rarely felt anything for Antigone aside from irritation, was gripped by a sharp pang of pity. "We will practice more today," she told her. "Maybe you will have some breakthrough."

Anti appreciated Jade's sudden compassion, but it was short-lived. Their tandem training day consisted of long lectures, led mostly by Harriet, but there were a few guest appearances by other members of the Orion Center research staff. The talks were on the nature of black holes, the mechanics of wormholes, Einstein-Rosen Bridges, the multidimensional nature of atomic building blocks called quarks, and mathematical equations relating to quantum physics.

The lectures also explained some practical applications, like the fact that the physical locations of Einstein-Rosen Bridges correspond to equivalent areas in other dimensions. Abraham would have landed near wherever the laboratory's similar site was in the next world. So, when they open the bridge, it would be near where Abraham was pulled in.

Anti grew bored while Jade listened with rapt attention. Anti expressed her boredom by getting up for coffee, going to the bathroom, and interrupting the lecture either to insert an unrelated anecdote about herself or to ask an occasionally pertinent, but more often off-topic, question.

Anti's first question, which she often repeated throughout the day, was, "Why do we have to learn this?"

Jade answered Anti's question the first time she asked it, but after that, she left it to the increasingly agitated lecturers. "I would like to know what is happening in case something goes wrong," Jade told her.

"What? Are you going to build a new wormhole machine if we get trapped in the other dimension?" Anti scoffed.

Harriet was the next person who attempted to demonstrate why learning quantum physics basics should be relevant to Anti. "When you first drive a car, you learn how the engine works, the mechanics of the brakes, and how the gears work. It makes you a better driver."

"I learned none of that about cars," Anti said with a laugh. "I just know where to put in the gas and which pedals to push."

At the end of their training, Harriet gave Anti a small, slick, black device about the size and shape of a remote control. It was like the equipment some lab technicians carried around.

"This device contains an Einstein-Rosen Bridge stabilizer," Harriet explained. "It will preserve a naturally occurring bridge for about half a day. If, for example, you find a portal to our world, but you haven't recovered Abraham yet, you can make sure the bridge home doesn't shift or disappear."

Anti grabbed the gadget and turned it over in her hands, looking interested in something for the first time that day. She took the time to ask the purpose of each button and gauge.

"This switch here," Harriet pointed to a switch, "turns on a universal translation field. If someone is speaking in a language you don't understand, turn on the switch. After they say a few hundred words, the translator should be able to translate the language into English, and, when you speak, it will sound like you're speaking in their own language. It may not work for all languages, and there will be some words that don't have an English equivalent. The translation field reaches for almost one hundred miles around the device."

"Finally, something with a purpose," Anti said after she made sure that she understood the device's operation. "It seems like the universal translator is on right now."

"Oh, does it?" Harriet took the device back and pressed the button a few times before handing it back to Anti. "It should be all set now."

A moment later, Kaylen the lab tech, wandered into the lecture hall, wearing a white coat and looking serious. "Antigone, we'd like you to look at one more simulation if you don't mind."

Anti rolled her eyes so hard head rocked backward, and she shuffled after Kaylen. "This is the last one, right?"

After ensuring Anti was indeed gone, Harriet approached Jade discreetly. Harriet stepped close to Jade and pressed an object into her hand. It was similar in size and shape to Anti's bridge stabilizer, but it was white and had a slight curve. Jade held it up at eye level, to examine it, and to force some distance between Harriet and herself.

"It's a focused antimatter cannon," Harriet told her. "Use it if you get into trouble."

"A weapon?" Jade stared at the gun for a few seconds before trying to give it back to Harriet.

"Look at this dial on the side." Harriet turned a small dial that, on another device, might have been a volume control. "On its lowest setting, it makes a steam barrier between the target and the antimatter. It just shoves the target aside." Harriet aimed the gun at the coffee machine resting on a nearby countertop. A wave of light burst from the end of the cannon and knocked the coffee machine. The coffee maker scooted to the left by six inches, and the leftover coffee sloshed around inside the carafe.

Harriet looked at Jade and waited for her to speak. When she didn't, Harriet turned the cannon's dial off and handed it to Jade. "Turn it up a little, and it will render a living target unconscious."

"What about the highest setting?" Jade asked. The cannon felt heavy in her hand, and she wanted to drop it.

"The antimatter will completely disintegrate the target, whether organic or inorganic."

Harriet took the cannon from Jade and pointed it at the coffee maker again, turning the dial all the way up and pulling a trigger on the underside of the device's curve. A quick pulse of black material shot out the end of the cannon. When the pulse hit the coffee machine, it disappeared, as if had never sat on the tan, laminate counter.

Jade gasped.

"We needed a new coffee maker away; it kept burning the coffee." Harriet shrugged and handed the antimatter cannon back to Jade. "Do you want to try it? We could use a smart board in here." Harriet eyed the whiteboard suspiciously.

"What do you really do here at Orion Center?" Jade gingerly turned the gun over in her hands. "This isn't the sort of gear I usually see at science facilities."

"We're quantum researchers," Harriet said. "We study quantum mechanics in action. It's that simple, and that complicated."

Jade looked as if she might like to say more but didn't.

Harriet waited before continuing. "The antimatter cannon only needs to be charged once every four hundred and thirty-seven years, so you should be okay. You don't need to load it; it makes its own antimatter from the electrons surrounding it."

Jade reluctantly slipped the cannon into her pocket. "Thanks."

"Oh, best not tell Antigone," Harriet added. "I may be wrong, but she seems imprudent."

Jade nodded.

In the hall outside of the multipurpose room, Anti stormed past with Kaylen trailing behind.

"I'm not standing around sniffing all day. You're all lunatics." Anti stopped, walked backward a few feet, and stuck her head into the room. "I'm done for today. I'm throwing in the towel," she said to Jade and Harriet. "See you in the morning," she added before bustling away.

Jade looked over at Harriet, who was scrolling through images on her smartphone. "What do you think about the kind with the little cups?" she asked as she held up her phone to Jade, revealing a picture of a high-end coffee maker.

"Perhaps we should all throw in the towel for the day." Jade's suggestion brought to a close their second day of training. The next day they would enter an unknown universe, using barely practiced skills and brand-new quantum devices to search for a lost colleague.

That evening was Friday night, and in Jade's home, Friday night meant fish for dinner. Her mother made grilled tuna with a zesty lime sauce. Jade, who usually had a hearty appetite, picked at the dish. Amber spent the entire meal picking at her plate as well, but for Amber that was par for the course. Amber monopolized the conversation, alternating between tales of the majesty of the musk turtle gala and lamenting the lack of pictures posted online of her in her green dress at said gala.

"I've found seven pictures so far," Amber whined, "and only five of them are taken on my good side."

Only Jade's father overlooked Amber's gripes enough to notice there was something wrong with Jade. "You've been working a lot lately," he said, raising his bushy eyebrows. "Two full days today and the day before, and you're going in again tomorrow—on a Saturday. I hope they're paying you well for all of this."

"Don't worry, Dad." Jade gave him a weak smile. "I'm being compensated."

Before she left the table, Jade gave both her mother and father a kiss and told them she loved them. Her mother thanked her and resumed her conversation with Amber, but her father gave her a quizzical look. "All right, dear?"

Jade, who wasn't used to this onslaught of attention, nodded and scurried to her bedroom.

That night, Jade couldn't sleep, and her usual bedroom pacing circuit did not seem wide enough, so she expanded it to include the hallway between her bedroom and the rest of the ranch-style house.

As she walked past her door, she saw the light on in Amber's room and heard the soft sounds of a television show playing. Jade stood outside the door, imagining she had a sister who she could tell her secrets to, a sister who would fling open her door and insist that they watch funny movies until dawn, just to keep her mind at ease.

Jade turned around and went back to her room, suddenly convinced just a small pacing circle was enough. She did not sleep that night.

CHAPTER 5
BENEATH A TECHNICOLOR SKY

Jade left her home early the next morning. She didn't want to wake anyone in her family, especially her father, who would certainly notice her unease. So Jade tiptoed out, grabbing a cereal bar instead of a toasted bagel and eating in her car.

Antigone woke up even earlier, as she had planned to take the bus due to an abundance of nerves that was making it hard for her to focus on driving. She lingered in the shower, though, so she ended up driving her hybrid, gripping the wheel all the way through her commute.

Both women arrived in the Orion Center parking lot, by coincidence, at 7:45 on the dot. They also parked next to each other. When Jade got out of her beat-up, but clean, navy blue Kia, Anti had already exited her pristine and luxuriously economical sedan. Anti was staring up at the sky, looking concerned.

"What's up there?" Jade asked, alarmed.

"A lot of gray clouds." Anti turned her face from the sky and looked into Jade's eyes with an unreadable expression. In a few quick movements, Anti reopened her car door, reached in and grabbed a pair of sunglasses from the dashboard, and closed the door again. She asked Jade, "Are you ready?" as if she hadn't just done any of it.

"No," Jade laughed and then said, "yes."

So, at 7:52 in the morning, Jade and Anti descended in the Orion Center elevator. Shortly after, they stood in front of the mouth of the collider, staring into its endless depths. Despite what seemed like a never-ending parade of Orion Center staff they had met over the past three days, there was only one technician in the collider room with the women. Jade noticed he was the young man named Marshall, the one with the rabbit named Lulu.

Jade wore a pair of jeans, sneakers, and a dark green hoodie over a green tee-shirt, because—after some debate—she had decided that green would be the best color if she needed to camouflage herself. The antimatter cannon sat heavy in the back pocket of her jeans.

Anti wore black boots, black leggings, an embellished purple tank top, and a heavy black cardigan. Jade discerned no rhyme or reason to Anti's outfit. Anti had also made a rubber thong to hold her Einstein-Rosen Bridge stabilizer and translation device, which she wore around her neck.

A bunch of the Center's workers watched from the observation deck. It was the same one that Jade and Anti had witnessed the accident from just a few days ago. About half a dozen Orion Center employees stood there now, with Harriet and her unmistakable hair at the front of the pack. Jade craned her neck to look up at her, and Harriet beamed and gave two thumbs up.

Marshall, the technician, pulled the lever, and the collider hummed. The entrance of the collider looked even more spine-chilling than it did from the observation deck. Anti looked down the collider and saw that behind the wall it was built into, the collider was vast and long; it stretched so far beyond the wall it seemed never-ending.

A bridge appeared in the opening while Anti was staring down the collider's tunnel; it was identical to the sparkly, globular portal Anti had seen during her training.

"Amazing," Jade said.

"You can see the portal?" Anti asked. "That's supposed to be my power."

"Jade can only see the bridge because the collider is making it stable. You wouldn't be able to see a natural bridge, even a stabilized one," Marshall said. "Are you ready to go through?"

"Not really," Anti replied, but Jade was already walking toward the bridge. Jade hesitated in front of it for the slightest of seconds. Then she stepped into the blob and vanished.

Anti said, "Fine. Here I go," and followed Jade through.

Jade was expecting a rush of air or a push, or maybe the weird sensation she felt whenever an elevator was about to stop, but stepping from one world and into the next felt just as commonplace as walking from the living room to the kitchen.

Despite the ease of her transition, the world on the bridge's other side was so bright it was blinding. She turned and squinted at Anti, putting her hands to her forehead, shielding her eyes against the brilliance of another world.

"Can you see the bridge home? If you find it, you need to stabilize it!" Jade shouted.

"Yeah, I'm working on it. And I'm right next to you, quit yelling." Anti had slipped on the pair of black sunglasses she'd grabbed from her dashboard. She took the stabilizer out of the thong around her neck and tapped away at its buttons. "I've got the bridge," she called to Jade. "It's stable."

Jade blinked her eyes at the area around Anti, but she could not see any evidence of a bridge.

"Don't worry," Anti assured her, "I know where it is. I can see it." Anti pointed to her sunglasses.

Jade's eyes adjusted to the unfamiliar world around them. They were in an area of lush vegetation. Tall grasses sprinkled with indigo flowers surrounded the women. About a quarter-mile to the left, the grass gave way to the gravel banks of a glittering, blue lake. Massive, white-capped mountains loomed in the distance. The sky was an intense blue, dotted with clouds of the purest white Jade had ever seen. A dense forest surrounded the grassy area on all other sides. Jade just made out the roofs of the buildings in a sizeable village across the lake.

"We landed in the right spot," Anti said. "Imagine if the bridge had been a few yards over." She nodded toward the water.

"You knew to bring your sunglasses."

"So, about that… I also knew that I should make you this." Anti pulled a second rubber thong out of her cardigan pocket. "It's a holster for the gun thingy Harriet gave you. You wear it around your waist."

Jade took the holster and examined it with suspicion before putting it on. "You overheard Harriet and I talking?" she asked Anti.

"No, but my powers are kind of working."

"You could have told me to wear sunglasses too."

"You could have told me you were carrying a deadly weapon." Anti looked hostile.

"Okay, okay. You're right." She searched for a way to change the subject. "Can you use your sense to tell where Abraham is?"

"Maybe. Shush." Anti closed her eyes and stood still. She dropped her arms down at her sides. Her stabilizer in its holster swung against her chest a few times before falling still.

Finally, Anti pointed to the village in between the lake and the mountains.

"Wow. You can tell that Abraham is in the village? Your sentience is developing.

"No." Anti shook her head. "I didn't see anything, but where else is he going to go? There's nothing else around here."

Jade and Anti strolled through tall grasses. They were headed to the forest that ran the length of the side of the lake. Jade marveled at the vividness and beauty of the flowers, the detail on each grass blade, and the air's fresh smell and taste.

When they left the field and entered the forest, there was little underbrush aside from luminous ferns and colored mushrooms. The forest was made of tall, thick trees with high branches forming a dense canopy. Despite the canopy, the woods were still so bright Jade had to squint, which confirmed her suspicion that the brightness didn't come from the sky—it came from the dimension itself.

"It looks like Lisa Frank threw up on a Care Bear cloud around here," Anti noted as she stomped through the forest.

"Who is Lisa Frank?"

"Come on," Anti jeered. "You're the same age as me. Don't tell me that your parents didn't buy you Lisa Frank stuff."

"My parents didn't buy a lot of toys."

"Right. Knowing you, your parents bought educational junk for Christmas and junior microscopes for all of your birthdays," Anti laughed.

"They didn't have money for anything," Jade said.

"Oh, sorry."

There was a minute of awkward quiet, and then Jade asked, "How does your extra-dimensional sentience work? How did you know to bring sunglasses? How did you 'see' the gun?"

"Starting last night, whenever I thought about going through the bridge, I felt a pain in my eyes, as if I was staring at the sun, and the only thing that would make the pain go away was imagining myself bring sunglasses through that bridge. And the gun, I saw Harriet give it to you, but not with my eyes. It was just a vision that popped into my head. I saw her disintegrate the coffee maker. I assume it does the same to people."

"You are correct, but there are settings. I could just shove someone aside or knock them out. I don't plan on using it to harm anyone. Ever."

"I don't like it. I don't care that you don't plan on killing. Accidents happen. In homes that own guns, you're ninety times more likely to die in an accident involving the firearm than you are to defend yourself with the gun."

"Listen to you rattle off statistics. You sound like a journalist," Jade smiled.

Anti didn't return the smile. "I'm not comfortable with weapons." She pointed to the antimatter cannon, now resting on Jade's hip in the holster that Anti had made. "And I don't like that you didn't tell me about it."

"There doesn't seem to be much you are comfortable with," Jade protested.

"When was the last time you went anywhere besides work or home? Since we're talking about comfort zones."

"I'm here, aren't I?" Jade asked. "Let's make a deal; you tell me what you know that I need to know, and I'll let you know what you need to know." Jade offered.

Anti considered this. "How do we determine what is necessary knowledge?" Anti froze. Her arm darted in front of Jade, blocking her path. "Something's coming," Anti said in a sharp whisper.

CHAPTER 6
HARPY MAGIC

A child stepped out from behind the trunk of one of the forest's massive trees. Well, she appeared to be a child until they looked closer. She was the size of a six-year-old and had youthful features, but her hair was white, and her pale blue eyes looked wise and ancient.

"Whoa. A ghost baby," Anti said.

The white-haired child spoke in breathy, melodic gibberish neither Jade nor Anti understood.

"Hold on." Anti pulled her stabilizer out of the thong around her neck and turned up the translation dial. "Can you say about ninety-seven more words?" she asked the child.

The girl blinked her elderly, blue eyes at them, and gestured for Jade and Anti to follow her.

"Should we follow her?" Anti asked Jade.

"Maybe she'll lead us to the village. It is in the direction she's going."

They trailed behind the girl, Anti fidgeting with her stabilizer for much of the way. "If you could just get her to say a few more words, I could get the translator on this would work, and we'd be able to communicate."

Jade looked at Anti, completely lost. She did not understand how to communicate with the otherworldly child.

"Okay. I'll do both then," Anti huffed. Anti stopped the girl and leaned down to meet her height. "What's your name, sweetheart?"

The girl stopped walking and stood, watching Anti.

"Where are you going?" Anti tried again. "Why is your hair white? Are you a baby ghost?"

Anti stood back up, and the girl maneuvered around her and continued walking.

"Make a tree or plant move with your ray gun," Anti turned to Jade and demanded. "That will get her talking enough for the translator to work."

"It's an antimatter cannon, not a ray gun. Five minutes ago, you weren't comfortable with me using it all," Jade said, bewildered.

"I'm adapting," Anti said. "It's a survival instinct."

"Fine." While they continued to follow the child, Jade pulled the antimatter cannon from her holster, triple-checked that it was on the displacement setting, and fired it at a large mushroom patch about fifteen feet in front of the girl. The mushrooms shifted three feet to the left, where they sat looking like they had grown out of that exact spot.

The child turned around and looked at Jade and her gun, which Jade holstered. When the girl spoke in her incomprehensible language, Jade imagined she was admonishing her for using antimatter to move the mushroom patch. While she spoke, Anti fiddled with her stabilizer, and after about thirty seconds, some of the girl's words began to make sense.

"Jibber, jibber tower, jibber, jibber, highlands," the girl said, turning and continuing to walk through the forest.

"The translator is working," Anti said.

"And we'll keep both of you in the Crystal Outlook until the Council meets on jibber, jibber day," the girl said.

Both Jade and Anti stopped dead in their tracks.

"I'm sorry you'll keep us where?" Anti asked.

"The Crystal Outlook, it's where we keep all prisoners outside of the village," she said casually. Hear insightful words sounded strange, coming from such a young child. "I didn't realize you spoke Uhlish."

"We just learned; we're quick studies." Anti discreetly removed the stabilizer from her thong and slipped it into one of her many cardigan pockets.

"Some manner of harpy magic, I'm sure." The girl was calm but suspicious.

"Is there anyone else in the Crystal Outlook?" Jade asked. "We're looking for a man named Abraham."

"No one has been in the Crystal Outlook for a jibber, jibber. I've been lonely," the girl said, sounding more childlike. "You will come to visit and stay for a long time."

Jade stooped down, so she was eye level with the child, mimicking Anti's stance from earlier. The child's blue eyes no longer looked ancient, but sweet and brimming with anticipation.

"A moment ago, you called the Crystal Outlook a prison and implied that we are prisoners. Which is it? A place you'd like us to visit or a place that we have to go?"

The girl's face turned red, at first, like she was blushing and then darker and darker red, the color of blood then a deep maroon. Her eyes changed to a shiny, obsidian black, and her entire body grew until she towered over Jade and Antigone. Jade jumped back from the girl as she transformed, and Anti let out an involuntary yelp full of fear and surprise.

"The Crystal Outlook is a place you have to go to." The monster girl's voice turned to a loud, raspy growl. She towered over them menacingly, a purple giantess in the fairytale woods, which were, apparently, *her* fairytale woods.

Jade pulled her antimatter cannon out of its holster, pointed it at the monster, and shot. She left it set to displace, so the giant only shifted a few yards to the right and a little closer to the women. Jade attempted to turn the cannon's dial to stun, but the giant grabbed it, her colossal, purple hand enveloping Jades and nearly crushing her fingers while extracting the weapon.

The giantess pinched the cannon between her fingers, brought it close to her face, and inspected it for a second before dropping it into her tunic pocket.

Jade never needed to use much imagination in her lifetime. She was a woman of peer-reviewed facts and natural law. Her guilty pleasure was watching a television show about millionaires looking for homes. An independently wealthy thirty-year-old was about as fanciful as it got in Jade's world, so she couldn't have imagined what another dimension might look like or dreamed the dangers that might befall her. For many people, such a lack of imagination may be a gift, but in this situation, it was a curse. How could a woman whose favorite book was *The Elements of Style* foresee this otherworldly danger or any other multidimensional mishap that might barrel down on her?

All of this flashed through Jade's mind, and she stared up at the giantess, still squinting her eyes at the brightness of the unfamiliar world. The abominable realization that Anti was her only hope of survival engulfed Jade's mind. Anti was fluidly creative; she was all instinct and reaction. Anti would have to be Jade's hero.

"Nope," Anti said, unheroically, after doing her own sizing up of the magenta monster. "I'm out." She turned and walked back toward the forest's entrance, headed for the stabilized dimensional bridge.

As soon as she realized Anti was attempting an escape, the monster sprouted half a dozen powerful tentacles, each as thick as a grown man's leg. She wrapped one around Jade's waist and another around Anti's upper thighs.

"Why?" Anti howled. "Why does the ghost-baby-giant have to be a secret octopus?"

Jade pushed at the tentacles. They were warm, thick, and scaly, but dry. The limbs also wouldn't budge an inch. Jade looked over at Anti, her eyes brimming with panic. Anti also pushed on the tentacles, wriggled, then shook her head in bewilderment.

The monster started walking, and with each stride, she pulled the two women behind her. She ambled along as tentacle beasts do on land, so Jade and Anti were able to walk upright and were not, thankfully, dragged across the ground.

"It turns out I don't like this place." Anti reached into her back pocket and turned off the stabilizer's translation function with some difficulty and maneuvering.

"She can't understand us anymore," Anti said.

"Does it matter? She doesn't listen to us anyway," Jade pointed out.

"You need to turn yourself into a monster. Copy her tentacle form and battle, or something."

"It's not smart to let her know I can change my form," Jade replied. "Let's see where this goes first." If she were honest, she was terrified of the giantess and couldn't envision a "battle" with her.

"Let's see where this goes? We're not on a first date with a guy wearing flip-flops. She'll crush us at any moment!" Anti roared.

"If she were going to kill us, she would have done so already. She could crush us, and now she has my antimatter gun. Why didn't you use your sentience to tell that the girl was dangerous?"

"It's not like your power. I can't turn it on and off; it just happens," Anti explained.

The tentacle beast girl stopped, turned around, and began squeezing them very hard with her tentacles as she jabbered at Jade and Anti.

"I think she wants us to speak in her language," Jade said.

Anti turned the translator back on, and they continued their uncomfortable journey through the dazzling forest. The woodland grew dense, and then sparse again, before opening into a long glade, at the edge of which there was a structure that had to be the Crystal Outlook. It was a crumbling, ruinous stone tower with a massive, crystal sphere on top. What looked to be the bottom floor was the only area with windows carved out, but all the windows were lined with rusty bars.

Jade attempted to hesitate at the doorway, but the tentacle monster tugged them both into the Crystal Outlook. The floor was made of packed dirt, and the tower's stone walls were even more decrepit than they looked from a distance. There were jail cells inside the bottom floor, but the bars that made up the cells were so rusted they were half red dust.

The tentacle monster put the women into the opposite cells and closed the gates. Once her task was complete, she shrunk down into her little girl's body, complete with glossy white hair and bright blue eyes. The antimatter cannon bulged in her tiny tunic pocket.

"I'm sorry about that. I was worried you wouldn't come to the Crystal Outlook. You have to be here."

"How long will you be here for?" Anti asked.

"You won't have to stay here forever," the girl said. "The Village Council will come by on jibber, jibber days."

"I'm sorry," Anti said, "but we can't understand you when you tell us how many days until the council comes. Can you show us with your hands?" Anti held up two fingers. "Is it this many days?" Anti held up three fingers. "This many days?"

The little girl held up both hands. Her palms spread out, more and more extensively, and her fingers multiplied. First, she had twenty fingers, then a hundred. Soon, she had too many fingers to count. The girl's fingers filled up the space in front of her and then surrounded her, fanning out in all directions.

"This many days," the girl said when her fingers stopped multiplying.

"That is gross and disturbing, but it's also a bit cool," Anti said.

"That is a lot of days," Jade said.

The girl contracted her hands, and they went back to their normal state of ten fingers. The girl stood, staring at Jade with her pale blue eyes for over a minute, before turning her head to stare at Anti. She repeated this several times.

"I wonder why she's doing that," Anti said as the girl turned her gaze for the fourth time.

"She's guarding us," Jade reasoned.

"I'm going to try talking to her," Anti said to Jade. To the girl, she said, "My name is Antigone, and this is Jade. Do you have a name?"

"I didn't know harpies had names. I'm Denodos."

"A lovely name for a lovely girl," Anti said. "I have another question for you. What does the Village Council look like? Do they look like you when you are a nice girl or do they look like you when you are a big, grumpy monster?"

"I am the only one who changes and gets big because I am the guardian of the Crystal Outlook. There are no other Outlooks in this village," the girl said.

"You poor thing," Anti said. "Denodos, you said we would be here for a long time. If we will make it until the Village Council comes, we will need food and water, and we're hungry and thirsty."

"Of course," Denodos said. "I will return." She performed one more set of long, warning glares before she left the tower.

"Okay, now turn into a tentacle giant and battle her when she comes back," Anti whispered the second Denodos was at a safe distance.

"Stop trying to get me to fight her, and let's think this through," Jade hissed. "We'll both have a better chance of staying safe if I can go unnoticed. I'll turn into a small animal, like a mouse, so she won't be able to find me if she goes after me. I'll run to the village where I can find Abraham, or at least find a Village Council member to reason with, and maybe I can get them here sooner than this many days." Jade spread out both hands and shook them, mimicking the girl.

"You're supposed to blend in with the surrounding fauna," Anti said in her best Harriet voice. "I haven't seen any mice around, have you?"

"No, but a mouse is small enough to hide. If I come across some native creature, I'll change into it."

"Fine. What am I supposed to do with little Miss Cthulhu while I wait for you to bring back the Village Council or Abraham?"

"Talk. Lord knows you're good at it."

Anti narrowed her eyes.

"Seriously, talk to the girl." Jade gestured out of the Outlook's door. "Find out what a harpy is and why she thinks that's what we are. Ask her about the Village Council." Jade directed as she shrunk down to mouse size. Soft brown fur sprouted all over her body, and two spoon-shaped ears popped out of the top of her head. The Jade mouse had a small stripe of black hair running from her forehead and down her back.

"So much cooler than my power," Anti lamented.

Mouse Jade bounded out of the tower just in time. A single second later, Denodos rounded the corner carrying a dented, blue pail full of water in one hand and a ripe apple in the other.

"Where is the other harpy?" Denodos asked, dropping the pail so that water slopped out over the edge.

"She escaped, I guess," Anti shrugged. "She doesn't tell me much."

Denodos bounded from the tower and stood in front of the Outlook, her head whipping as she surveyed the landscape for Jade.

"You might as well stay here with me," Anti called. "You don't want to lose both of your prisoners."

"Harpy tricks." Denodos stalked back into the Outlook. Her face turned red again, and Anti expected another transformation into the tentacle beast.

"Hey, hey, hey, relax." Anti made a lowering gesture with her hands. "It seems like you've been alone here for a while. I know what it's like to be alone. Do you want to talk about it?"

Denodos's face returned to normal, and she looked at Anti with frank curiosity.

"Yes. I want to talk about it," the little girl said after a lengthy pause.

CHAPTER 7
GOAT YOGURT

Jade remained a mouse until the Crystal Outlook was out of her sight, then she surveyed her surroundings for a native animal to shift into. Anti was correct; there were no mice, at least not in the forest. The first creature Jade came across was an elegant squirrel. This squirrel looked crafted by the gods themselves, its gray fur shone in the spots of light that dappled the forest floor, its tail was bushy, and his sharp black eyes sparkled.

When she shifted, Jade did her best to capture the attractiveness of the squirrel paragon, but she couldn't quite match his magnificence. Jade bounded the rest of the way to the village as a not quite exemplar squirrel. On her way, she saw several other animals, all of them impeccable versions of earth animals. A gorgeous fox with a lustrous orange coat ran past her, chasing a handsome, high jumping toad.

Jade soon came to the remains of a crumbling, brick road that seemed to lead from the edge of the forest into the village. The trail led to a ruined rope bridge crossing a narrow, but deep creek bed. Jade could not cross it in her squirrel form, so, after a quick look around, she transformed into a bluebird and then back to a squirrel once she landed on the other bank.

The dilapidated brick road gradually turned into a passible country lane with signs of civilization lining it, including decorative flower and herb gardens. One neatly planted herb garden caught the senses of the squirrel part of Jade, so she stopped to munch on some leafy basil plants.

Full of basil, Jade, the squirrel, carried on until she reached the actual end of the forest and saw a farmhouse. The farmer himself was carrying two buckets of water, slung in yolk over his shoulders. Like Denodos, he had white hair, but he looked like he might be much younger otherwise, in his mid–twenties, perhaps. He wore long, flowing robes swirled with rainbow colors. He brought the buckets to one of his crops and watered rows of a root plant that Jade could not identify.

Three children played in a fenced-in area in front of the farmhouse. Like the farmer, they all had white hair and wore multicolored robes. Snow white goats of all ages frolicked in another large enclosure while the children laughed and fed them long strands of grass.

Squirrel Jade watched the scene for half an hour, building up the courage for what she knew she had to do next. Scientific interviews were the only occasions Jade had to talk to strangers. Then there was always a purpose. She came in prepared with a list of questions, and when the pre-determined questions were over, the conversation was over. The interviewees were often as unaccustomed to chatting as Jade was, and the entire exchanges were predictable as if she had scripted them.

Jade tried to plan out her rapidly approaching conversation with the farmer as if it were one of her interviews. However, guessing the replies of a being from another world was not as simple as she had hoped. Perhaps she would begin with some softball questions; she'd ask him about his plants or enquire about the names of the goats. Eventually, she'd work her way up to the whereabouts of Abraham and then segue into questions about the Village Council. Too much time had passed by then, though, and she knew her planning, though incomplete, had to be over.

Jade changed into her human form, taking care to make her hair as lily-white as all the other inhabitants of this plane. She couldn't match their hair's silky luster, and she hoped it was enough to convince the locals. Jade also dressed in an outfit like the farmer's, a rainbow swirled poncho reminiscent of a 1960s hippie. She took a few deep, relaxing breaths and headed toward the farm.

When he saw Jade approaching from the forest, the farmer let out a gasp and dropped the yoke from his shoulders. He stood and watched Jade with a curious expression that made Jade think perhaps she should run back into the forest. Maybe Denodos had lied, and all the people of the dimension were hidden monsters. A second before Jade bolted, the farmer reached out his arms and walked toward her, smiling, readying an embrace.

Jade was not a hugger.

"Traveler!" he said, squeezing Jade and pulling her in with his outstretched arms. "You startled me. It is a rare day when a traveler comes from the direction of the Thorotia Empire."

The stranger's hug mortified Jade, but she realized she had to relax in his arms, lest she give herself away.

The farmer released Jade, looked into her eyes, and said, "Well met."

It took Jade a moment to realize he was waiting for her to respond. "Well met," she said, guessing at the proper response.

"Indeed." The farmer seemed satisfied. "I'm called Rupus," he said. "Can I offer you some yogurt or wine?"

"No, thank you. I'm called Jade." She mimicked his affectation. "I'm hoping you can answer some questions for me." She mentally got out her reporter's notebook.

"Of course," Rupus said, "But you must have some yogurt. Our goats make the most delicious milk in the entire village."

She mentally put away her reporter's notebook.

A few minutes later, Jade sat inside Rupus's farmhouse, belly up to a polished, wooden table. The farmhouse was simultaneously sunny and cozy, with huge windows, plush furnishings, and a massive hearth with a crackling fire. The walls were full of paintings, a mix of pastoral landscapes, and painted portraits of the Rupus family's white-haired ancestors.

Rupus placed a large wooden bowl in front of her. It was full of white, creamy yogurt and topped with bits of candied orange. The farmer's three girls (at least Jade thought they were girls because they all had the same long, white hair and knee-length tunics) had lined up along the wall like spectators to the yogurt eating.

Rupus handed Jade a carved, flat stone, which she supposed she should use as a spoon. He was correct in his declaration of the yogurt's deliciousness, Jade had never tasted anything so good. The yogurt was light and creamy, and the bits of candied orange were little bursts of intense, citrus, and sweetness.

"Rupus, this is…" Jade continued to eat, "this is unlike anything I've ever had before," she said.

Once Jade's bowl was empty, Rupus waved his children outside and sat across from her. "I'm sure you have questions for me, as I have many questions for you. I have never seen someone from the West. Forgive me for my asking, but I thought the Thorotian Empire had collapsed many hundreds of years ago."

She had been hoping to ask a few questions first, to gauge the situation. In interviews, the interviewee doesn't ask questions. The yogurt had thrown her off. Jade's thoughts scrambled, and she had to work to the right of them.

Rupus took her brief silence as an offense. "Sorry," he said, "I should not have asked."

There was the upper hand Jade needed. She smiled. "It's all right. Before we speak any further, I'd like to meet with your Village Council."

"That will be difficult as we haven't had a Village Council for decades. We govern ourselves. What were you going to discuss with them?"

And there goes the upper hand. Jade gave up and got right to the point. "Has another traveler come through here recently from the same direction? Someone called Abraham?"

Rupus laughed out loud this time. "As I said, the village has many travelers, but you are the first traveler I've ever seen come from the Thorotia side of the forest."

Jade was close to despair, but she had a sudden idea. "Are there any travelers with brown hair?" Jade touched her own, shape-shifted, white hair.

"There is just one person in the village with dark hair, but he's not new to the village," Rupus said.

"Is he called Abraham?" Jade asked.

"No, he's Christian. Such a strange name." Rupus laughed again.

"Can you bring me to him?"

CHAPTER 8
THE TATTOOIST

It was about a mile walk from Rupus's farmstead to the village. While they walked, Rupus sang in his rich voice, a lighthearted song about a bird who flew from the lake to the mountain. Entranced by his voice, Jade continued to marvel at the striking beauty of the landscape; each leaf was symmetrical, every flower was a work of art, and though there were clouds in the sky, they never seemed to blot out the sun.

The village itself was much larger than it had looked from across the lake. There must have been over a hundred squat, tan buildings, but the streets were broad and easy to navigate. All the villagers had the same stark, white hair, and wore colorful robes. Everyone seemed to know Rupus. He stopped to hug each passerby, and, once he introduced Jade as a traveler from Thorotia, they would try to hug her. Jade gave into these unwanted hugs, but from that day forward, the villagers always spoke of the people of Thorotia as being unfriendly with hugs, like wet noodles.

Rupus led Jade to a plain, one-story house surrounded by hedges. Like most other homes in the village, it had a lovely garden out front. A handmade sign hung above that door read: Tattooist.

When they approached the door, Jade heard a light argument coming from inside.

"You must pay today, or I can't complete it," the first man said.

"But I've known you my entire life, couldn't we make a deal, Christian?" A second man said.

Rupus shrugged and opened the door, revealing the owners of the voices. Jade looked the men up and down. One of them had dark brown hair, with a touch of gray at his temples, and the other had white hair. They both wore the customary rainbow robes. At first, Jade was ready to dismiss the idea that either of them was Abraham, but then she realized that brown-haired man was Abraham, but he was decades older.

"Well met, Christian. Well met, Renard," Rupus said to each of the men.

Abraham stopped arguing and looked at the newcomers. Recognition flickered over Abraham's face, followed by surprise, which he hid. "Well met, Rupus. Who is your friend?" Abraham asked.

Without thinking, Jade rushed toward Abraham, full of relief at finding him and curiosity about what had aged him thirty years in the past three days.

"Sorry, ma'am, but I'm not taking any more appointments today," Abraham said as Jade advanced on him.

She stopped for a moment and looked around the compact room. Beside Abraham was a table with primitive tattooing equipment, a small hammer, a needle, and pans of colored ink. She saw that Abraham had been using these instruments to tattoo a crude rowboat, afloat on a thick clump of waves, on Renard's shin.

"I'm Jade. We met at the Orion Center a few days ago," she said to Abraham. "I'm from the *Journal of American Sciences*. At least, I think it was a few days ago."

"You must be mistaken." Abraham's mouth twitched.

"What did she say?" Rupus furrowed his brow at Abraham. "I couldn't understand what Jade said to you."

Words like 'Orion Center,' and 'Journal of American Sciences' had no translation to Rupus's native language, Jade figured.

"I was speaking Thorotian," Jade lied. "You've been helpful, but I'd like to speak to my old friend Christian alone, please."

"So strange," Rupus thought out loud.

Abraham gave him and Renard a curt nod, indicating they should listen to Jade and leave the tattoo shop.

Rupus and the tattooed Renard left the shop, exchanging quizzical looks with each other and with Abraham, who shut the door behind them and watched them go through a curtained window.

"Aside from the hair, which I guess is a disguise, you look the same as you did thirty years ago. Did they come up with a miracle anti-aging pill?"

"Thirty years?"

"Give or take. There are two suns here and the nights are short. It's hard to figure out the relative passage of time."

"Flowing time," Jade said half to herself. During their training, Harriet brought up the possibility of flowing time incongruity, but she said it was only theoretical. "To me, it has only been a few days since the collider accident. How long has it been for you here?"

"One moment, I was standing in the booth watching the experiment, and the next, I was standing in a field next to a little lake." Abraham sounded tired.

"Orion sent Antigone and me to recover you. We have a stabilized portal to our home dimension. There's been a complication, though. We have to free Antigone from a rogue prison warden in the forest, and then we can get you home." Jade spoke breathlessly.

"I don't want to go home," Abraham scoffed, ignoring Anti's imprisonment. "This is my home."

Jade gave Abraham her best incredulous schoolteacher look. "This is not your home."

Abraham sighed, picked up a rag, dipped it in a nearby solution, and used it to clean a tattoo needle. "The first five years that I lived here, I thought I had died during the collider malfunction, and this was heaven. Everything was so beautiful; everyone was so nice. The weather is always perfect, and the food tastes so good. I only suspected the truth when I realized I was aging. You don't age after you die."

"This still isn't your home, Abraham. You have people in your actual home who love you and miss you."

"Do I? What would they say if they saw me like this?" He raised two ink-stained fingers to the hair graying at his temple. "I decided a long time ago that I belong here. I'm not going anywhere."

"Fine," Jade said in a way that let Abraham know it was not fine. "Can you at least help me free Antigone? She's stuck in the forest's Crystal Overlook, guarded by a creature that looks like a child but can transform into a monster. The monster said it will keep us until the Village Council visits it, but Rupus told me the village doesn't have a council."

"He's right. We haven't needed a council in decades. Sounds like you ran afoul of the Crystal Sentry, though. That thing is so old. I'm surprised it still functions. It's a relic of the war our village had with these humanoid and bird hybrid creatures who live on the mountain."

"That explains why she called us harpies."

"Yes. I suppose you're the only thing the Sentry has seen with dark hair, besides the harpies."

"And you. You have dark hair." Jade pointed out, "

"Me, I never met the Crystal Sentry. When I came here, there were patrols all around the lake. A pair of guards brought me into the village, assuming I was from Thorotia too." Abraham paused. "Honestly, I'm not sure there is a Thorotia, it's just a tall tale about what lies to the west."

"Do you know how to get Antigone out of the Crystal Outlook?" Jade interrupted his rumination.

Abraham resumed cleaning his tattoo equipment, signaling he had little interest in helping aside from providing information. "You can just turn it off; it is just a machine." He hesitated as the buried science journalist in him emerged. "But things don't follow natural laws here, or at least our natural laws. If I believed in magic, I would say this place is magic. In case turning off the machine is more complicated, you will have to go to the Tomes, which has books with information on the Crystal Outlook and its Sentry."

"Great. We can do that when you're finished cleaning up." Jade chided, then smiled. "Is there anything I can do to help?"

Abraham looked at Jade wearily, set down his equipment, and plodded over to his traveling cloak, which hung on a wooden peg by his door. "Let's go."

CHAPTER 9
CHRISTIAN'S EUPHORIA

Christian led Jade through the village, which was desolate due to it being one of the village's several mealtimes, to a street called the Avenue of Heroes. The Avenue of Heroes was lined with statues of the culture's greatest champions, artists, explorers, and thinkers. The Tomes, the village's book depository and library, was located among the monuments.

Jade was disappointed when she realized she couldn't read the engravings on the statues.

"Our translation field must not extend to written language," she said as she squinted at the hieroglyphics on the monument's base.

"This one tells the tale of Allyope, whose paintings of sunsets were so magnificent she earned the nickname 'Sky-Stealer,'" Abraham read.

"That's so interesting. What does this one say?" Jade pointed to a statue that held links of sausages in one hand and a meat cleaver aloft in his other hand.

"That's Hosta. He invented 1,417 ways to cook boar meat."

Every few paces, Jade would find another statute fascinating, and she'd ask Abraham to read it for her. Abraham pulled a reluctant Jade from the statues and led her into the building called "Tomes," which looked like his tattoo shop from the outside, squat and cozy. The inside, though, was stuffed with as many bookshelves as could fit in the modest, one-story structure. The room had only one long desk, pressed up against the far wall, and enough space to move in between the shelves. Looking around, Jade didn't see any curator. The Tomes appeared to be open to the public.

"Your Tomes needs renovation," Jade noted. "Some extra rooms, at least."

"I've been saying that for years." Abraham knew what he was looking for and headed to a shelf to the slight right of the entrance. "Once I learned the language, I spent a lot of time in here. Learning as much as I could about the culture and history. It was fascinating, and I wanted to assimilate. Here we go."

Abraham held up a book, opened it, and began scanning through the pages with his finger, flipping through them until he found what he was looking for.

"I knew it. You *can* turn off the Crystal Outlook and put the Sentry to sleep. No one's done it because there's been no need to use the Sentry, and we don't go to that part of the forest anymore, so we haven't thought to do it."

Jade's opinion of the Sentry shifted. She imagined the creature alone and forgotten for decades. "How do we turn her off?"

"This." Abraham extracted a scrap of metal, shaped like a wonky puzzle piece, that was embedded in the book's thick pages. He held it up. "It's a key. You climb up to the Outlook's crystal orb and insert this key into a slot in the base. It should shut everything down."

"You'll go with me, right?" Jade asked. "You are the expert."

"I am not an expert. I know the people here and the culture, but the science of this place is a total mystery to me, still. Generations of engineering families used word of mouth to pass down the inner workings of the Crystal Outlook and similar devices. Most of the knowledge here is oral, or lost. The books in the Tomes are the *only* books. Since you have seen it and interacted with it, well, you know more about the Sentry than I do."

Jade stopped and gathered her thoughts before speaking. She was a weak salesperson and often failed at even the most rudimentary negotiations. She couldn't get doorbell evangelists to quit her front porch and often ended up agreeing to attend exotic church services just to get them to shove off.

Not for the first time that day, Jade longed for Anti's sharp tongue. She said, "You're right, I know more about the Outlook and the Sentry. I know that no matter how bad you think the creature is, it is worse."

"Well, now I'm definitely not going," Abraham chortled.

"Please let me finish."

Abraham nodded and gestured for her to go on.

"Antigone and I went through extensive training and risked our lives to come and rescue you. We had no comprehension of what we were walking into when we crossed over into this world. We didn't know so much time passed for you in this dimension. You don't have to come home with us, and I understand your reasoning, but you owe us some help."

"Of course." Abraham deflated. "I'm happy to help an old, old friend."

On their way out of town, a group of villagers carrying makeshift, stringed instruments ambushed Jade and Abraham.

"What's happening?" Jade whispered to Abraham.

"Hugs," he said.

"Who is your unknown companion?" a plump, smiling woman asked.

"A friend," Abraham said.

"From where? We have so few visitors."

"The West," Abraham said, uncertainly.

The small crowd babbled with impressed murmurs before advancing on Jade with outstretched arms.

"What do I do?" Jade asked Abraham.

"Hug them," he said, confused at Jade's question.

Jade agreed to half a dozen awkward hugs, after which one of the instrument bearers asked Jade if she'd like to hear a heroic saga, sung by the troupe.

"Yes, of course," Abraham said, but Jade gave him a sharp look, "but another time. We're just off to the woods. I'm walking my friend home."

This farewell triggered another round of hugs, after which Jade was ready for a long, solitary shower.

The troupe's song faded while Jade led Abraham to the forest entry point on the other side of Rupus's farm. While they walked, she stayed introspective, choosing to marvel at the brightly colored countryside, soaking in the strange plane. To Jade's relief, Rupus appeared to be away and did not rush at them with open arms and bowls of goat yogurt. Perhaps he was tucked away inside his farmhouse, enraptured by his marvelous hearth.

Once they passed the Rupus homestead, Jade felt comfortable enough to ask Abraham a personal question. "Why tattoos?"

"It is my gift to them." Abraham kicked an invisible rock out of the way. "About a year after I came to this place, I realized that there were all these artists, but no one had tattoos. They hadn't created tattoos yet. There's no equipment, so I used a method I saw on National Geographic once. I'm terrible at it—you saw my boat this morning—but they don't know that here. They gave me the title 'Most Celebrated Artist.' I'll have a statue on Hero's Avenue when I die. And, eventually, I'll pass down tattooing to someone who is actually a decent artist."

"The boat tattoo today was not that bad," Jade lied.

"Thank you. You have to understand why I don't want to leave. What's for me at home? No statues, no recognition, and mediocre food."

"Your family?" Jade suggested.

"My family is scattered across the entire country. None of them even live in Worbridge. They're all religious. Besides, what do you think they would say if I came home aged by thirty years? No one would understand my explanation. My family would just say it was God. Do you know what I like the most about this place? There's no God here. I spent my first twenty-seven years on Earth with God. He walked with me and judged my every move."

They had arrived at the ravine with the broken rope bridge, the one Jade flew across as a bluebird earlier. It now presented a problem, as Abraham could neither transform nor fly.

"Oh, I forgot about the bridge," Jade said, happy to change the subject. "Or lack of a bridge, I should say."

"You crossed this on your way to town?"

Jade nodded.

"Well, this will be slow going for me. I'm a sexagenarian." Abraham climbed down the steep edge of the ravine, taking measured, slight steps and steadying himself with branches from tree roots. In solidarity, Jade decided not to transform into a bird, and she climbed down the ravine after him instead. Since they also had to cross the creek, it was a muddy, sluggish crawl to the other side of the creek bed.

Jade and Abraham were a soggy mess by the time they got to the Crystal Outlook. When they saw it in the distance, Abraham quickened his pace, rushing toward the crystal sphere-topped stone structure.

"Gorgeous," he said. "It's a pity the townsfolk forgot about this place. I'll have to remind them."

"Hold on!" Jade called after him. "The Sentry thought Antigone and I were harpies because of our dark hair. It will think the same thing when it sees you."

"Harpies?" Abraham slowed. "How should we approach it then?"

"I think it's best if you try to access the controls with your key from outside while I distract it."

They were now close enough for Abraham to inspect the crumbling tower while Jade paced around the base of the Outlook.

"You seem like you'd be a better climber." Abraham grabbed an outcropping of the Outlook's decaying stones to test its stability.

"The monster knows me," Jade reasoned. "She will attack you immediately."

"Fine." Abraham patted the Outlook key in his pocket. "But, for the record, I was much better off before your attempted rescue. I was just about to have scones and tea. Then I was tattooing the image of someone's cat on a lady's thigh."

"Noted." Jade turned and headed through the open arch and into the Outlook. She found Anti with the Sentry, both inside Anti's prison cell. The Sentry was in her little girl form, and Anti was braiding her long, white hair.

Jade gaped at them, too stunned to speak.

"We're friends now," Anti explained. "As long as I don't leave before the Village Council gets here." Anti looked Jade up and down, observing her damp and disheveled state. "Serves you right for eating delicious yogurt without me. Yeah, I saw that." She added, "My sentence works well here."

"Yogurt? Your power is so selective that it's practically useless," Jade rubbed her temple.

"That was mean," Anti said. "You know I have power envy. And, speaking of that, what is with the tie-dyed poncho? It looks the 1960s threw up on you."

"It's what they all wear here," she said. She looked down at her distressed poncho and attempted to smooth it out. After a moment, Jade noticed that the Sentry was ignoring her. She spent a minute inspecting the Sentry before concluding.

"It thinks I'm a villager," Jade said. "I don't look like a harpy. I can just walk in and out." Jade demonstrated this by exiting and entering the prison doorway a few times.

"Good for you," Anti grumbled. "But I still look like a harpy, so I'm stuck. Hey, did you ever find Christian?"

There was a sudden, deafening rumble, and, in a quick burst, the Outlook transformed. The rusted bars turned to solid, clean metal. The stone walls looked as though someone set them in the last year.

Jade and Anti stood on a floor made of solid masonry, where there had only been dirt a second before. The Sentry herself changed. She was no longer a little girl, but a hearty-looking adult woman, although she still wore a flowing, white gown and the two plaits Anti wove in her hair.

"The Village Council must be here," the fully grown Sentry said with unabashed joy. "They are early!"

"What happened?" Anti asked.

"Abraham *is* here. He was turning it off." Jade heard moaning from outside. She ran out of the Outlook and found Abraham lying on the ground, cradling his ankle.

"I found the base and put in the key, but the building turned smooth. I lost my footing, and I slid down the side. I may have broken my leg."

Jade knelt next to him, examining his leg. "You didn't turn it off. The Sentry and the Outlook appear even stronger than before. And now, it will be much harder to climb up and put in the key."

Abraham looked at her sheepishly. "I'm sorry. I didn't realize it would go so wrong."

"Did you do this on purpose?" Jade dropped Abraham's leg, which she had been holding.

"Everything was happening too fast. I needed some time to think, and I didn't expect you to understand."

"I don't."

"I hadn't thought it through, obviously. I want to stay, but maybe I should go home. I miss other Earthlings; I miss shared history and experience. If you stayed a little longer here, you'd want to live here too. I was trying to buy time."

Before Jade could respond, the Sentry rounded the corner, expecting to find the Village Council and was disappointed. Finding Abraham instead, she screeched, "Another harpy!" She examined Abraham and added, "This one is wounded."

The Sentry picked up Abraham like a sack of annoying potatoes and carried him into the Outlook's prison. She set him down on one of the two cots that had recently appeared in Anti's cell.

"At least it's more comfortable in here now," Anti said from the other cot. "Hello Christian, you're looking old and weird."

"It's Abraham's fault that this place is more secure. He was supposed to turn it off, but he was trying to trap us here." Jade had followed the Sentry back into the Outlook. It appeared the Sentry either couldn't see her or didn't care about Jade as long as she appeared as a villager.

"You surprise me, Christian," Anti said. "I wouldn't suspect you capable of treachery. You never seemed that interesting."

"You know, I could have gone the rest of my life without hearing you take another swipe at me." Abraham adjusted himself on the cot, wincing at his attempt to ease the pain in his swelling leg.

The Sentry left the cell and closed the gate behind her. There was a whirl, and a click as the lock slid into place. Jade went to inspect the exterior of the tower. She figured there must be something to use to climb up the Crystal Outlook's control panel.

This left Abraham and Anti alone in their cell with the Sentry keeping guard. She stood in front of the entryway, blocking it while staring into the cell that held Anti and Abraham. This was even more disquieting than the last time the Sentry took this stance because, this time, she was looking at them with an adult's determination and capability.

Anti stood up and inspected the cell's renewed bars. "I didn't mean to take a swipe, Christian," she said to Abraham. "I thought it was a compliment."

"Why do you call me 'Christian?' You know my name."

"Because you work for a Christian Science Magazine, and it's funny."

"I don't think I'm religious anymore, but still, it's not funny."

"Maybe I used the wrong word." Anti stopped inspecting the bars and turned her full attention to Abraham. "I should have said 'ugly,' not 'funny.' Religion is ugly... Abraham. It is the oldest and meanest con. Religion absolves every person who believes of any shred of accountability for their actions. Your sins are always someone else's fault, either a sinner or the devil. They are never your own fault, and when you run out of people to blame, it turns into God's plan. God is the most dangerous kind of nonsense."

"I would tell you I changed my name to Christian here. It was the first thing I thought of when I didn't want to give my actual name, but now that I know where the name comes from, I'm having second thoughts. God is not dangerous nonsense."

"I thought 'no God' was the best part of being in this place. Or, at least that's what you told Jade half an hour ago."

"What? Did you two discuss my religious doubts while I was climbing the tower?"

"You're not that interesting, Abraham. And since you're now defending your god—you may thank me for solving your crisis of faith."

"How did you know about what I said to Jade?"

"Shh." Anti ignored his last statement. "Jade has an idea, and it might be an excellent one."

"How do you know *that?*"

"I said, 'shh.'" Anti glared at him, and the added, in a whisper, "I have sentience. It's a great multidimensional superpower… the greatest… better than Jade's."

True to Anti's prediction, Jade reentered the Outlook with a determined demeanor. She paced around next to the Sentry for a few seconds.

"I couldn't get up to the top of the Outlook. The stone is too smooth now," Jade explained. "I have an idea, though."

"Just make yourself big to reach it. Like Alice in Wonderland," Anti suggested. "You know, 'Eat me.'"

"I can only replicate organisms I've seen, and I've never seen myself big, so, no. My idea is to give the Sentry what she wants." Jade turned to the Sentry and said, "I am from the Village Council. Can I help you?"

The Sentry responded as if someone flipped a switch; her vacant stare lit up, and she appraised Jade. "Wonderful! We'll convene on the status of the harpy prisoners once the remaining seven Village Council members arrive," the Sentry said.

"She needs the other seven council members. Nice try, Jade," Anti said. "It looks like you'll have to change into a tentacle creature and battle her."

"What's she talking about?" Abraham peered around the Sentry to ask Jade.

"I'm sitting right next to you, Abraham, you can just ask me what I mean." Anti narrowed her eyes at Abraham.

Abraham declined to ask Anti any further questions for the time being. He slipped into a pensive silence. The Sentry resumed her vigil, and Jade slunk down onto a bench in the open cell.

"I can't take on the Sentry's monster form, it's too complex for me," Jade said after a few quiet minutes.

"You say 'I can't' a lot," Anti offered. "I have yet to see you try."

"I *am* trying." Jade's eyes flashed.

"I feel bad about all of this. I'm a mature, older man, and all of this has turned me back into a twenty-seven-year-old with a chip on my shoulder," Abraham said. Anti looked at his sudden intrusion into the conversation with frank curiosity. He continued, "I hope we can still be friends. Come sit next to me." Abraham sat up and patted the empty spot next to him on the cot.

"Chip on your shoulder?"

Abraham eyeballed her and continued to pat the cot next to him as if he were beckoning a stubborn cat.

Anti took the hint and sat down next to him while she kept her eyes on the Sentry, who was looking straight ahead as usual. It was difficult for Anti to tell if the Sentry was watching them or if she was in some off duty trance.

When Anti sat down, Abraham held her hand and pressed a small, puzzle piece-shaped object into it. He made a slight nod toward the locked prison cell gate. On the other side of the bars, Jade watched them closely.

"It's amazing that you're *opening up* like this to me, Abraham." Anti gave Jade a meaningful look.

The Sentry continued to ignore her prisoners' odd posturing. Truth be told, she was not great at her job, but, in her defense, she had no occasion to practice her craft.

"If we ever get out of here, please take me with you, even though I'm injured, and it will be difficult for me to walk. I will be slow to get up."

Jade moved from the other cell and stood just behind the Sentry.

"Abraham Christian," Anti patted his head with false levity, "you poor lost soul." Anti stood up and walked, at a measured pace, toward the cell gate, and looked into Jade's eyes. "You can," she said. "You have to."

When Anti was just a few feet from the lock, Jade shouted, "Now!"

Anti darted forward and slid the puzzle-shaped key into the cell's lock, then swung the gate open. Abraham jumped up and hauled himself over to the open cell door, as fast as he could—which was sluggish because of his advanced age and a broken leg.

The Sentry morphed into her tentacle beast form and reached for Anti, but Jade had already transformed herself into a matching monster. Monster Jade reached out one of her massive tentacles and used it to hold the beast back long enough for the others to escape, with Abraham leaning on Anti as she guided him out the door.

"What was that?" Abraham leaned against the outside of the Outlook, panting.

"It's just a thing she does," Anti told him. "How do we turn the tower off?"

"There's a control panel on the underside of the Crystal part of the Outlook. You slide the key in there, and then you can command the Outlook. The yellow switch reboots it, and the green switch turns it off," Abraham explained.

"How do I get up there?" Anti craned her neck up at the top of the tower. The newly restored outlook was made of smooth stone, and the crystal orb sat in the curve of a U-shaped structure at the top.

"According to my reading, there's a way to activate stairs on the inside of the structure. It's too complex to explain; I have to do it."

"I just hauled you out here," Anti panted in exasperation. "Now, we have to get you back in?"

"I thought it was more important we get away from the beasts."

"What's going on out there?" Jade, the monster, called to them. Her monster voice bubbled like she was gargling.

"Is there any way you ladies could battle out here?" Anti shouted. "Abraham just informed me that we have to get back inside."

Jade used her thick purple tentacles to pull the Sentry outside, and they continued their fight in front of the Outlook. Jade and the Sentry were an even match, and they received each blow or grab from a tentacle with replicated force, but Jade was tiring.

Once inside, Abraham hobbled to the far wall and touched eight bricks in a pattern that repeated three times. Anti wondered how he remembered the design but then realized out loud, "It's a song!"

"The opening bars to what you might call our National Anthem. A song called 'Euphoria.'"

A set of shallow steps appeared. They looked as if they had always been carved into the wall. Once Anti climbed them, she found herself at the top of the tower, looking up the through the round of the crystal sphere. The crystal's surface curved and distorted the tops of the trees.

As Abraham had promised, there was a control panel on the lip of the stone curve holding the orb. She slipped the puzzle key into the slot at the bottom of the board, but Anti forgot which color switch Abraham told her to press.

"Hurry," Jade yelled, "I can't do this for much longer."

Anti shook herself out of it and flipped the green switch. The commotion below ceased. Everything was still, and, as always, bright.

"I think you did it," Jade called. "I don't see it anywhere."

Anti took a moment to absorb the landscape, realizing she would never again be at the top of a crystalline tower overlooking the woodlands of a different dimension. She took a slow, deep breath, so quiet and so profound she tempted the emerald green trees themselves to sway in her direction. *I love this*, she thought. *I want more.*

Anti climbed down and met Abraham and Jade in front of the Outlook.

"Look." Jade held up her antimatter gun. "It just fell to the ground where the monster was standing."

"Your monster fight was the only incredible thing I got to see," Anti complained. "And I missed most of it dragging lame Abraham around. You saw the entire village and ate magic yogurt. I had to sit here, braid hair, and listen to the Sentry whine about how she never gets any prisoners."

"Well, now I guess it's your turn to do the whining. Besides, the yogurt wasn't magic," Jade clarified. "It was just good yogurt. Are we ready to go home?"

"I guess," Anti turned to Abraham. "Are you coming?"

"No. I have decided that my life *is* here. Sorry about trying to trap you here. I panicked."

He reached out to shake Anti's hand. He was relieved when she took his hand after a lengthy pause.

"Apology not accepted," Anti said. "It's Jade's apology to accept. I suffered none of the consequences. She turned into a monster for you."

"Forgive me," he said to Jade with a brief bow. Jade smiled and shook his hand.

Both women stood and watched him as he limped off toward the town.

CHAPTER 10
FUN... FOR SCIENCE

Jade and Anti made their way back to the swirling dimensional bridge. They were a little bruised, but no worse for the wear. The women stood in front of the portal, taking in the dimension for the last time.

"Too bad we have to go. I would have liked to explore this place," Anti said. "It is our job to observe and report. Weren't you the one who said something about journalistic duty?"

"I know. My eyes were just getting used to the light here," Jade replied. "I was starting to be able to see."

"Why don't you just form some sunglasses for your face?"

"Organics only."

"But you made clothes."

"They were cotton."

"That's ridiculous."

"I don't make the multidimensional flux rules; I just obey them."

They continued to stand in front of the dimensional bridge, neither woman making any moves to step through.

"The Center expected us to retrieve Abraham, and we since couldn't fulfill that obligation, we should attempt some journalistic accomplishments before we leave. For science."

"Are you suggesting we have fun, Jade?" Anti laughed. "I don't believe it. If we're staying, get me some of that yogurt."

"If I'm having fun, it's only for science," Jade reproached.

"Okay, whatever," Anti chuckled.

Jade led Anti back through the forest, past the now-defunct Crystal Outlook, and down the cracked and nearly non-existent brick road. It was on that road that they met Abraham, dragging his wounded leg. They helped him, with much griping from Anti, to get to Rupus's farm. Rupus patched up Abraham, and Anti got her yogurt, which she raved about. Rupus was much more satisfied with Anti's response to his food than Jade's.

In fact, all the villagers responded positively to Anti even though she dressed like an outlander. Anti's red hair made her an instant celebrity; the villagers had never seen or heard of anything so alien. Anti wanted to listen to every one of the troupe's songs, which captivated her, and she accepted every hug with grace.

Full of songs, hugs, and yogurt, Anti allowed Jade and Abraham to lead her to the Avenue of Heroes. "This is the best place," Jade explained.

Anti leaned in to look at a plaque on the base of a statue. "What does it say?"

"Adamort," Abraham read. "He was the first person to throw a discus."

Anti looked at Abraham quizzically. "They made a statue of the first person to throw a frisbee? I guess that's cool, but why is this the 'best place' here?"

"These are our equivalent of scientists and inventors," Abraham explained.

"This is what we would study if we had time to study this place," Jade added. "This and a place called the 'Tomes' where they keep all the books. That's on this street as well."

"Fine," Anti said, "We did my thing, let's do yours."

Anti waited while Abraham read the plaque on every statue, and Jade listened with rapt attention. Some figures were confusing and likely had something to do with the strange, magic-like science that seemed to govern this dazzling world. The women learned about Grandea, for example. She flew with wings made of ether, and Tel, who was taller than the tallest tree. His statue was of just his leg, as his whole figure would not fit on the Avenue.

They had only reached the Tomes, which Anti was looking forward to enormously, as books were her both her wheelhouse and her choice comfort when Jade realized they'd been in the dimension for at least fourteen hours, but there was no sign of a setting sun.

"The days here must behave differently," Jade determined. "More daylight just means more daylight. I'm not too worried."

"It's the two suns," Abraham clarified.

So, they spent a few more hours in the Tomes flipping through the pages, looking at fascinating pictures and listening to Abraham as he read strange passages, and sorting through odd objects stuck in the pages. Jade located the book that the Crystal Outlook's key came from and stuck it in a chunky page's puzzle-shaped space.

"What does it say about the Sentry?" Anti asked as she handed the book to Abraham.

"It says that there are dozens of Outlooks all the world. Not all of them are crystal; some are obsidian. Ancient people made them using forgotten magic. Hm."

"What?"

"It says that Outlooks are best left alone as the Sentries are irrational, protective, and hard to turn off."

"That's why you should always read the user's manual."

The suns did begin to set, about twenty hours after they'd first arrived, but they set so slowly that Jade and Anti made it all the way back to the dimensional bridge while there was still some light. Somehow, the world was still bright, even in twilight. Their journalistic curiosity satisfied; the women stepped through the dimensional bridge.

CHAPTER 11
MORE THAN ONE BITE OF VEGETABLE OMELET

Jade and Anti returned to a collider laboratory room identical to the one they left nearly twenty-four hours ago. Marshall still stood a few feet from the bridge in the collider opening, and Harriet was still at the front of the pack in the observation deck, her hands locked in the same thumbs-up she treated them to as Jade and Anti left the dimension.

"Virtually no time has passed here," Jade said to Anti.

"What happened?" Marshall asked. "You couldn't get through?"

Before either of them answered, Harriet's voice sounded over the intercom, "Is there a problem, ladies?" She was no longer in front of the observation deck and had hustled over to the communication pad.

"We were gone for almost an entire day in the other dimension!" Anti shouted, mimicking the loud intercom.

"The other dimension had flowing time. You discussed the possibility during training," Jade explained.

"Aside from the time difference, was the other dimension similar to ours in any way?" Harriet asked.

"No. Not at all," Anti said, shaking her head.

"Was it a city?" Harriet asked.

"No. There were woodlands and a primitive village."

Harriet released the intercom and paced in the observation box.

"Were you able to find Abraham?" Marshall asked.

"Yes, but he wouldn't come with us," Anti said. "He likes it there."

Marshall looked confused, but before he could ask any more questions, two technicians burst into the lab and swept Jade and Anti up and down with their handheld devices.

Harriet's voice came back on the intercom. "These engineers are checking your dimensional stability. Once you're deemed stable, we'll meet in the ready room for a debrief."

"No one's ever deemed me stable," Anti winked. Jade pursed her lips, signaling she did not appreciate the joke.

The staff indeed deemed Jade and Anti stable. It turned out, to no one's surprise, that the "ready room" was the same break room the Orion team seemed to use for everything. There was still an assortment of doughnuts out, but no coffee since no one had time to replace the destroyed coffee maker.

Harriet took notes and asked questions while Jade and Anti narrated their experiences on the other plane. Jade got the impression that Harriet was much more interested in the nature and the features of the different dimension than of the failure of their mission to retrieve Abraham. Although she supposed that she couldn't hold Harriet's interest against her.

Jade and Anti described the new dimension as beautiful and luminous, so the Orion staff named the plane Luster. Anti protested, however, as she wanted the world named for Rupus, or something related to his yogurt.

"At the very least, we should name it after the Sentry," Anti suggested. "She was a casualty of this whole thing. She may never get turned back on."

Harriet looked at Anti as if she had sprouted purple tentacles herself before dismissing the suggestion and continuing with the debriefing.

By the end of the interview, Jade and Anti were exhausted, considering that, to them, they'd been awake for an entire day. When Jade returned home that afternoon, she barely had the energy to greet her parents before collapsing on her bed.

The next day was Sunday. Jade told her parents she was not feeling up to attending church with the family and instead took the early morning empty nest as a time to recuperate from the previous day's adventure. When her parents and sister returned, Jade hid in her room with her laptop, cataloging everything she'd seen in the other dimension. She had a section of notes for plants, animals, people, culture, and "other." The Sentry and her Outlook fell under "other." Jade stayed engrossed in her cataloging until her mother called her for dinner. The evening meal was the first time Jade noticed that something was wrong with her family.

Her mother made vegetable omelets for dinner, as it was the family custom to have breakfast for dinner on Sunday evenings. For a few minutes, Jade ate happily, although all food would always pale compared to Rupus's orange candied yogurt. But then, she had the creeping feeling something was off. Jade looked around the table at the faces of each of her family members. Her mother had the same face as always, perpetually cheerful, but with solemn eyes. Her father was balding with a circle of curly, receded black hair that ringed his head like a reverse halo. He had a benevolent look to him, although he could grow hard and frightening when necessary. Thankfully, Mr. Hill rarely found it necessary.

When Jade's eyes fell on her sister, she realized why she was so unsettled. Amber was eating her omelet. She couldn't remember the last time she'd seen Amber eating at the dinner table, or eating anything anywhere, for that matter.

Jade almost dropped her fork in surprise, but she caught herself and put her fork down and studied her younger sister. Amber looked prettier than the last time that Jade had seen her—just a day ago. It took Jade a moment to realize it was because Amber put on some weight. She now had a youthfully plump layer of fat underneath her skin instead of her normal gaunt, stretched skin covered with copious amounts of makeup.

It didn't seem possible for Amber to have gained that much healthy weight in the past two days. Then, Jade noticed something far more disturbing than Amber's vegetable omelet eating; Amber did not have her heart pill at the table. The small, white pill sitting next to Amber's water glass, waiting for her to swallow it, was missing. Every night at dinner, Amber would force down one bite of food because she had chronic tachycardia and took her heart pill with food. But, for the first time in almost a decade, Amber was sitting at the dinner table without her medicine.

"Where is your pill?" Jade asked with visceral anxiety.

"Who are you talking to?" Amber smirked and took another bite of omelet. "What pill are you talking about?"

"You." Jade's voice rose. She studied her sister as if she were a volatile chemical mixture that may erupt. "The heart pill you take at dinner."

"I don't take heart pills." Amber's face flushed. "You're not good at jokes, Jade. I don't know why you even try them."

"Leave your sister alone," Jade's mother chimed in absently, with the air of a woman who has broken up three-thousand arguments between her daughters.

"I didn't mean it in a bad way." Jade realized that, with no way to explain herself, she ended the conversation there.

Jade finished her omelet and ran to her room, where she tried to calm herself. She took rapid, shallow breaths while she reasoned through what could be happening. Amber's tachycardia was as much a part of her sister's life as her acting career, her freckles, or—Jade thought with mounting dread—her refusal to eat more than a bite of dinner.

Amber hadn't been born with heart issues, nor was her tachycardia the result of an illness, at least not a physical illness. From the time she was in middle school, Amber always exercised too much and ate too little. Everyone in Jade's family tended toward leanness, so no one said much about Amber, aside from Jade's mother's occasional insistence that Amber "eat something, for God's sake."

In her sophomore year, Amber collapsed on the track field at school while preparing for a meet. The kindly family physician, Doctor Lavra, diagnosed her with anorexia. Jade had suspicions before the foggy and alarming family counseling session at the doctor's office, but she didn't want to frighten her parents or aggravate her sister. Their mother's lighthearted insistence that Amber eat turned to grim battles over nutrition shakes, dark battles that their mother had lost more often than she had won.

Jade had been in the library, working on an assignment for her community college's newspaper when she received a sober call from her mother. Since Amber was still a minor, Dr. Lavra gave Jade's mother Amber's medical results to pass on to Amber. The doctor told her mother that Amber's anorexia had weakened her heart. Amber would have to be on medication and monitoring for the rest of her life. Her sister would also have to give up being on the track team, which wiped out her chances for a college athletic scholarship.

"I haven't told your sister yet," Jade's mother said as she'd choked back tears. "We will talk to her together tonight when your father gets back."

"Why would you tell me before Amber or Dad?" Jade was positive everyone in the library was watching her on her phone as she tried to hold back her tears. They were not.

"I don't want to be the only one who knows," Jade's mother said. "And you can handle it," she added.

That afternoon, Jade returned from her classes and sat on the edge of Amber's bed, while Amber did her homework at her desk. Amber was oblivious to her condition. For all she knew, she was a typical sixteen-year-old working on an essay for Global Studies and prepping for a track meet that weekend.

"What's up?" Amber paused her homework and turned to her sister.

"Nothing," Jade tried to smile. "How are you feeling?"

"Fine, but I have a ton of stuff to do." Amber turned her back on Jade and continued to study.

"I'm just going to read a book in here, if that's okay," Jade thought up an excuse. "It has small print, and the light in here is so much better."

"Yeah, fine."

Jade sat next to Amber, holding *Ulysses* and pretending to read. Those were the last hours Amber would have as a disease-free teenager, at least as far as Amber knew. Soon, her sister's identity as a track star would vanish.

Jade wanted to hold that healthy version of Amber forever in her mind, even if it was only an illusion brought on by ignorance. She cried and did her best to hide her tears from her sister. For over an hour, Jade sat, crying while attempting to focus on the book. That was the last time she ever read *Ulysses*. She donated her copy of the book to a consignment shop later that month.

The memory of the day that Amber found out about her heart condition was clear in Jade's mind. The only way Amber could be free of the chronic disease would be if Amber were another person—or, Jade reasoned, another Amber.

While she at on her bed, mulling, Jade glanced at her bookshelf and saw her old copy of *Ulysses* displayed prominently.

CHAPTER 12
BOAT MURDERED

Anti's evenings were all similar. She had a routine established over the six years she had lived by herself in her cavernous apartment. Each evening began with changing into gym clothes as soon as she arrived home from work if she went to work; otherwise, she started the routine at five in the afternoon. She would download an episode of one of her current favorite television shows onto her tablet. Then she'd walk down three floors to her apartment building's gym, carrying a water bottle, headphones, and her tablet. She'd watch the freshly downloaded program while she pumped up and down on the elliptical.

It barely even felt like exercise. Anti didn't like it when work felt like work.

Anti would take a shower after her workout, and then she ordered takeout from one of five different restaurants unless it was Tuesday. She tried new takeout restaurants on Tuesdays, hoping to find a new place to add to her restaurant rotation. Anti would've liked to expand her list to eight whole takeout joints. She chose these five restaurants based not only on the quality of the cuisine but on the demeanor of the host and their willingness to chat.

If the weather was mild, she walked to pick up her food. Otherwise, she had it delivered. She read a book while she ate dinner, believing she was maximizing her enjoyment of both activities. Once a week, usually Sunday, she called either her mother or her father, on alternating Sundays. Other days, she read some more, wrote and researched for work, or watched a movie until she fell asleep.

She didn't choose this routine; instead, it chose her. If it was up to Anti, life would be all parties, group vacations to warm beaches, and drunken escapades with her band of attractive, witty best friends. But Anti had grown up a flower in the hothouse of her parent's academia. By some trick of luck, perhaps brought about by reading Burroughs' *Naked Lunch* at a wholly inappropriate young age, Anti's personality clashed with every person who came within shouting range. The tennis playdates her parents set up for her as a teen ended in tears for all parties involved. Her brief stint as a sorority sister was thwarted by a bowl of punch Anti spiked to near poison. After years, her loneliness had become a matter of habit.

The Sunday after Anti returned home from her adventure at the Orion Center, she put on a moisture-wicking tank top and yoga pants, and searched for a program to download. She planned on downloading *Boat Murdered,* a true-crime program about people who were murdered on boats. However, it was two seasons in, and the producers were running out of boat murders, so sometimes the crime just involved a ship at some point, or the occasional canoe.

Anti couldn't find the next episode of *Boat Murdered.* She searched online to see if the network canceled the show and couldn't find any proof *Boat Murdered* had ever existed. But, she knew it had, and she could state, by memory, about a half dozen of the boat murders and the circumstances of the aquatic crime.

Her research into the missing program took up almost her entire workout time, so she skipped it and called in her favorite kebab shop for dinner. Except the phone number didn't call a kebab shop. It was an authentic British pub staffed by expats from England. The hostess did not want to chat with Anti at all.

Later that evening, Anti sat on her sofa, eating unpalatably greasy fish and chips, making bets with herself about how long it would take Jade to realize that they were in the wrong world. Early the next morning, Anti awoke to a text from Jade. *Is anything strange going on with you?*

I think we returned to the wrong dimension, Anti typed back in response. She wanted to type more but waited to see what Jade had to say to her puzzling announcement. When Jade didn't respond, Anti called her.

The phone's ring jolted Jade, who had been staring at the words "wrong dimension" for the better part of five minutes. Her phone seldom rang, so it took her a few moments to orient herself to the noise.

"Antigone?"

"Yeah, some bizarre stuff," Anti launched into the conversation as soon as Jade answered. "*Boat Murdered* has vanished. I tried to stream it, and it was just gone. Not that it wasn't streaming anymore, but it never existed. All the other *Murdered* shows were still there. *Murdered by Love, Fire Murdered*—"

"Okay," Jade interrupted her, "There is also something way off in my house."

"What is it?" Anti asked. "You should look it up online. I looked up *Boat Murdered* online, and I'm not the only person who remembers the show existing, even though there's no record of it."

"I can't look up what happened to me online. My family members are the only people who would know about this," Jade told her. She took a deep breath. "My younger sister isn't sick anymore. She's had a serious health problem since high school, and it's just gone."

Anti was quiet for a few seconds. "Maybe that's not so bad," she said at last, "if she's better."

"But it means that my actual sister, the one with the heart condition, could be out there waiting for me to come home to some other dimension," Jade figured.

"Or, some other version of you might have come home to her."

"No matter what, we have to go back to the Orion Center and report what has happened," Jade concluded.

"I was hoping you wouldn't say that, but I knew you were," Anti griped. "Because of my sentience," she added.

CHAPTER 13
POTENTIAL SIDE EFFECTS

Anti was already waiting in the Orion Center parking lot when Jade arrived. She was leaning against her dark green hybrid, travel coffee cup in her hand, saddlebag slung over her shoulder, and sunglasses on. Jade checked her dashboard clock to make sure she wasn't late. She was not.

"You're not late. I'm antsy," Anti called to her as Jade shut her creaky car door. "This place is creepy to me now."

I agree, Jade said, but not out loud. She thought it.

"Did you just agree with me in your mind?" Anti asked.

Jade nodded.

"My powers getting better," Anti beamed. "Let me finish my green tea, and we'll head right over. Maybe they can stick us back in the right dimension. All of this is giving me an awful headache."

"Tea?" Jade eyed Anti's cup.

"Coffee makes me anxious." Anti took a sip of her tea for emphasis.

"Antigone," Jade gasped. "I think whatever it is might be wrong with you too. You drank a ton of Orion Center coffee last time we were here."

"No, I'm not alternate dimension Anti. I quit coffee today. I don't need any extra heart palpitations."

After Anti finished her tea, the two women found themselves once again ushered into the Orion Center's break room. Harriet met them, looking both as severe and as ridiculous as ever with her stern expression and mile-high hair.

Harriet listened to Jade and Anti's recounting of their experiences over the past few days. She did not seem surprised by the developments in the lives of the journalists. She nodded and spoke when they'd finished.

"Dimensional dislocation is nothing to worry about, really," Harriet said. She prepared to leave the break room and head back into Orion's depths. "It happens all the time."

Jade furrowed her brow, close to tears.

"We are worried though, really," Anti mimicked her affectation.

"We move in and out of other dimensions constantly," Harriet explained while pressing her fingers to her forehead as if she were explaining why the earth is round to a pair of seven-year-olds. "It's a fact of life. This happens either by crossing naturally occurring dimensional bridges or because we've walked through an area where the environment fused the two realities. Most of these dimensions are so close in makeup to our current dimension; we don't even notice the difference. And, to that end, our consciousness assimilates to the new reality before we see anything has changed. Occasionally, residuals from other worlds stick in our minds. I assume your knowledge is rooted in the dimension you left from when you first went to the dimension we're calling 'Luster' to retrieve Abraham. You may grow accustomed to your new plane of existence and come to forget the old one, or you may always notice when you naturally shift from one dimension to another. It is all potential side effects of interdimensional travel."

"You might have warned us of this side effect," Anti said.

"Why?" Harriet asked, indifferent to the answer.

"You don't find it disturbing that we're in another dimension?" Anti pressed.

"No. It happens all the time; you are just unaware of it occurring all around you. Like bees pollinating or cells regenerating."

"What cells?" Anti asked.

"Any cells. Now, I'm late for the start of an important experiment. Do you have more questions?" Harriet asked this in a way that let the women know there had better *not* be any more questions.

"I'll never see *Boat Murdered* again," Anti said as she and Jade made their way through Orion's labyrinthine passages back out the parking lot.

"That's all you got out of the conversation?"

"And that Harriet is a liar."

"Is this your extra-dimensional sentience? What do you think she's lying about?" Jade stopped walking so she could study Anti's face while she responded.

"I'm not sure. Nothing Harriet said is sitting right with me, and I don't know enough about quantum physics to figure it out. Do you?"

Jade thought for several seconds. "Maybe."

Anti ran her hands through her thick, red hair. "Let's go someplace and work through this. My place? Your place?"

Jade's mind filled with thoughts of her mother and father hovering while she entertained her guest at the kitchen table. Her mother offering homemade bread and her father, asking endless questions. Worse yet, Jade pictured trying to hold a discussion in her bedroom, with the only sitting surface being her bed, the conversation reminiscent of teen study sessions.

"Yours," she said.

•   •   •

Anti's neighborhood surprised Jade. The two women had identical jobs at similar science journals. On her own, Jade couldn't afford anything but a studio apartment in a hazardous part of the city. Her salary was one of the driving forces that led her to stay with her parents.

Anti's apartment was in the upscale Southern Tier neighborhood, full of parks, posh restaurants, and museums. The location of Anti's flat may have confused Jade, but the interior stunned her. Anti's apartment was large and airy with high ceilings and ample windows. The flooring was a vibrant hardwood covered with stylish throw rugs. Her furnishings were upscale and comfy. She had a wall-mounted flat-screen television, a desk covered with high-end electronics, surfaces decorated with eclectic art, and shelves teeming with books. When Jade asked to use the restroom, she noticed that the hall led to two bedrooms.

"Who lives here with you?" Jade asked when she returned from the bathroom, her hands still smelling like Anti's pricey lavender hand soap. Jade was hoping to get some explanation for Anti's lap of luxury life; perhaps she had a wealthy roommate tucked away in one room.

"Just me." Anti was sitting on massive sectional, scrolling through a website on her phone. "The other room is for guests."

Since Jade was too polite to ask how Anti could afford her trappings, the conversation moved on to Harriet and the Orion Center.

"I've been considering what Harriet said, and you're right. It isn't adding up with what I know about how the multidimensional travel works."

"See. I knew you'd figure it out. You're so much better at science than I am."

"I only paid attention during the Orion Center lectures when they were prepping us. "It's not a matter of who is 'better at science,' if you'd only focus, Anti."

Anti rolled her head back, "I didn't understand most of it. Not my forte."

"I'm not holding it against you, I'm trying to help." Jade sounded a little irritated.

Anti made a 'hurry' gesture at her. "Go on. Lecture me some more."

"Well, from what I understand, Einstein-Rosen Bridges occur in nature, but they should not be everywhere, at least not so much so you'd walk through them all the time without noticing, as Harriet suggested. Without more information, that's all I can say for sure."

"I figured you might say that, so I already came up with a plan." Anti scooted to the edge of her sofa and leaned toward Jade as if she were imparting classified information to a secret agent. Jade looked around to see who Anti might safeguard against. "You're going to have to shape-shift into Harriet, go into the Orion Center, and swipe her files, or her computer, or anything that might hold the information we need."

Anti reclined on her couch again, satisfied that she had delivered a foolproof plan.

"I don't know where Harriet's office is inside the Center," Jade reasoned, unimpressed by Anti's master plan. "The Center is a massive building, with a lot of underground halls and walkways."

"So," Anti thought for a moment, "shape-shift into Marshall, or a turn into a bug, or something. Follow her until you know where it is. Then, wait for her to leave, go in, and take whatever we need before she gets back."

"Why do all of your plans involve my doing something hazardous while you relax someplace safe?" Jade reproached.

"Because you got the better power," Anti rationalized. "Anyway, I won't be relaxing. I'll be nearby using my EDS to let you know if I see any trouble."

Jade folded her hands across her chest and said, "Fine." In a flash, Jade transformed herself into Harriet. She gave Anti a huge, fake smile and two thumbs up.

Anti howled with laughter. "You got her, but your hair still isn't big enough."

"Really?" Jade put her hands up and felt around the updo.

They decided that Jade would shape-shift into the technician Marshall to get into the Orion Center before locating Harriet and shifting into her. Jade practiced turning into Marshall a few times in front of the long mirror next to Anti's door.

"It works," Anti said. "Not as good as Harriet, though." She lowered her voice to indicate a scandal. "How does it feel to be a guy, with you know, all the trimmings?"

Jade, as Marshall looked confused for a moment and then said, "I didn't do that part."

"So, you're all original hardware down there? Why?"

"Because I don't have to." Jade was suddenly angry and embarrassed.

"Fine. Fine. It seems like you're missing out on some entertainment, though."

"We have different definitions of entertainment."

CHAPTER 14
HARRIET'S MORAL HAZARD

Marshall Thomas walked into the Orion Center for the second time that Tuesday. The security guards at the front desk might have noticed that Marshall hadn't left after the first time he'd entered, if they were the perceptive sort. The security guards were instead the sort who watched hilarious wedding fail videos on their cellphones, so they overlooked Marshall's second ingress.

Taking this as a sign of expert shape-shifting, Jade stopped at the receptionist's desk, sitting just past the security kiosk, and asked the receptionist where she could find Harriet, using her best version of Marshall's voice.

"Why?" The receptionist asked, not bothering to look up from his computer or stop typing.

Jade had not prepared herself for this question.

"I have to file a report with her?" Jade said, in more of a question than a statement.

"Where's the report?" He stopped typing and looked up at Jade, his bald head catching a spark of the sun filtered in through the entryway's skylight.

"What?" Jade's heart raced.

"Where's the report?" The receptionist's voice was warm and helpful, not meant to induce the panic Jade felt. "I'll give it to Harriet."

Jade's phone rang, and she nearly jumped out of her Marshall skin. She pawed through her bag, searching for her phone while monitoring the receptionist in case he realized she was a Marshall imposter. When she found it and answered it, Anti was on the other end.

"I see you're having some trouble with the guy at the front desk," she said.

Jade looked at the receptionist. "Yes," she told Anti, "I am."

"Act bothered by this call and then ask him where Harriet is again."

"I see." Jade picked up the ruse. "That is deeply troubling."

"Deeply troubling?" Anti echoed with a snicker. "That's what you say when you're bothered?"

Jade no longer had to pretend that the call annoyed her. She moved her phone away from her ear and looked pointedly at the receptionist. "Sorry, where did you say Harriet was?"

"In her office," he said. The phone diversion worked. "The one on lower level three; her private office, not the lab one."

Jade gave a curt nod of thanks and headed into the Orion Center, acting as if she had a clue where she was going. All she knew for sure was how to get to the break room and the elevators. She vaguely remembered how to get in and out of the lab where she'd been subject to the failed experiment and subsequent failed rescue attempt.

The halls of the Orion Center were labyrinthine, and the lower third floor was underground, with no windows, which made navigating even more difficult. Jade found Harriet by discreetly peering into the frosted glass windows of each office until she saw a silhouette resembling Harriet's sharp chin and a high bun. Then, Jade stood around the corner and waited for Harriet to leave her office. At about half an hour in, Jade wondered if Harriet would ever clear out.

With all the searching and waiting, Jade had been in the Center for over an hour, growing more anxious every minute. The wait and her nerves made it harder for her to hold Marshall's form. Jade noticed her skin color darkening, resembling Marshall's pale freckles less and her own skin tone more.

She was ready to abort the mission when Harriet stood and left her office. As soon as Harriet was out of view, Jade shifted into a Harriet lookalike and entered the woman's empty office. Jade reached up and touched the top of her Harriet's hair, just to make sure it was all there.

Harriet's office was a mess of potential clue sources, including a desktop computer, two laptops, a tablet, stacks of notebooks, and a filing cabinet filled with piles of paper instead of file folders. Jade's phone rang again, startling her and causing her to slam a file drawer closed.

"The marble notebook." Anti didn't even bother to with a greeting. "It's on the left side of her desk." Anti hung up before Jade responded.

As Anti had predicted, there was a marble composition notebook on the left-hand side of Harriet's desk. It was under a few manila folders and loose sheets of paper. Jade opened it and flipped through the pages. She knew immediately Anti was right—the notebook had the information that they needed.

Jade realized the scope of Anti's growing powers shouldn't surprise her, but it unsettled her, nonetheless. Having held the form for too long, Jade's red Harriet bun broke apart, and her own curly, black hair fell over her forehead as she inspected the notebook.

Jade took a moment to shift her hair back to Harriet's style, grabbed the notebook, and left—keeping herself as Harriet and figuring she could navigate through the Center as Harriet easier than she could move through it as Marshall. Once she was in her car, she shifted back to her own body and took several minutes to calm herself.

"This isn't me. I can't do this," Jade whispered to herself, almost in awe that this *was* her; she *was* doing it.

Harriet's notebook was a horrifying confessional. Jade read it but didn't finish. She realized the journal was something she wanted to read only once, and so she saved it to look over with Anti, in the comfort of her swanky apartment, accompanied by expensive brie and toasted crackers.

So, forty-five minutes later, Jade chewed nervously while Anti read aloud, punctuating the more alarming revelations with raised eyebrows and shaky breaths.

March 28th, 2019: Alternate Reality Number 322

This is at least the third time I have written an account of the following events. I am hopeful, but I doubt this will be the last time I have to make a record of what has happened to me. Follow these directions, and you might escape our grim fate.

Harriet, if you read this, believe it. You will not remember it. Believe it anyway. After you read it, you will put this notebook down and walk away. You will forget it all over again. Read this regularly to remember. You will forget why you keep this notebook with you. Keep it with you anyway.

This is happening to you because you are the victim of constant interdimensional transference. You are dimensionally unstable, Harriet. Every few days, sometimes every few hours, you shift into a new dimension, which causes you to lose the memory of your life in previous worlds. Therefore, you need to read and accept the contents of this notebook and update what you can remember as you move through times and realities. Documentation may be your only memory.

March 29th, 2019: Alternate Reality Number 306

What happened, at least what I can piece together of it from my limited memory and the accumulated contents of other journals, began about a year ago. A year ago, I was—we were, rather—happy and complete. Although perhaps I was so busy that I never took the time to realize or enjoy my happiness.

I was married to Frank, whom I miss dearly when I can remember him. Frank and I had three children: Adaline, Cora, and Cornelius. Through a mix of luck, schooling, and bringing myself to the brink of exhaustion, I became the research director for the Quark Collider Project at the Orion Center. This position and this place have been the only constant in my never-ending trip through the multiverse.

The Center was cautious in our early Quark Collider experiments. There was about a year between our initial attempts, and the first time we successfully created a synthetic black hole. We forged this hole within the depths of the machine. None of us could see it, being close enough to look at it was deemed too dangerous. Instead, we just sensed it with our tests and measurements. We realized we had not made a synthetic black hole, but an actual wormhole—an Einstein-Rosen Bridge to another world. As surprising as it was, the bridge was open for mere seconds and useless for anything aside from observation. Regardless, we made more of the wormholes—we are scientists, after all, and scientists replicate experiments.

Like a mother who knows she is pregnant, but only feels parental joy for the first time when she hears the baby's heartbeats on the Doppler, we knew the Einstein-Rosen Bridges were there; we had identified other worlds. Still, we didn't understand until we saw the readings on that first collision. The next step was bringing our creation from the Collider's womb into the world.

We began the work of making the bridges safer and more stable, as the news of our discovery spread. Industry wanted to use the bridges for transport, the military wanted us to develop weapons for them, and we just wanted a chance to glimpse into another world. To keep the grant and investment money coming, we harnessed some of the Collider's power. We developed equipment for our backers, items like antimatter cannons for the military, and instant translation devices for businesses.

Even with these other commodities, the bulk of our efforts went into answering our most elusive question—how can we make the Einstein-Rosen Bridges safer? The problem we had is the nature of the dimensions. It is the nature of a universe to expand. Left on its own, an Einstein-Rosen Bridge will grow to encompass the entire dimension, eating the old world and replacing it with whatever world was on the other side. This might happen in an instant, or it could grow slowly and take days or decades to encapsulate the old world.

Our Quark Collider kept the bridges from increasing beyond the machine's massive tubes, and we could destroy any fast-growing bridge within the pipes the moment it posed a risk. The downside was that we never interacted with the bridges, and the ability to create holes into another world became a useless novelty. In this alternate reality, the wormholes still are a harmless curiosity. I'll continue to document once I'm back in a reality where the wormholes have developed into the dangerous anomaly that separated me from my family.

June 1st, 2019: Alternate Reality Number 13

It has taken me over two months for me to drift back into a dimension where Elizabeth discovered a method to stabilize the bridges. She's able to take dangerous bridges and develop them into the type that takes years to devour a host dimension, as opposed to seconds. We could bring the bridges up to the surface of the Quark Collider; we could look at them, and then we could investigate them, eventually gaining the ability to pass objects through them.

There is a psychological trick Frank told me about once called a moral hazard. The idea is when you make something safe in one way, you may inadvertently ignore other related dangers. For example, the advent of seatbelts correlated to an increase in speeding, and some speculate that it led to an escalation in traffic-related deaths.

Elizabeth's bridge stabilizer led to a moral hazard—or, at the very least, a blind spot. Who knows how much havoc it caused until it did something so drastic I had to pay attention?

I first noticed the dimensional rifts when I came home from work, and my youngest child, my son Cornelius, no longer existed or had ever existed. My family, who assumed I was deranged, told me I only had two daughters, and I had never had a son. As unacceptable as losing Cornelius was, I had no choice but to move on. I assumed I had, perhaps, gone mad.

Then, one day, I came home, and there was just Frank. He told me we had had no children, only two Corgis named Cora and Corni. He had photo albums and social media profiles full of proof of our childless life. I knew I wasn't crazy, and there was only one thing I could think of that was powerful enough to erase an entire life.

I poured over the readings and data from the Quark Collider experiments, and I found our moral hazard. Every time we created an Einstein-Rosen Bridge, whether inside the collider or out, whenever it stabilized, we shifted our entire dimension into a new one. We hadn't noticed because we were so focused on the bridge that we ignored what we should have been looking at the entire time—everything but the bridge.

These dimensions were very close to own, almost imperceptibly so. Most people have not noticed the shifts, aside from people who have contact or are near an Einstein-Rosen Bridge stabilizer. I do not understand how many variations I have experienced, but I didn't realize it until Elizabeth created the stabilizer. When I realized the danger of the situation, I was faced with a choice.

I made the wrong one.

June 5th, 2019: Alternate Reality Number 341

After a brief trip into an advanced universe, I'm back in a dimension where the stabilizer does not yet exist. In fact, Elizabeth had already discovered the stabilizer in few worlds I've come across, so I've often had to help her along. To make matters more complicated, in the absence of a functional dimensional stabilizer, my consciousness assimilates to the new dimension. Luckily, I've noticed anomalies and can catch it before it happens. This is one purpose of this notebook. I rewrite it whenever I encounter a dimension where I have not written it yet, just in case I forget.

My first inclination was to shut the entire Quark Collider project down, but I realized if I shut it down, I'd be trapped in a dimension without my children. Increasingly, I find myself in a world bereft of the technology needed to create or stabilize the bridges. It's hard to qualify if I'm doing the right thing by *allowing, and sometimes aiding, the Orion Center's wormhole program when I find myself in a dimension bereft of the technology, or even the project.*

In the following pages, you will see what I can remember of the schematics for the collider and the stabilizer. There's enough information there that if you give the design to Elizabeth, she should be able to complete and carry on with the Quark Collider experiments.

Our situation is getting more and more desperate. I woke up a few days ago, and Frank was not in bed next to me. This all-encompassing hole in reality had wiped out my husband of seventeen years. According to my family, friends, and social profiles, I have always been a single woman with no children. I still have the two corgis, though.

Harriet, if you ever read this in a world where you have forgotten, please know your children and your husband are worth it. They were beautiful and amazing. They still are out there being beautiful and amazing, and you have to get back to them.

Anti finished reading the notebook passage, and the two women stared at each other, their faces blank with shock.

"Harriet has been traveling from universe to universe making reality-altering wormholes," Jade summarized, "on purpose."

"To find her family. I'd do the same thing," Anti added. "Anyone would."

"I wouldn't." Jade jumped up from Anti's sofa as if she electrified it. "She's putting the entire universe in jeopardy. Multiple universes."

"No, she's not. No one even notices unless they're from the Orion Center."

"I can't believe what I'm hearing. What Harriet is doing violates every scientific and moral precedent," Jade fumed.

"So, you'd just abandon your family?" Anti stood, upsetting the cheese plate on the coffee table.

"Her family isn't abandoned. They are fine living with their own versions of Harriet. She's the only one abandoned," Jade reasoned.

"You have a family. You don't understand," Anti hissed.

"You have a family too, Antigone. Who pays for this apartment?" Jade had a vague awareness that the argument was drifting away from the matter at hand but seemed unable to wrangle her words.

"Money doesn't equal love. My parents are divorced, and they don't like me." Anti seemed to shrink and contort. She stood with her hands balled into fists and her hair falling over her face in ragged strands. Jade had never seen her look so unlovely.

"Maybe if you weren't so hard to like." Jade regretted saying it before she even finished.

Anti sat back down and looked at her hands as if her purple, polished fingernails were incredibly exciting. "Yeah, maybe if I wasn't."

"I have to go." Jade snatched her purse from the chair and hustled out the door.

"There's more in the notebook," Anti said, but Jade had already left.

CHAPTER 15
A HARRIET-SHAPED HOLE

Anti flipped through the remaining pages of Harriet's notebook on her own. The technical aspects of the journal, which included schematics for a stabilizer and detailed drawings of an antimatter cannon, increasingly frustrated her. Following the technical drawings were two more journal entries, dated within the last few days.

January 5th, 2020: Alternate Reality Number 5

There has been a development in my current dimension. Two reporters observing a recent transport experiment have gained abilities related to being in proximity to the Quark Collider during a dimensional rift. Subject A has dimensional sentience, and Subject J can fluctuate her atoms at will. A third subject, Subject W, was from this dimension. His existence is only remembered by those in proximity to the stabilizer during the event. I believe he may have shifted into whatever universe we opened during the experiment.

As far as I know, this is the first dimension where the event surrounding these three journalists has occurred. Although there have been other incidents, these are the first circumstances that could prove beneficial to my mission.

The abilities of Subjects A and J and the disappearance of subject W seem providential. A's ability allows her to explore a dimension and return to her home through bridges invisible to everyone else. J's shifting ability will help her mimic any distinctive species or unique characteristics, should she cross into a dimension vastly divergent from our own. I can use W's disappearance can as a catalyst to propel the two into an adjacent dimension, and I can unwittingly enlist them in the search for my homeworld.

When she finished reading this passage, Anti's hand twitched toward her cellphone as she considered texting Jade to tell her about Harriet's further manipulations. But Anti was determined to find something salvageable about the woman on a quest to find her lost family; she didn't want to call Jade and tell her she'd been right about Harriet. Anti read on:

January 7th, 2019: Alternate Reality Number 326

J and A have returned from their own dimension; the realm the women traveled to was not remotely like our own world. Even worse, this dimension contained subject W, so there will be no further expeditions to search for him, which means I must create another guise to convince them to travel to additional dimensions. Since they have had contact with the stabilizer, they will notice any subsequent dimensional shifts. However, I should be able to use their dimensional volatility to convince them to pursue further exploration.

Harriet had stapled dozens of pages of Quark Collider data readout following this journal selection. It was again unintelligible to Anti.

"All right, fine. Harriet is awful. You were right," Anti said to no one, but she may have been practicing saying it to Jade, so the words would be ready the next time she saw her.

After several minutes of deep thought, Anti stood up and put on her long, tan peacoat. She left her apartment and drove straight to the Orion Center. She used the drive to ready herself for confrontation.

When she arrived in the Center's Lobby, Anti saw the same bald receptionist Jade had encountered just a few hours before. Then, Anti had seen him in her mind with her sentience. It was strange to see him in person, unaltered by her dimensional perception, which made everything look like a hazy dream.

"Where's Harriet?" Anti choked out at him before she was close enough for him to greet and welcome her to the Orion Center.

Ryan, the receptionist, was overloaded with work because the semiannual file audit was next week. He had less than forty-five minutes left in his shift, and he did not want the poisoned dish Anti was serving.

Ryan paused, his long fingers hovering over his keyboard, as he turned to Anti. "Can I help you?"

"Harriet." Anti gestured around the top of her head, alluding to Harriet's memorable updo. "You know."

"What are you doing?" Ryan looked alarmed.

"I have to talk to Harriet. The research director." Anti leaned forward over the edge of Ryan's high counter.

Ryan's hands subtly moved from his keyboard to the security call button stuck to the underside of his desk. "No one named Harriet works here," he said. "At least, not as long as I've been here. Five years."

Anti focused hard on Harriet's image in her mind, hoping to use her sentience to seek her out. The best Anti could feel was a Harriet-shaped hole in the dimension.

Anti wondered if Harriet might have taken the dimensional shift problem with her when she disappeared. However, she could not be sure, since she was far from an expert in multidimensional physics.

She supposed that Jade would want her original sister back. Although, after their last interaction, perhaps not. Anti decided to shoulder on selflessly, even though Jade didn't want to be her friend. They didn't have to be friends to stabilize the multiverse together.

Anti spent the rest of the evening scheming and shuffling all the pieces of her grand plan into place. Late that night, Anti called Jade with the good news that she had convinced the one person who had any hope of helping them set the dimension right.

"Doctor Osborne?" Jade looked at her phone incredulously, forgetting Anti couldn't see her reaction. "The Internet Psychic?"

CHAPTER 16
WET PAPER AND PEOPLE FOOD

Jade drove to Anti's suite the next day. The previous afternoon she had spent several hours wallowing in an odd mix of despair and guilt over her confrontation with Anti. Jade was not a "people" person, so Jade did not understand Anti's need for approval. It would make everything so much easier if she were ambivalent toward other people's opinions. It would suit her personality.

Still, Anti cared, and Jade had hurt her. Jade had been stewing in the bedroom, trying to figure out an excuse for calling Anti so they could continue their investigation when Anti called to tell her that Harriet had vacated their current dimension.

"I know you're not my friend," Anti had said, "but we're in this together, and we have to see it, though."

"I didn't mean it like that. I was just shocked about Harriet—" Jade started, but Anti cut her off.

"I think I know who can help us," Anti said, ignoring Jade's attempt at an apology.

That's when Anti mentioned Dr. Osborne, a psychic famous for his internet videos wherein he probed various phenomena, including mansion hauntings, yeti sightings, and parallel universes. Anti had somehow finagled an appointment with Dr. Osborne for the following afternoon.

After an evening dinner, during which she wrung her hands while her sister heartily ate spinach quiche, Jade spent a restless night in a state of half-sleep. Then she sped over to Anti's apartment the next morning, hoping to convince her to call off her session with the paranormal investigator.

"Before you say anything," Anti greeted her at the door, clutching Harriet's notebook, "there's more." She handed Jade the notebook. "I didn't want to explain on the phone."

While Jade read the two additional entries and flipped through the device schematics, Anti continued to talk, which made it hard for Jade to concentrate on reading. Still, it was a little too soon after their last altercation for Jade to feel comfortable telling Anti to zip it.

"So, when I found out Harriet was gone, I thought, 'problem solved.' Hopefully, she landed in a dimension with her husband and kids. I figured you could shift into Bill Gates and drain his bank account. We could split the money and spend the rest of our days in Thailand."

Jade scowled.

"Not together, since you hate me. You can be on one side of Thailand, and I'll stay on the other."

There was so much wrong with Anti's statements that Jade was unsure of where to start, so she said, "Thailand is politically unstable."

"Is it? Anyway, I realized our problem is ongoing. *Boat Murdered* is still gone, Harriet's notebook is still here, my stabilizer is still here, and so is this thing." Anti pointed to the antimatter gun sitting next to a vase of fake sunflowers on the side table next to her door.

"Harriet made all this. So why is it still here when she isn't?"

"The dimension is probably unstable. Perhaps the Orion Center is still conducting the wormhole experiments without Harriet. It's a good thing. If we slipped into a dimension without these things, it might trap us," Jade concluded.

"Right. I'm having a hard time getting a grasp on this. I figured we could use some outside input, considering no one at the Orion Center would understand now that Harriet has vanished."

"You know Doctor Osborne doesn't talk to ghosts and travel to other dimensions, right? It's for his show, Antigone." Jade knew Anti was a little touched, but until now, she figured she at least had a few peaches in her cobbler.

"He's a world-renowned quantum physicist, Jade. Until the internet show, he lectured at the same college my dad works for, Pinewood."

Jade gave a tiny, involuntary gasp. The University of Pinewood was prestigious, practically Ivy League. She was simultaneously shocked that the University was Anti's father's place of employment and that the quack Dr. Osborne had lectured there.

"Oh, pack it in," Anti said when she saw the astonishment on Jade's face. "I sent the doctor pictures of the machines in Harriet's notebook and gave him the highlights of our recent escapades. He said the soonest he could meet was around lunchtime today."

"Your father is a Pinewood lecturer?" Jade overcame her awe.

"Yeah, Greek Literature. That's where I went to school. I feel like I told you that before." Anti was typing on her phone and didn't look up. "No one listens to me."

"*You* went to Pinewood?"

"You don't have to say it like that. I got in on a family scholarship and almost flunked out." Anti held up her phone and waved it. "I've just ordered lunch for Gustavo and us; how do you feel about chicken shawarma?"

"Gustavo?" Jade felt unmoored. If Anti attended and graduated from the University of Pinewood, then anything was possible.

"It's his first name. It's Gustavo. You can't say 'Gus,' okay?"

Dr. Gustavo Osborne arrived before the chicken shawarma delivery, dressed to the nines in a three-piece, dark blue suit. He was a short man with a full head of wavy, salt and pepper hair, a matching mustache, and a kind face. Dr. Osborne had a graphing paper notebook in one hand, and underneath the other arm, was a chubby, grinning, bright white Maltese.

"This is Eliot," Dr. Osborne said, setting the small, white dog on the ground after he had greeted Jade and Anti. Eliot was as fastidiously groomed as Dr. Osborne; he looked like a snowball with eyes.

"Hello, Eliot." Anti knelt to pet by Eliot while Jade wondered if Dr. Osborne was planning on explaining why he'd brought his dog to a serious meeting.

"Well, you girls are in a pickle." Dr. Osborne settled himself in one of Anti's paisley chairs. He spoke in the same deep and gravelly voice he used to add weight to his internet videos.

Anti settled on the sofa. Jade remained standing. She kept her arms folded and held a rigid stance while Eliot frantically licked her ankles.

"I'm not sure you can help us," Jade said.

"Well, I saw some cellphone photographs of the illustrations in the notebook. Anti told me what you two girls went through at the Orion Center. I have a theory."

"Women," Jade interjected.

Dr. Osborne didn't quite understand. "I'm sorry?"

"Antigone and I are women," Jade corrected him. "I'm twenty-seven years old. I'm not a girl."

Anti chuckled. "She has a point."

Dr. Osborne cleared his throat. "Right. I'd like a look at the notebook in question, just the same."

Anti handed over Harriet's notebook while Jade sat in Anti's other chair. To her horror, Eliot jumped on to Jade's lap, turned twice, and settled down.

"Looks like you've made a friend there." Dr. Osborne looked up from the notebook and raised an eyebrow.

The four sat in silence for a while, though Anti's apartment intercom announcing the chicken shawarma delivery interrupted them. The sudden noise caused Eliot to rocket out of Jade's lap and run around the living room, madly barking with excitement. He was even more excited once they opened the Styrofoam takeout containers. He bounced from person to person, like a gigantic tennis ball, soliciting bits of chicken and pieces of pita.

"Eliot only eats people food," Dr. Osborne explained.

After several more minutes of eating and Eliot feeding, Dr. Osborne set Harriet's notebook down on Anti's coffee table with a dramatic flourish. "I have some good news and some unfortunate news for you, ladies."

"Yeah," Anti encouraged through a mouth full of hummus.

Dr. Osborne tore three tiny pieces of paper from a blank sheet of Harriet's notebook and set them in the center of Anti's coffee table. He grabbed his cup of takeout ice water, wrenched off the top, and poured it onto the table. The flowing water swiftly swept away the paper bits and left them in a puddle on the floor.

Anti grabbed her magazine from the table, narrowly saving it from the spreading water. "It's the latest issue of *Cuisine and Cocktail.* I haven't read it yet," she said. "What was that for, anyway?"

"You two, and Harriet, are the pieces of paper," the Doctor explained. "The water spill is the anomaly at the Orion Center; the table is your original universe. Your original universe is fine, but you have been swept away. As long as you're caught in the wormhole's wake, the dimensional shifts you have experienced will continue to happen at a more rapid rate. You will experience shifts to stranger and more foreign dimensions, just like the water carried the paper farther and farther away from the original spot of the spill. You will get carried away to a point where the very fabric of the multiverse is weakened and…" Dr. Osborne made a falling off the table gesture.

"We'll die?" Anti clutched her copy of *Cuisine & Cocktail* to her chest.

"I wouldn't say *die*. More like transformed into unrecognizable dimensional debris." Dr. Osborne fished the paper fragments from the puddle on the floor. They were now wet gobs resembling spitballs.

"What's the good news?" Jade scowled at the spitballs.

"Well, I'm here to help you, for one." Dr. Osborne grinned. Jade turned her scowl full force toward him. "And, secondly, Harriet is wrong. The wormhole isn't the dimensional spill; Harriet is the spill. Her trip through the multiverse is causing the shifts. Get her back to her original dimension, and it will clean up the spill as if it never happened. Well, except for you two." He glanced at the paper wads. "You'll be left with the multidimensional effects."

"I don't want to be wet paper," Anti lamented.

"Technically, we already are wet paper," Jade said. "If he's correct, the abilities we gained from the first Orion Center experiment are irreversible."

"I have more good news," Dr. Osborne added. "I will investigate your story for my show. We might even make it into a two-part episode."

Jade said, "I'd rather not."

Anti looked elated. "What's the plan?" She asked.

"You two… *women*… will need to follow Harriet into whatever dimension she has flowed into. Use the same plan Harriet laid out in her notebook, except, instead of finding Harriet's home dimension, you'll find her. Antigone, you'll use your senses to find Harriet's dimensional bridge. Jade, you can change forms as needed to locate Harriet. Once you find Harriet, Antigone will use her sense to pinpoint Harriet's original dimension and bring her back there."

"That's lovely, Gustavo," Anti said. "But, you have overestimated my abilities."

"You'll just have to get better." Dr. Osborne stood up and tore Elliot from Jade's lap. "He loves you," Dr. Osborne laughed. To Anti, he said, "Practice your sentience tonight, and I'll be over in the morning with a camera crew."

"I didn't agree to anything," Jade pointed out. Both Anti and Dr. Osborne ignored her.

After the doctor left, the women spent several hours poring over Harriet's notebooks and investigating with their leftover Orion Center artifacts, Antigone's translator and stabilizer, and Jade's antimatter mini cannon. Then Anti tried to use her sentience to find Harriet while Jade practiced shifting into a variety of shapes, including Eliot, to Anti's delight.

Around seven, Jade's phone rang incessantly with calls and texts. It was her mother, concerned that Jade had not come home in time for dinner.

"Tell your mom you're spending the night here," Anti called to Jade, who was talking on the phone with her frantic mother. At the mention of "dinner," Anti had retreated to the kitchen to throw together a quick chicken Caesar salad. "I just cleaned the sheets on the guest bed," Anti shouted to Jade.

This was only partially true—Anti's guest sheets were clean, but because no one had ever slept on them, not because she'd just cleaned them. Jade agreed to stay the night, though she had to put up with half a dozen suspicious questions from her mother. However, Jade was not spending the night so they could hone their skills; she refused to be a part of Dr. Osborne's show. Her plan was to find the dimension Harriet had traveled to that night and leave early in the morning before the doctor—and his camera—arrived the next morning.

"That sounds like a monumental amount of work," Anti said over her wilted Caesar salad. "I don't even know how to find Harriet. We don't have the Orion Center to help us, all we have is your antimatter cannon and my stabilizer. What if the bridge to her current dimension is a thousand miles away?"

"It's the same amount of work as it would be if Dr. Osborne were here, but with fewer dogs and video streaming. And Harriet's dimensional bridge will be close to here because she is discordant with the dimension; she caused the bridge to open before she went through it. We just go through it after her, get her, bring her back to this dimension, find the bridge to where she belongs—"

"And shove her back through it," Anti finished. "I'll be right back." Anti disappeared down her offensively long hallway and reappeared holding a pair of yellow pajamas, a tee-shirt, and pants covered in miniature unicorns and rainbows.

"Here, have some spare jammies." Anti handed them to Jade, who took them as gingerly as she would a grenade.

"We should get started tonight," Jade said.

"No. Who knows how long this will take. We need to sleep before we do anything."

"But Doctor Osborne—"

"Will be here around breakfast. We'll get an early start."

Jade changed into pajamas and found that they were garish but surprisingly comfortable. When she returned to the living room, she saw that Anti had also changed into pajamas, although hers were black patterned with blood-red roses.

Jade sat down next to Anti on the sofa and asked, "Have you tried focusing your sentience on Harriet? Can you see where she is?"

"I said I'd start in the morning. We need a break. Do you want to watch a movie or something?" Anti picked up the remote and searched through the cable menu. "*Encino Man* is on. I love Pauly Shore."

"No," Jade stood up. "If we're going to just rest, I'd rather go to bed."

Anti deflated. "Why do you hate me?" She asked in a small voice. "You yell at me, say I'm hard to like, you won't watch a movie with me, and you wrote a mean critique about my menstrual cup article."

"Fine, I'll see the movie." Jade flopped back down on the sofa and rubbed her forehead with her hand as if she were soothing a headache and trying to shield her eyes from Pauly Shore.

Anti did not watch the movie. Instead, she glared at Jade until she forced Jade to respond.

Finally, Jade said, "We're about to search through the multiverse for a rogue researcher, because we will be turned into multidimensional debris if we don't find her, and you're worried because I challenged one of your articles. Is that correct?"

"Yes," Anti said. "That sums it up. I don't want to do this with someone who hates me. It would be easier if I understood why you do."

Jade sighed and straightened up. "I don't hate you. This," Jade motioned up and down her body, which was accidentally comical because of the unicorn pajamas, "is my default. You are uncomfortable for me to be around because, not only do you speak nonstop, you somehow involve me in whatever nonsense you're blabbing about. As far as the article, I was disinclined to tell you in person because it is easier for me to write out a rebuttal than it is for me to speak to someone in person."

Anti thought through the tirade, which was more than she'd ever heard Jade say at one time. "You don't like me because you're shy?"

"Yes." Jade sagged on the sofa, relieved to be understood at last. "I'm shy."

"That makes sense." Anti nodded. "We can work on that. We'll get you used to talking to strangers and do some public speaking aversion therapy."

"Absolutely not." A floodgate had opened in Jade, and she found herself unable to stop talking. "Toward the end of my Bachelor's degree program, it became apparent I would likely be the Valedictorian of my class. The thought of having to give a speech frightened me so badly I purposely got a 'C' on my final paper in my Public Relations class. Valedictorian went to someone else, but at least I didn't have to give the speech. That's how bad it is."

"I'm sorry, Jade. If it makes you feel any better, I got a ton of Cs, and none of them were on purpose."

"That does not make me feel better."

"Well, if you want to work on it, I'm here. I'm fantastic at self-improvement, especially other people's self-improvement." Anti smiled encouragingly.

"I think the Orion adventure is helping. I was genuinely amazed by myself in the last dimension we went to, because of all the strangers I talked to without feeling too afraid to speak. Then I realized it was because I wasn't myself. I wasn't Jade, I shifted my form and changed my hair and clothes. I feel like being a different person is the only way that I can be confident."

Anti put her hand on Jade's knee. "That's just sad and untrue. Let's go to bed, we have a Harriet to hunt tomorrow."

CHAPTER 17
ASH AND STONE

Anti woke up the next morning to delightful cooking smells coming from her kitchen. Jade was cooking breakfast burritos; she had already sautéed peppers, onions, and mushrooms, and she was just finishing up scrambled eggs with cheese.

"Jade, this looks and smells amazing," Anti beamed. "Where did you get all of this food? Did you go shopping at six a.m.?"

"Yes." Jade placed an overfilled burrito in front of Anti. "We have a big day. We'll need nourishment."

"Okay. I would have just gone to a café on the way, but thanks." Anti picked up her burrito and took a big bite. Cheese and egg dribbled down her chin. "I mean it."

"Don't mention it. Have you found Harriet yet?" Jade sat down opposite to her at the kitchen table and ate her burrito with a knife and fork.

"Yes. I can see Harriet, and I think I've even found a bridge to where she is, but I'm getting some nasty vibes about the place. I'll bring my lucky pomegranate."

"I'm sorry, I thought you said, 'lucky pomegranate.'"

"I did."

"The fruit? You're bringing fruit?" Jade paused mid-bite.

"Nope, it's a necklace." Anti pulled a chain out of her pocket. At the end of it was a pomegranate made from cut, red crystal and set in silver.

"Why?"

"Pomegranates are lucky, my dad gave this necklace to me, and the next day I found eight dollars in a garbage can."

"Did you have to reach into the garbage can? You know what, don't tell me."

"Another time when I was wearing it, I got pulled over for ignoring a stop sign and the cop just let me go with a $100 fine."

"So, that's about minus ninety-two dollars' worth of luck," Jade figured.

"I'm wearing the pomegranate," Anti said. "You can't stop me."

Half an hour later, shortly after dawn, Anti navigated while Jade drove her well-kept, late model sedan into the dusty, industrial area of the city. According to Anti, this area held the bridge to Harriet's current dimension.

"Okay, park here," Anti said as she directed Jade to park in a row of diagonal spaces in front of a drab, concrete warehouse.

The women met around the back of Jade's car. Anti was wearing her pomegranate necklace and carrying a blue and white striped folding umbrella, even though the skies that day were clear. Her dimensional stabilizer bulged in the front pocket of her designer messenger bag, which cost about a month of Jade's wages.

"What is the umbrella for?" Jade had asked her earlier when they were getting in the car.

"I can just tell you we will need it." Anti tapped her temple. "It's my sentience. I only have one umbrella, so we'll have to share." Anti stowed it in her bag.

Anti walked about twenty paces from the car, her shoes crunching on the loose gravel from a parking lot that was last paved around the turn of the millennia. She approached the chain-link fence surrounding the warehouse and pointed to a spot about a hundred yards in front of the wall.

"The dimensional rift is there," she said. "It looks like a pile of shifting ash."

Jade couldn't see a thing, but she was ready to give a sigh of relief at the fact that they wouldn't be hopping any fences that morning when the sound of an approaching car startled her.

It was a dark gray Tesla, small and slick. Jade knew immediately who was behind the wheel. The driver parked next to Jade's rust bucket, making it look even more shoddy in comparison. The door opened, and a little puff of white fur popped out and trotted over to Jade.

She instinctively reached down to pet Eliot, even though she was unhappy to see him.

"Starting without us, ladies?" Dr. Osborne approached them carrying an expensive handheld camera. "It's a good thing we saw you leaving this morning and followed your car." He beamed. "Or else we may have missed your dimensional shift."

"Jade doesn't enjoy being on camera, Gustavo," Anti explained.

Dr. Osborne turned himself and his camera toward Jade. "I must record this in the name of science. You of all people should understand that," he said.

"More like in the name of view counts." Jade turned from the camera.

"We'll cut that part," Dr. Osborne said.

Jade, determined to get this over with as fast as possible, said, "Antigone, where is it? Right here?" Jade lurched forward and felt in the space in front of her.

"Let me stabilize it." Taking Jade's cue, Anti pulled the stabilizer from her pocket.

"Can you please explain what you're doing?" Dr. Osborne called. "The audience deserves an explanation."

"I'm stabilizing the dimensional portal so we can get in and out of it." Anti waved her arms more dramatically than was necessary as she circled the bridge with the device.

An outside observer would see a warehouse parking lot empty, aside from a man in suit recording two women, one of whom was thrashing around in the air as if fighting invisible demons as a tiny dog ran from person to person, desperate to be part of whatever was happening. Thankfully, there were no outside observers that morning.

A gray portal appeared about five feet to the left of where Anti flailed around. To, Anti it looked like an upright pool of water swirled with dust and sparkles. Once it was stabilized, Jade stepped through it without hesitation. Anti turned to Dr. Osborne, smiled, waved, and followed Jade through. Eliot barked and tried to follow, but Dr. Osborne scooped him up with his free arm.

On the other side of the bridge, the women stood on a barren, rocky crag. They were close to the edge of a cliff, and Anti had to pull Jade away from the drop-off. An ominous feeling overcame the two women, but it was hard to say of it was due to the dimension or the fact that they were perched on a mountain ledge. The air was crisp and dry, and an occasional harsh wind swept through, howling and making them shiver.

Anti stabilized this side of the portal. "I'll turn the translator function on before we meet anyone. We'll be able to understand everyone almost right away this time, I hope."

On another mountain ledge, about a mile away, a large city loomed. The city covered every spare inch of the plateau, with some buildings built on jagged scaffolding overhanging the bluffs. There was a twin city on another plateau below them, and in the distance, they saw similar cities built into other mountainsides. The towns and the mountains were all ringed with thick, dreary mists, and there seemed to be no foliage, aside from an occasional, struggling pine tree, attempting to grow at an angle in the rocky soil.

"Which city is Harriet in?" Jade asked once she had gotten her bearings.

Anti cheerlessly pointed to the city on the ledge above them.

"How do we get up there?" Jade wondered out loud.

"The stairs." Anti walked around a nearby boulder and revealed a shallow staircase carved into the side of the mountain. She looked up and down and cringed. "I wish I hadn't been skipping step aerobics."

There was no rail or wall. Time and wind had worn the steeps smooth, so the footing was precarious, and the climb was slow. When they were halfway up their rise to the city, Anti paused, removed the umbrella from her messenger bag, and opened it. The bright blue and white umbrella contrasted with the bleak surroundings.

"You'll want to get under this," Anti said.

Before Jade could ask why, snow fell from the clouded sky. But, Jade realized, it was too warm to snow. Upon closer inspection, she realized that she was not looking at snow. She reached her hand out from under the umbrella to touch one of the white flakes.

"Don't," Anti said, but it was too late.

The flake landed on the back of Jade's hand and burned it. Jade recoiled her hand in pain and shock.

"I said, 'don't.' Were you hoping to write up another peer-reviewed rebuttal about why I'm always wrong?" Anti sniped.

"Ash," Jade said. "It's raining hot ash."

"Yeah," Anti replied, holding tight to her umbrella. "This place is about as much fun as your peer-reviewed rebuttals. Let's get to the city up there. They should have cover from the falling ash."

Climbing the stairs was even slower with the umbrella open. With nothing to brace against, the women swayed back and forth and couldn't stay under the umbrella, so they dealt with the occasional flake landing on their arms or faces.

At first, the stings were a painful nuisance, but they realized that the ash stings added up and would turn into actual burns if enough landed on their bare skin.

Jade did her best to focus on avoiding slipping or being burned, but a nagging question broke her concentration."Harriet's journal said that she was moving through dimensions like our own, but this one is dissimilar, how did she end up here?"

"Maybe it's like Doctor Osborne said. The multiverse is pushing us farther and farther away from the familiar."

Jade and Anti reached the top of the staircase, and, with great relief, they saw a stone awning erected to shield the entry to the city from the falling ash. Their respite was short-lived, however. A group of three armed guards stood under the awning, blocking the entrance to the city.

Two of the guards approached the women, and the other held his place under the canopy. One of the approaching guards had curly, blond hair, and the other was bald, aside from some black stubble around the base of his neck.

"What's going on here?" the blond guard grumbled.

"Just out for a morning stroll through the acid flakes, sir."

"Sergeant," the blond guard corrected Anti, "Sergeant Phim."

"If that's all, Phim, we'll be on our way."

"I doubt that. We have several violations. Your clothing is inappropriate. I don't know what this item is," Phim gestured to the umbrella, "but we do not allow it. And, I will need to see your permit to climb the stairs."

"We don't have a permit to climb the stairs," Anti said, closing the umbrella since they were safely under the awning. "I lost it. I had it out and ready to show you, and then there was a sudden gust of wind, and it just fluttered away down the mountain." Anti used her hands to show both the wind and the fluttering.

"You are under arrest," the bald guard said.

"I've never been arrested," Jade said.

"Me either, Jade. You said that like you assumed that *I* have been arrested before," Anti accused before Phim shushed her.

The guards stood behind Jade and Anti and used their long rifles to nudge the women into the city. Once inside the gates, Jade understood why the guards deemed their clothes improper. All the citizens were wearing thick leather garments banded with metal plates, and leather caps or metal helmets with similar banding.

"Which court should we bring them to?" Phim asked.

"Well, we could bring them to the Vesture Court for the clothes or the Contrivance Court for their contraband. Then there's the Permit Court..." the bald guard trailed off. "Let's take them to the Aggregate Court; that will take care of everything."

As the guards led them through the city, Jade noticed an abundance of courthouses with wide, steep steps and imposing domes. The guards led Jade and Anti up a set of stone steps and forced them through a massive marble archway into a richly appointed courtroom.

The bald guard went to speak to a clerk. Phim gestured for the women to sit down on a black bench carved from a single piece of obsidian. While the guards talked, Jade and Anti watched the current court case unfolded.

The judge was an older woman with long, white curls. Instead of a judge's bench, she stood on a high stone pedestal and loomed over the accused. The defendant stood on one side of her and the plaintiff on the other. When it was time for her to hear the argument from either of them, her entire pedestal lifted and turned so she could only see the person who was speaking. There didn't appear to be any lawyers, as both men were advocating for themselves.

One man had some severe facial swelling and bruising, one of his eyes had puffed shut, and he nursed an injured jaw, causing him to mumble. The judge's pedestal turned toward the wounded man. "State the nature of the injustice," she said.

The two men were neighbors. The injured man was a greenhouse owner, and he claimed the other young man had asked to plant some onions in his greenhouse, and in exchange, the onion owner would split the crop with the greenhouse owner. All was well and good until it was time to harvest. The onion owner accused the greenhouse owner of harvesting onions ahead of the shared harvest and taking more than they agreed upon. The onion owner had then confronted the greenhouse owner and beat him within an inch of his life.

"We have two issues," the judge said, once she had used her perch to isolate and interrogate each of the claimants. "Crop theft and assault. And since you are from the city of Lower Brimstone, onion theft is the more serious of the two charges."

"I wonder why they're in court here if there from another city," Anti whispered to Jade, who shot back a dangerous, warning glare.

Phim, the watchman, had returned from his conference with the clerk and had overheard Anti's question. "Agria is where everyone comes for justice. We have the best justice in the nine kingdoms. Why don't you know that?" He looked at Anti with suspicion.

"I knew that," Anti blurted. "It's a game we play, asking questions we already know the answer to."

"Pipe down," the bald watchman interrupted their whispered conversation.

Jade and Anti directed their attention back to the trial. The judge seemed ready to deliver her verdict. Her pedestal swung, so she faced out into the courtroom.

"For the crime of unanswered assault, I sentence Mister Rei to one regular beating, lasting no less than three minutes, and no more than five minutes. His accuser, Mister Yutzi, may administer the beating himself, or appoint a proxy to administer the beating. For the crime of stolen onions, Mister Yuzi must buy seventeen onions and deliver them to Mister Rei; alternatively, he may pay Mister Rei the replacement value of seventeen onions, which is, approximately, 4,781 Credits. As always, if either of these punishments is unsuitable, you may choose execution at any time."

The men thanked the judge, although Mister Rei looked upset at the verdict. Neither of the men chose execution, so they filed out of the courtroom.

"That wasn't so bad, aside from the execution part. I wonder if the judge meant you could choose to be executed, or you could choose to execute the other person?" Anti speculated aloud.

"It's mutual," Phim explained, finished with wondering why Anti didn't know basic legal concepts. "They can have each other executed."

"Over onions." Anti shook her head and clicked her tongue.

The next case seemed even less severe. There was no injured party, only a defendant on trial for feeding a family of stray foxes.

"Do you have a retort?" The judge asked after the bailiff read the charges.

"The kits could have died. I had a bit of extra meat." The defendant seemed resigned.

"If everyone fed every kit, the foxes would overrun us in a few months," the judge said.

"Yes. I understand. I am so sorry."

"Since you seem so concerned about feeding, I sentence you to death, and we'll let the foxes devour your corpse."

"Please," the defendant begged, but the judge turned her platform away. The defendant reached for the judge's robes, "Mercy."

"I am offering mercy. I could have the foxes eat you alive so you could enjoy watching them dine one last time." The judge walked down from her platform, and two guards advanced on the guilty woman.

Jade gaped at the scene in horror, and Anti asked, "What's the punishment for climbing the stairs without a permit?"

"Well, you'd get thrown down the stairs or off the cliff altogether," Phim answered. "If you're found guilty, that is. Is this your question game?"

The judge walked to the clerk, who handed her paperwork and nodded toward Jade and Anti on the bench.

"What are we going to say?" Jade asked, "We don't understand what's going on here, and I'm guessing that ignorance of the law is not a valid excuse to these people."

"I know. I've thought it all, though, and I've decided that the only thing we can tell the judge is the truth."

"We can't tell them we're journalists from another dimension." Jade looked terrified. "They either won't understand us, or they will think we're crazy."

"We are crazy; look at where we are. That's beside the point." Anti slipped her pomegranate necklace over her head, the large red pendant swung across her chest. "For good luck." She held up the chain before dropping it back down.

In the courtroom's front, the judge climbed back up onto her pedestal. The guards shuffled Jade and Anti into the defendant area, then they took their place in the area designated for plaintiffs.

"West Gate Watchmen versus these strangely dressed women," the judge announced.

The judge's pedestal rotated, so she was facing the watchmen. "What charges are you bringing against these women?" she asked.

"Your Draconian Wonder, we bring the following charges: improper dress, unregistered gadgetry, and climbing stairs without a permit." Phim said, he tried his best to sound loud and confident, but his voice shook a little.

The judge's pedestal swung around so she was facing Jade and Anti. "What is your defense?" The judge looked them up and down, seeing the women for the first time.

"We're not from here," Anti explained, but the judge cut her off by swinging her pedestal to face out into the courtroom.

"Case dismissed," she said. "These women are wards of Zofia Noghana, Admiral of The Red, and therefore under Red Protection, except for grievous violations, including murder, high theft, and breach of contract. This concludes the ruling."

The judge stepped down from her pedestal again and addressed the guards, "Escort them to the Red Citadel, please, and make sure no tries to litigate them on the way."

"Yes, your Draconian Wonder." The bald guard gave a curt nod.

"Why are we protected by the Admiral of the Red?" Anti asked as the watchmen hustled her and Jade out of the courtroom. "What's a Noghana?"

The bald watchmen pointed to Anti's necklace. "You're wearing the Admiral's sigil. What is the matter with you two? Why you didn't show me before?"

"Lucky pomegranate," Anti whispered to Jade.

Jade rolled her eyes. "It's not luck, it's your extra-dimensional sentience. You somehow knew the necklace would be our only way out."

"Yeah, well, what will happen when we get to the Admiral's house, and he realizes that we're not his wards?" Anti asked.

Jade shrugged. "Tell him, or her, the truth. It worked last time."

The guards marched Jade and Anti through the maze of masonry that made up Agria's streets. As they were under the protection of the Red Admiral, Anti was allowed to keep her umbrella open to shelter them from the falling ash, which registered some incredulous looks from the locals. It stopped raining ash about halfway through their trek. Anti folded the umbrella and put it back in her bag.

Aside from the domed courthouses, the buildings in Agria were all tall and pointed, built to resemble the surrounding mountains. Everything in the environment, from the architecture to the people, seemed to be washed in a dreary gray. This had the effect of making the women feel rather downhearted and tired.

It greatly relieved them when the watchmen stopped in front of a gargantuan stone gate, and Phim said, "Welcome to the Red Citadel."

"It's not red," Anti observed.

"Some days it is," the bald watchmen said cryptically.

"We don't have to go in, do we?" Phim wondered.

"No," the other watchmen shook his head. "We brought them here, and this is as far as we need to go."

The watchmen left Jade and Anti on the steps of the Citadel. As he left, the blond watchmen called, "Bye, nutcases. Hope you enjoy The Red." He gleefully made a slitting motion across his throat.

CHAPTER 18
THE RED ADMIRAL

"Can you feel if Harriet is still in this city?" Jade waited for the guards to be out of earshot before she asked Anti. They stood on the Citadel's stairs, neither making a move to enter the place or move from its steps.

"Yes. Harriet is still in this city," Anti told her.

"Let's just go find her," Jade offered. "There's no reason for us to go inside this place."

Before Anti agreed, the door to the Red Citadel opened. The doors were almost as tall as the building, soaring past several floors and pointed at the top, like everything else in Agria. When the doors opened, they got a glimpse of the inside, it was dark and grand with arches and a marble floor.

A little man stood at the entrance. He was older, just a little taller than Jade, and much shorter than Anti. He wore a white suit and a floppy white hat. Jade thought he looked like a Smurf. When his eyes rested on Anti's pomegranate pendant, he seemed bothered.

"The Admiral wasn't expecting any wards today," the man said.

Anti sized him up and said, "We were not expecting to be here today either. I'm Antigone, and this is Jade."

"You may call me Nillo. Follow me, please."

Much to his continued annoyance, Nillo led Jade and Anti into the Citadel. Almost everything inside the Citadel entryway was made of polished, black marble, with spare, white streaks. Here and there were some dark red accents, such as red cushions on a marble bench, and red and black patterned tapestries on the walls. As they walked, their footfall echoed through the cavernous space.

"Any vampires around here for us to interview?" Anti chortled.

"I'll throw you off the cliff myself, ruling or no ruling," Jade hissed.

"You'd have to come too—*mutual execution*," Anti mimicked the voice of the judge.

The staircase was the centerpiece of the grand foyer. It was carved marble, like the rest of the Citadel, with a deep red runner slicing through the middle. When Nillo climbed the steps, Jade and Anti were reluctant to follow.

"You will have rooms," Nillo said, having misunderstood their hesitation. "Wards have rooms, even when they're not expected. Although the current wards' chambers are not completely empty."

Nillo was far enough up the stairs that Jade and Anti had to follow him.

"Who else is in there?"

Nillo chuckled, it was an unsettling sound. " *What else* is in there."

When they reached the top of the stairs, Nillo led them down a long hallway lined with grand, carved doors. Most of the doors were closed, but when one was open, they could peek inside and see more of the same, carved stone, black marble, red accents, and enormous fireplaces.

The wards' chambers were similarly appointed, with a circular central sitting room, ringed by three bedrooms and a grand bathroom. Nillo waved his hand, and a roaring fire sprung to life in the sculpted fireplace.

"Magic," Anti whispered, and Jade elbowed her.

"Enjoy your apartments," Nillo said as he left. "The Admiral will arrive this evening, I'm sure she'll be overjoyed to reunite with her mislaid wards." With the last line, Nillo hinted sarcasm.

Anti didn't pay him any attention. She was busy inspecting the fireplace, looking for the mechanism that caused the fire to spring to life with the wave of Nillo's hand.

"Magic isn't real." Jade explored the rest of the quarters. "In any dimension."

"After all we've seen and been through, it's hard to believe you could think magic isn't real. Everything is real, there are endless dimensions and endless possibilities." Anti sat down in a high-backed chair in front of the fireplace. "Are there any books around here? I feel like I should read a book in a chair like this."

"You know we can't read books with the translator," Jade reminded her as she wandered from room to room. The next second, Jade screamed, and Anti bolted into the bedroom after her.

"What's the matter?" Anti looked around the room. It had a red-curtained bed, another fireplace, several stone chairs, and an empty bird perch.

"It flew right at my face!" Jade pointed at a small white bird fluttering around the ceiling.

They both watched as the dove ceased fluttering and settled on the wooden perch next to the window. Anti looked at the perch with curiosity. It was the first piece of furniture she'd seen in the Red Citadel not made of stone. The bird was a cream-colored dove with a strange, red marking around its throat.

"This bird has a lucky pomegranate necklace too," Anti observed. "Good thing there are three bedrooms," Anti noted. "It seems the dove claimed this room already."

Jade calmed herself and investigated the dove. "The bird must be what Nillo meant when he said the chambers weren't empty."

"We could use this bird," Anti said. "If you ever needed to hide, you could change in it."

To practice, Jade studied the dove for a few minutes and then shifted into a nearly perfect replica of the bird, aside from the red necklace marking and a single, shiny black feather running down one wing.

"I'll never get over how cool your power is," Anti said to Jade the Dove.

The gray light spilling from their chamber's few windows turned dimmer and dimmer until the sky outside turned an inky black. Nillo came around nightfall and presented them with trays of food.

"Normally, you'd dine with the Admiral, of course, but she has not returned from her day at the courts." Nillo gave a curt nod and left the room. The plates Nillo brought were piled high with a fried fruit, resembling bananas, and a lump of stringy meat covered in honey, with a piece of sweet bread on the side.

"I miss Rupus's yogurt," Anti said through a mouth full of honeyed meat.

Throughout the meal, Jade and Anti debated whether they should attempt to go to sleep or try to escape the Red Citadel to find Harriet. They stayed, which led to an argument on what to say to the Admiral.

Anti suggested telling the truth. Jade balked, however, so they compromised. They would pretend to be wards, with the hope the Admiral had so many wards she couldn't keep track of them. They would tell the truth only if the lie failed. If neither plan worked, they'd flee.

"I don't think we're prisoners. There may be nothing stopping us from just walking out of here," Jade suggested.

"And into the city streets at night?" Anti retorted.

"There are so many laws and watchmen here, I think nothing will happen to us. Even if it does, just flash your necklace, and someone will bring us right back here. The night may be the ideal time to move through the city unhindered while we search for Harriet," Jade said.

"Who is Harriet?" A woman had slipped into the room while Jade and Anti were talking. She was small and pale and wore black and blood-colored robes, which obscured her hair.

Jade and Anti froze, too shocked to act.

"I'm Zofia Noghana, Agria's Red Admiral." She touched her hand to her chest. "Which you would know if you were my wards, which you are not," Zofia spoke softly and dangerously.

Anti took a step towards her. "I'm Antigone, and this is Jade. We were in the courts, and I had a necklace that looks like your sigil. It got us out of a lot of trouble, and we wound up here."

Zofia held her hand up, signaling Anti should stop. "What language do you speak? It sounds foreign when you speak it, but I can understand the words by the time they reach my ears."

"That's our translation equipment," Anti said. "You are the first one to notice it. You must be very intelligent."

"Where did you come from?" Zofia narrowed her eyes.

"A place that differs greatly from here." Anti put her hands out in an open gesture. "If you will allow us some time, we can explain."

"And if I don't allow you time?" Zofia asked.

"We'll vanish, and you'll never have the chance to know."

"Why doesn't that one speak?" Zofia nodded at Jade.

"She's shy."

Zofia laughed; it was surprisingly melodious. Anti was almost ready to laugh along with her, but then Zofia halted.

"Follow me," Zofia said, giving no sign of if she intended to hear Anti out any further.

"Zofia is spooky," Anti hissed at Jade as they left the wards' chambers. Jade nodded.

She led them through the Citadel's cavernous halls to the center of the structure.

The room at the heart of the building was an open, circular, reception hall, surrounded by a dozen fireplaces. The reflective marble, coupled with the multitude of fires, made the entire room glow red. The room had rows of seats beside the fireplaces, and the middle of the hall was a sunken pit with a drain in the center.

Zofia sat down on one bench and gestured for Jade and Anti to do the same. "Do you know what happens in this room?" she asked in her treacherously, gentle voice.

"You are an executioner," Anti trembled. "I can see it." Her words snagged in her throat, and she could not continue.

"Are you going to kill us?" Jade asked, her voice was much steadier but no less terrified.

"She speaks! I cannot murder you. We follow the law in this land. We wouldn't execute you without a trial. That you do not know this, tells me you are very much strangers to Agria. You are lucky. I have had dealings with strangers like you. I have a soft place for them in my heart."

"Thank you." Anti was unsure if this was an appropriate response, but thought it was better than nothing.

"If you were familiar with our laws, you would also know I am putting my position, and even my life in danger by not turning you two over to the courts. So, you have a responsibility to explain yourselves to me. First, who is the Harriet you were discussing, and why have you come to Agria to find it?"

"The Harriet." Anti threw her head back and laughed.

"You are standing in an Executioner's pit that has seen the reaping of a thousand souls," Zofia said.

Anti stopped laughing. "Look, we are from another place. Not a distant city; not another country, we are from a whole other realm of existence," Anti paused, trying to read Zofia. "Are you understanding? Another dimension."

"Yes." Zofia looked at Anti like she was dense. "We've already established you are the Strangers." Then Zofia said something in a language they didn't understand, followed by "One of the Baedes. We see your kind often."

"You have other multi-dimensional travelers here?" Jade interjected, wanting to make sure she understood what Zofia was saying.

"Not here as much, unless they come for the courts. The Baedes come from the city of Flurcross because it leads to the World of All Gates. How did you get here if you didn't come through the All Gates?" Zofia stood, and though she was a small woman, the shadows cast by the fires made her an imposing figure with a shadow flickering in all directions.

"We didn't come through the All Gates," Anti said cautiously. "We came through our own gate; we made it ourselves."

"Explain!" Zofia demanded.

"Jade will explain," Anti said wearily. "She's the one who paid attention during Harriet's lectures."

Jade spent the better part of the next half an hour describing the Quark Collider and the wormholes to Zofia. She discussed the accident, and Anti's newfound ability to sense dimensional rifts, though she was careful to leave out Anti's occasional foresight and her own ability to shift. Jade finished her discourse by describing Harriet's letter and the reason they were in Agria searching for her.

"If Harriet is here, she won't be for long. Either she will be imprisoned for being an unregistered Baedes, or she will have left for Flurcross."

"Why would she have left for Flurcross?" Anti asked.

"No one travels to this realm on purpose. Fire springs from the hands of our people, hot ash rains down from the sky, and our justice is constant, swift, and deadly. The only reason to come here would be to travel through here to someplace else or to buy justice from the courts. You will find the Harriet in Flurcross unless she has already gone into The World of All Gates."

"So, we'll head on over to Flurcross and then to All the Gates," Anti agreed. "Can you give us a permit to climb the stairs and some proper clothes? We got in trouble the last time."

"You'll never make it to Flurcross without me," Zofia said. She sat down on one bench along the rim of the execution pit and seemed to relax a little. "I'm going there tomorrow, anyway. My current husband is holed up there, and I must invite him to our divorce hearing."

"Sounds like a blast," Anti joked.

"It will be a sorrowful occasion," Zofia said. "For him," she added with an uncharacteristic smile.

Before Anti could ask if divorce in Agria led to execution, Nillo arrived to take Jade and Anti back to the wards' chambers. He shuffled in, looking disappointed that there was no blood swirling down the execution pit's drain.

Zofia stopped Jade and Anti before they left the hall. "I believe every part of your story. However, there are some details you have left out of your adventure."

Jade and Anti looked alarmed but did not respond.

"I understand if you cannot tell me. But there is another story I don't believe, and neither should you. That story belongs to Harriet."

"We already know Harriet's a liar, but thanks for the tip."

"Here's a tip for you: she is not here by accident, she's here by careful design, and I'm sure you are too."

CHAPTER 19
THE LORDS OF ALL WISDOM

The beds in the wards' chambers were comfortable, with the surrounding curtains drawn and the fire warming the room. Jade so was cozy in her cocoon that she almost forgot where she was and why she was there.

Jade awoke when Anti pulled the curtains back, to let the gray light of Agria stream onto her bed so harshly that Jade had to squint her eyes against it. She immediately remembered where she was, and her heart sank. Jade didn't want to chase after Harriet in Flurcross or in the World of All Gates. She wished to stay in her cocoon bed, or even better, she wished she could fly away.

Out of instinct and urge, Jade transformed herself into a replica of the dove and flew to the ceiling.

"You'd better knock it off, Jade," Anti called up to her. "You don't want her majesty Admiral of Spooky Scarlet to come in here and see you like that."

Jade, the dove, landed on the wooden perch, next to the real dove, who reacted badly to a counterfeit dove invading his personal space. He snapped his beak forward and jabbed and stabbed Jade in the cheek. Jade shifted back into human form, with her hand pressed against her cheek and blood running through her fingers.

"I told you that was an awful idea," Anti said self-righteously. "Let me see your face."

Jade pulled her hand back and revealed a deep gouge that had a steady stream of blood pumping out.

"Yikes," Anti said. "That looks awful. But face wounds always bleed a lot and look worse than they are. Maybe you can transform it away."

"I don't know." Jade left and went into the bathroom in search of a mirror. Anti followed her. "I don't think so, or else the wound would have disappeared when I changed back from the dove."

Jade looked at her reflection in the bathroom's ornate mirror. She grabbed a washrag and pressed it against her cheek; the blood-stained the rag.

"I'm telling you, use your power. Try to make it stop." Anti said. "You control your own matter; imagine your face without a cut."

Jade removed the rag and stared hard into her reflection in the mirror. As she focused on the cut, the blood faded from her face, and then the wound itself closed until it was as if it had never been there. Only a small, white scar remained.

Anti smiled and put her hand on Jade's shoulder. "See, I knew it. You'll have to learn how to heal yourself faster, though. In case you get badly hurt." Anti left the bathroom. "Now, where did that bird go? I'll shoo it out the window into the ash rain. Nobody pecks at my friend."

"Leave the bird alone." Jade sighed as she followed her.

Jade could convince Anti the bird posed no additional threat, nor did it need to be taught a lesson, and all was calmed by the time Nillo grumpily brought the women breakfast. This morning's breakfast was an improvement on the honeyed mystery meat from the previous evening, though not by much. With no flourish or explanation, Nillo served a syrupy baked apple covered in sugared nuts.

"Why is all of your food so sweet?" Anti asked Zofia when she came to collect them.

"It's not sweet to me," Zofia answered. "I supposed if I visited your city, all of your food would taste bitter."

That morning, Zofia was dressed in blood-red robes tied open to reveal a skimpy black dress. She wore a towering ruby headpiece and her pitch-black hair flowed from under it.

"That's one hell of a divorce outfit," Anti noted.

"These are my ceremonial garments. I'm executing someone this morning before we leave."

"Oh," Anti said. She and Jade exchanged worried glances.

"Come." Zofia stepped out into the hall and beckoned them to follow, confirming their worries.

"To the execution?" Anti wheezed.

"Of course. You are my wards. Officially, the reason you are here is to witness. Come on now. Try to act like you've seen a slaying before."

The execution hall looked the same as it did the previous evening, except for the several dozen spectators sitting on the curved benches. The circular room had no windows, so it was dark as midnight and lit by fire only.

Jade and Anti entered behind Zofia, and the crowd became silent the instant they entered. Zofia motioned for Jade and Anti to sit in the last row of benches as she descended into the pit in the middle of the room. Inside of the hole was a man dressed in clothing that mirrored Zofia's. He wore a black robe over a red loincloth. Instead of a cowl, someone had wrapped thick black bands around his head, obscuring his eyes and most of his face.

"I don't want to see someone die," Anti squeaked. "Can we stop it?"

"How could we, without getting ourselves executed in the process?"

"It feels wrong; we have powers," Anti pleaded.

"Your lucky pomegranate won't save him," Jade whispered sadly.

Zofia read off an extensive list of crimes of the accused. Her perilously soft voice echoed in the chamber, sending chills down Jade's spine.

"General counterfeit, specific harassment, consumption without a permit, solicitation with a permit, sports fraud…"

"I'm closing my eyes," Anti muttered.

"We can't. The audience will know we're not wards," Jade replied.

"… and murder," Zofia finished.

"See. Zofia is killing him for a reason. He's a murderer," Jade reasoned.

"So's she," Anti pointed out.

From the depths of her robes, Zofia drew a long and thickly bladed machete. Anti closed her eyes. When she opened them, she saw Zofia, splattered in blood, standing next to what looked like a pile of black robes. The silent crowd stood and filed out in an orderly queue. Jade and Anti followed the congregation.

"I didn't look," Anti said as they filed out. "I'm sorry. I couldn't."

"Me neither. I don't think anyone noticed, though. It's dark in there, and the audience was focused on someone else."

Zofia met them moments later. "On to Flurcross," she said and rushed past them, her boot heels clicking and bloodied robes flowing behind her.

"She's not going to change? Or at least wash up?" Anti raised her eyebrows.

"Looks like she's not." Jade and Anti followed Zofia through the Citadel and into the streets of Agria.

There was no falling ash that morning, so the people they passed on their trip through Agria dressed a little less defensively. Most wore gray or black robes. The occasional person wore colored robes, but they seemed to be dignitaries. On their way through Agria, many citizens acknowledged Zofia with a curt nod, but not all of them. Several people averted their eyes, and some went as far as crossing the thoroughfare to avoid her.

"Relatives of the executed," Zofia explained when she saw Anti had noticed a couple avoiding her.

"Lovely," Anti said. She tried to match Zofia's forward-looking stance.

When they reached the edge of the city, Jade and Anti passed the city watchmen, and Anti gave them a snooty look. She glared at Phim and made a slicing motion across her throat.

"I'm not looking forward to climbing down these stairs. It was hard enough to climb up them without falling," Jade mumbled.

"We won't be climbing the stairs," Zofia told her. "Stair climbing is archaic. It's only used for punishment or by those afflicted with a sentimental longing for the old ways. We will use discs to travel."

The three women walked for ten more minutes and rounded another city gate, which opened onto a launchpad. At regular intervals, half a dozen people climbed up onto room-sized discs. Once everyone had climbed on, the discs rose off the launch pad, hovered over the ground, and then lifted off into the sky, propelled by flames engulfing the underside of the circle.

"I'm not riding on one of those," Anti protested. "I'll fall right off the edge of that thing. What happens if it tips?"

"Climbing is not an option," Zofia insisted. "Besides, if anything injures you, it will be flames flickering over the disc's sides. The discs don't tip."

Jade didn't want to ride the discs either, but the stone steps were even less inviting. She also assumed arguing with Zofia was fruitless. "It's fine. We'll ride them."

Anti frowned at Jade and vigorously shook her head. "Since when do you speak for both of us? Or speak at all, actually."

Everyone forgot Anti's worries, aside from herself, as the overly courteous disc conductors attended to the executioner and her wards. They readied a private disc and delayed the flights of crowds of passengers so Zofia, Jade, and Anti could board.

Zofia stood at the head of the disc, faced forward and stared regally into the air in front of them, her lengthy, black hair and robes flapped in the wind. Afraid of the edge, but still wanting to take in the view, Jade stood several paces behind Zofia. She wrapped her gray cardigan around herself to protect from the stinging winds. Anti sat in the approximate middle of the disc with her legs crossed and her hands over her face. Occasionally she'd peek through her hands and regret it. Zofia attempted to rouse Anti from her seated position by telling her she was "disgracing herself," but she could not move Anti.

The flame that lifted the disc off the ground also heated it with a pleasant warmth. Zofia called their destination to the conductor, and their saucer rose higher before soaring forward. It moved at a comfortable clip through gray clouds and over mountain cities.

Jade took in the majestic scenery, but she also spent some time contemplating how she'd come to be standing on the edge of flying disc, in another dimension, and how she might proceed once they arrived in Flurcross.

Occasionally, Zofia offered geography lessons from her perch on the bow of the disc. She pointed to a mountainous city as they passed over it. "Nulgol. The city of Commerce. They have the best shops in the world. Then banks and lenders are there as well. The lenders come to Agria for justice often."

"What's at the bottom of the mountains?" Anti asked as she peeked from under her hands. Below the disc, a thick layer of clouds prevented them from seeing what was at the base of the peaks that held the cities.

"Fertile land farmed by a more primitive society. They bring their goods to Nulgol, and we buy the food and distribute it."

"That explains why the food is so sweet," Jade said. "It goes through a lot before it gets to you. The sugar preserves it."

"Oh, look at that place!" Anti exclaimed. Ahead of them was a city full of brightly colored buildings, haphazardly arranged on a sprawling plateau.

"New Halo. It's the City of the Arts," Zofia said, disapprovingly. "Theater, painting, sculpture, music, it's all contained there."

"I wish Harriet brought us there instead of the murder court city."

"Are you referring to my home?"

"Sorry, Zofia." Anti reburied her head in her hands.

The journey took about an hour. Jade was surprised to find herself disappointed to see the end of the disc ride. Anti, however, was frantic to get off the disc once it touched down on Flurcross's landing pad. Flurcross's disc conductors treated Zofia's party with anxious respect.

"I found my new least favorite way to travel. Before today, it was the municipal bus after dark."

"Pay attention!" Zofia snapped her fingers in Anti's face. "A minor mistake here could cost you your life."

"As opposed to Agria, where they almost executed us for hiking up the stairs and carrying an umbrella."

"Yes, because you're no longer under my protection here." Zofia gave Anti a chilly glance. "Entry to Flurcross is not the same as it is in Agria. Here, there is one gate and no watchmen because the city is personally guarded by members of the royal family."

The city's stone wall loomed over the disc landing area, and they could see an imposing gate in the distance. A well-kept road hugged the wall and led from the disc landing pad to the portal.

"Why do royal family members guard the city gate?" Anti asked. She was still getting her bearings after her terrifying disc ride.

"You may ask them yourself when we pass through the gate," Zofia suggested. "But I don't recommend it. When we pass through the gate, *they* may ask *you* questions. Answer to the best of your abilities. Always address members of the royal family as Lord or Lady of All Wisdom."

"What if we can't answer their questions?" Anti worried.

"Tell them your story. The royals are used to Baedes here. Flurcross is the edge of the universe. The Lords of All Wisdom are interested only in collecting knowledge. I have never learned of your world, and I imagine they have never heard of your world either. They'll be happy to collect your knowledge, and we'll be able to move freely throughout Flurcross."

"That's why you brought us," Anti accused her as they neared the city gate. "Not because you have a soft spot for strangers. You needed to get into the city, and you wanted to make sure you pleased the Wisdom Lords with your offering of fresh knowledge."

"Yes," Zofia didn't try to hide her manipulation. "We'll all get into the city. You can find Harriet, and I can find my husband. Here, we've arrived. Answer the Lord and Lady's questions and say nothing further. Remember, your lives hang in the balance."

"Oh, good," Anti said, as Jade nudged and shushed her.

The Flurcross gate was a short tunnel through the city's thick wall. It was just long enough for seven people to stand across both sides. Jade could see into the town on the other side of the tunnel. The streets were made of cobblestones, and the buildings were dark brown brick. It was hard to tell from the mouth of the tunnel, but the roads seemed to lead uphill at a rather steep angle.

The people lining the walls of the tunnel were dressed in fine clothing. Their pants had dozens of tiny patches sewed onto them, and they covered their shirts in jewels of various shapes and sizes. Each resplendent figure wore a sword, sheathed on their hip.

"The Red Admiral of Agria," one of the male figures announced. Jade couldn't tell who was speaking because the darkness of the tunnel obscured everyone's faces in shadow.

"Yes," Zofia said, sounding hesitant for the first time since Jade and Anti had met her.

"These are two of my wards. They are also Strangers, or Baedes, as we call them in Agria."

"Speak your names and titles, Strangers," one of the female royals spoke this time.

Anti cleared her throat. "I am Antigone Pagonis, a science journalist for the *American Science Journal.*"

There was total silence while everyone waited for Jade to speak. She knew what she wanted to say, she had practiced it in her mind while Anti spoke. But it wouldn't come out, the words were caught in her throat, and, with every second that went by, Jade's mouth grew dryer, her hands sweatier, and her eyes wider.

Anti elbowed Jade, then looked at her face for some sign of what was happening. When she saw the stage fright, she said, "For Christ's sake, Jade."

Anti grabbed and shook Jade with so much force, she shocked her into speaking "Jade Hill," she said, without believing that she was speaking. "I'm a freelance science journalist... as well."

None of the royals noticed Jade's delay, or if they did, they ignored it. "How do you speak in two languages at the same time, Strangers?" an unfamiliar female voice asked.

"A machine," Anti answered, "from our home world."

"How did you get here if not through the gate to the World of All Gates?" Yet another voice asked this question, and Anti realized that they were asking their questions in order of where they stood along the tunnel wall, and when they answered each question, Zofia took another step forward. Jade and Anti followed her lead.

"We don't have access to the World of All Gates. We make our own gates, or we find them in nature."

"What is the name of your world?" The next royal in line asked. If the royals on the other side of the cave stayed silent, Anti figured they only had three questions left.

"We call our planet Earth and our country America," Anti answered, waited for Zofia to take a step forward, and then took her next step forward.

"How do you make your own gates?" Another female royal asked.

"We have a machine called a Quark Collider," Anti said, hoping that would be enough of an explanation.

"Clarify," the same female voice asked. Zofia did not move forward. Anti's answer was not enough.

"Tell them, Jade," Anti whispered to Jade. "I seriously don't know how it works."

"You know how the collider works," Jade hissed. "You were at the Orion Center reporting on it."

"I was going to look up how it worked after; I learn best from online videos," Anti confessed.

"I've explained it to you half a dozen times since," Jade said desperately.

"Is there a problem, ladies?" Zofia arched her eyebrows.

The entire royal family, on either side of the tunnel, unsheathed their swords and raised them high enough to gleam in the semi-light that ran down the center of the passage.

"Um… the quarks collide inside a tube." Anti did not sound confident in her response. "The gates sparkle?"

The royals on both sides of the tunnel took a step forward, closing in on Zofia, Jade, and Anti with their swords.

"Einstein-Rosen! People say that a lot," Anti tried.

"The Collider takes advantage of the multidimensional nature of the quarks, which are the smallest building blocks of atoms," Jade said. Initially, her voice shook, but it became louder and steadier the longer she spoke. "The collider separates a quark from its counterpart in an adjacent dimension, then it smashes them together. At first, our scientists thought they were creating black holes, but they were making an Einstein-Rosen Bridge, which is what you would call a 'gate' to other worlds."

The royals lowered their swords and took a step back toward the tunnel wall. They didn't sheathe their swords, though, and instead held them unsheathed at their sides. Zofia took a tentative step forward, and Jade and Anti followed suit.

"Why have you come to Flurcross?" A male voice said, at last.

"I have come to speak with my husband to begin separation litigation," Zofia said. "He educates at the Academy." Zofia didn't step forward.

"Anti and I are here looking for a woman named Harriet from our world. She was part of an accident with the Quark Collider, and her existence in other dimensions threatens our own."

"Grievous business," the last royal said, and all the royals sheathed their swords.

Zofia walked the rest of the way out of the tunnel, unhindered, but two imposing royals barred Jade and Anti's way. "We will discuss the nature of your knowledge," a royal said. "We may require you to donate your wisdom to The Academy."

"Yes, that sounds marvelous." Anti was eager to leave the suffocating tunnel. "I'm very charitable. I donate all the time; sick kids, stray cats, the works."

When Anti agreed, the two royals stepped aside, and she and Jade were let into the city. The obscured view from the tunnel was accurate; all streets in Flurcross sloped up steeply toward a castle in the center of the city, which sat atop the sizeable central hill. The roads were made of moderately well-kept cobblestone, though occasionally a piece of it would tumble down the incline.

"I suppose that's The Academy?" Jade said as she craned her neck at the castle.

"It is," Zofia said. "What did the royals stipulate on your way out of the city gate?"

"They said that we may have to donate our wisdom at The Academy," Anti said. "I figured they mean for us to talk to a researcher or something."

"Yes, it may mean you may have to speak with an Academic, or it may mean they will remove your head and dissect your brain," Zofia said coolly.

"What is wrong with this place?" Anti moaned.

"I will leave you to find Harriet. I have some business to attend to here," Zofia said over Anti's moans. "If you run into any issues, tell them you are my wards, although that carries much less weight here than it did in Agria. If you want to travel back to Agria with me, I will meet you at the disc conductor's station at sunset. If you are not there, I will leave without you."

"Okay," Anti said.

"If Harriet has gone into the World of All Gates, as I suspect she has, you will find the access point in The Academy. It's one of their most famous exhibits," Zofia added.

Jade and Anti thanked Zofia, though they were both relieved once they were no longer in her company.

CHAPTER 20
A DROP TO DRINK

"Do you sense Harriet here?" Jade looked at Anti.

"She's up there." Anti pointed to the Academy perched high atop the city. "Zofia was right."

The two women started their trek up the hill to the impressive castle. As they climbed, the reason for the rough cobblestones became apparent. The steeper parts of the streets were made of shallow steps, which helped pedestrians climb up to The Academy.

While they climbed, Anti unleashed a litany of questions and comments that Jade disregarded. "Why does it seem like we're always climbing in this dimension?" And, "How do people sleep here without rolling out of their beds?" And "Zofia was probably just kidding about the chopping off our heads thing, but those royals were no joke."

Once they arrived at the apex of the hill, they still had to climb a set of stairs before they reached The Academy's doors. Jade sat down on the first few steps to catch her breath.

"Why aren't there any people here?" Anti asked, and this time Jade paid attention. "We saw more people inside the tunnel than we have on our whole climb up this mountain."

"You're right." From her vantage point, Jade had a view of the entire east side of the city. She counted four people out on the streets, but the town was packed with homes, inns, and shops.

"We're so close to Harriet, though. We can figure it out later."

The women didn't need to wait long to understand. As they approached the castle, they heard a cacophony of voices. When they walked through the open, arched entryway to The Academy, they found it packed with people.

The vaulted entrance hall opened all the way to the roof of the castle through seven floors of balconies. Every open surface was crowded with people. Many of them carried stacks of books held together by straps, and others sat reading in chairs or on the floor. The castle held endless classrooms and lecture halls off the main entrance hall and little rows of stairs leading from one balcony to the next.

Like the royals, the people wore pants with patches and shirts with jewels, but the number of patches and jewels varied from person to person. One woman would be so encumbered by gems that she could barely walk, and the next might have a single ornament attached to her shirt with a stray few patches on her pants.

"How will we find Harriet in all this?" Anti lamented.

"The passage to the World of All Gates," Jade said. "Zofia guessed that's where she was headed. I think we should look there first."

Anti agreed. She walked up to a youthful woman sitting on a cushioned bench, reading.

"Hi, there," Anti said to her. "Sorry to interrupt, but can you point me to the passage to the World of All Gates?"

The woman looked up from her book, considered Anti, then laughed and continued reading.

"Excuse me," Anti said a little louder, which, since she was already attempting to be heard over thousands of voices, was ear-splitting. "Can you show me to the passage to the World of All Gates?"

The reading woman laughed again and pointed to the far end of The Academy.

Jade and Anti made their way to where the woman had indicated. Moving through the crowd was slow going because, with their eyes on their books, many people were not paying attention to where they were going. Tons of people sat on the floor or spilled off furniture, and even more walked encumbered by vast stacks of strapped books.

A glass dome big enough to fit a luxury R.V. was in a roped-off area in the far end of The Academy. A white mist swirled around inside of it, making the dome look like a huge snow globe.

"This is the gate," Anti said. "I can feel it. It's making my entire soul vibrate."

A square of thick, velvet cords, confined the snow globe and four attendants, dressed in jeweled regalia, stood at each corner of the rope. Still, a crowd pressed near to the globe and formed a loose line in front of it. Stairs led up to the globe's platform and a little, closed door carved into the glass.

"When can you go inside the glass?" Anti asked a lady milling around the back of the line.

"When everyone else finishes coming through the other side," she said.

"Which is when?"

"In two hours or so, I guess," she shrugged.

They watched as two men materialized is the globe's swirling mist. An attendant near the stairs walked up and opened the globe's doors. He escorted the men from the sphere, down the stairs, and through the crowd.

"What are we going to do for three hours?" Jade asked as they backed away from the congregation.

"We're in the universe's biggest library in a city dedicated to accumulating knowledge. Let's read some books."

"The translator doesn't work on written words," Jade reminded her. "We can't read any of it."

"Water, water everywhere and not a drop to drink," Anti philosophized.

"That's clever," Zofia said. Jade and Anti gasped. At some point, she had crept up behind them. Zofia looked less horrifying than earlier, though. She had washed off the blood from the execution and closed her substantial robes.

"Zofia! We're so glad to see you again," Anti said through her gritted teeth.

"I'm here to collect on your debt to me."

"I thought you already did when you used us to get past the Wisdom Masters."

"That was for my first favor—not killing you on the spot for impersonating my wards. This is for my second favor—not turning you over to the Lords as a clairvoyant," she said to Anti before turning to Jade, "and a shapeshifter," she finished.

"How?" Jade sputtered.

"The dove in your chambers is another ward, a *real* ward. Whenever I want, I can see through her eyes and hear through her ears."

"You pecked Jade," Anti accused.

"I don't always control the bird. I use the bird's senses sometimes. Besides, you never would have discovered your healing abilities if it weren't for my dove's sweet little kiss." Zofia caressed Jade's cheek.

Jade recoiled; Anti glared.

Zofia went on, "And once you've completed this simple task for me, I'll get you a book from here you *can* read."

Anti looked at Jade, who turned to Zofia and said, "I will not agree to anything until you clue us in on this 'simple task.'"

●   ●   ●

A dozen academies, each dedicated to a different scholarly subject, encircled the vast library. A set of dormitories carved into the hills trailed down the slope behind every school.

The High Scholar of Dead Languages, Professor Twist, had a temporary room in the dormitories behind the University of Linguistics. This room was only supposed to house him until he sorted out the unpleasant business with his wife.

The University of Linguistics dormitories had a winding and confusing layout because they were built over time as a series of additions carved further and further into the city's mountain. The halls and rooms were damp, windowless, and unnumbered. The architecture was often maligned by the University's students, particularly the young students who spent their early months wandering around the passages, afflicted with colds, and complaining that their studies were suffering. However, the covert and confusing nature of the quarters were ideal for a man attempting to hide.

Professor Twist was an insignificant man with thinning hair and round, watery eyes. He didn't seem like the sort to spark any kind of lustful attraction, but he had a darkly beautiful wife, who, until recently, was devoted to him.

He also had a mistress. His research assistant was young, bubbly, and equally devoted. Or, at least, she had been until her recent, sudden, and unexplained death. Twist hadn't spoken to Zofia since the campus staff had found his mistress's body crumpled at the bottom of the University of Linguistics' grand central staircase. Still, he was confident their next interaction would include the initiation of divorce proceedings.

Divorce proceedings with an executioner usually lead to, well, execution. Ignoring divorce proceedings with an executioner was equally deadly. Twist's plan was to avoid the issue for as long as possible, which he figured would be quite long, considering he was protected by the University and the Lords of All Languages.

The professor was rooted in the bowels of the dormitory, studying the texts of the long-departed Scurqix people from the Malli Universe when a timid knock on his bedroom door startled him.

"Hello," he called out without standing.

"Professor Twist?" The voice sounded familiar.

"Yes?"

"It's Emlyn from your Languages of the Great Drought class. I have some interesting... um... information on the... ah... languages."

Twist opened his door a crack and peeked through. The hall was dank and lit only by a few weak ensconced candles. Emlyn stood in front of his door with her eyes wide, and her long blonde hair spilling down her back. She was clinging to a stack of papers.

He opened the door wider. "What do you have there?"

"I should show you," Emlyn said as she stuffed the papers into his hands.

He glanced down at the papers and realized his mistake. He looked back up and Emlyn; her hair was too blonde, her eyes were too wide, her lips were too full. She turned and ran back down the hallway.

Professor Twist sat down at his desk and read through the divorce papers with a worried grimace.

• • •

Jade, still disguised as Emlyn, met Anti and Zofia in an alleyway a few blocks over from the University of Linguistics dormitory.

"Was I right about which room? Did you find him?" Anti asked.

"I don't have the papers anymore, do I?" Jade snipped. "I think he realized I wasn't his student after I handed him the papers."

"Good, then he won't blame her next time he sees her," Anti said.

Jade began the process of fading out of the Emlyn form and back into her own body.

"Satisfactory work," Zofia said. "You should go back to the library; the Gate should open soon. This will be the last time I see you."

Zofia handed Anti a slim book with a stiff, blue cover.

"What's this?"

"It's the Almanac of the Abyss."

Anti looked at her quizzically.

"It's your 'drop to drink.'" Zofia offered a rare smile.

CHAPTER 21
MORE ADVENTURE

"Check this out." Anti held the Almanac of the Abyss up to Jade's face, making it even harder for her to navigate the hazards of the library.

"Why does everyone here wear clothes covered in patches and gems?" Anti asked.

The Almanac's page, which had been blank, now filled itself with hand-drawn images of the Flurcross residents' unique garb alongside informational paragraphs.

Anti pulled the book away from Jade's face and read, "The patches are badges representing familiarity with a certain topic or subtopic. For instance, a light green patch means the person knows about Interdimensional Culinary Arts. The gems mean they have mastered an entire discipline."

"It's like an Internet search in a book."

"A magical internet search."

"Magic isn't real." The enchanted-looking Gate the women approached dwarfed Jade's antimagic protest. As Zofia had predicted, the Gate attendants were now processing outgoing travelers.

People lined up to climb onto a platform and step through a small door on one side of the dome. One at a time, they stepped into the bubble, the mist enveloped them, and they disappeared.

"It looks like we can just go in there, if we need to," Anti observed.

"Do we need to?" Jade asked. "Can you sense where Harriet is?"

"I don't need to feel her, I can see her." Anti pointed to Harriet, who was in line to be the next person to enter the dome. Bejeweled attendants helped her up the stairs to the platform.

"Harriet!" Anti called as she rushed up to the ropes around the dome. An attendant blocked her.

"You need to get into the line, and the passage costs nineteen Confederate Ducats," he said in a bored voice.

"We're wards of the Red Admiral," Anti said hopefully, she dangled her pomegranate necklace in the attendant's face. He looked less bored.

"All right, then we'll charge your passage fee to the Red Admiral, but you still have to get in line."

"Harriet!" Anti called again.

Harriet, who was approaching the dome's glass door, turned when Anti called her name. Her eyes locked on Jade and Anti. She gave a broad smile, and her signature double thumbs-up before she walked into the dome and vanished in the mist.

"Aw, what the hell Harriet," Anti grumbled. "Let's get in line. At least it's free."

About two dozen people stood in line in front of Jade and Anti, so they had time to talk through some looming issues.

"We know that there is a natural passage back to our dimension from Agria," Jade reasoned. "But we don't know if there's one from this World of All Gates. I'm afraid we could get trapped there."

"So, we could wait for the sunset. Zofia will take us back to Agria, then we go back through the bridge to our world, then we try to find a bridge to the World of All Gates and hope that Harriet is still there. But, if Zofia is right, why would you travel to the Gate World if to wasn't a layover for someplace else? It would be like going to the airport just to get some overpriced candy bars." Anti said. "Plus, my multidimensional sentience is getting stronger, I bet I could find us a way back out of there."

"But, I'm afraid—"

Anti interrupted Jade, "I'm afraid, too." She held onto Jade's arm. "You started this entire trip when you sent me that text saying, 'I think we should go.' And I didn't want to go find Christian, but I went anyway because you convinced me that this is what journalists do. Now I'm all in. You're coming with me because it's all your fault."

"You're right," Jade admitted. "Harriet is ignorant, or she doesn't care that she's sweeping us farther and farther away from our home dimension. I don't think we will get another chance to stop her."

The women watched as a family disappeared into the mist; a mother, father, and an adolescent girl. A man in line in front of them turned to face them, wearing the leather hats banded with metal popular in Agria.

"First time through the Gate?" he asked.

"How d'you guess?" Anti smiled.

"You have that look." He nodded to the book in Anti's hand. "A gift for your little ones?"

"Huh?"

"I think he means the Almanac," Jade chortled. "It must be a book for children."

"No," Anti said. "It's for me." She flipped through the almanac again before tucking it into her messenger bag.

"All right." He turned away from the women to watch more people step through the Gate.

Before he stepped up onto the platform, he turned to Jade and Anti and said, "There is no more beauty in the wilderness than there is in our own home, but there is more adventure." He winked, turned, and walked through the dome's glass door, and the attendant closed it behind him.

"Why did he say that to us?" Jade asked.

Anti smiled. "I think he wanted to say it to someone, and we were standing in the right place."

Jade and Anti climbed up the platform two minutes later. Then they walked through the delicate glass door and let the mist of the World of All Gates surround them.

CHAPTER 22
SO BIG IT NEVER ENDS

When the mist cleared, Jade and Anti walked through a door that closed behind them. They were in a long hallway, resembling one in an upscale hotel lined with what could be the doors to a hundred hotel rooms. Jade turned to look at the door they had just walked through. It was a white door with black lettering.

"The City of Flurcoss," it read in a black, block font, and underneath it read, "World of Ninoxis."

"I wonder why we can read it," Jade said. "The translator hasn't worked on written language before."

Anti opened the Almanac. "Where are we?" She asked the book. "I just want to see if it works in other dimensions," she explained to Jade.

Jaded nodded.

Anti read from the Almanac for a few moments. "It says we're in Aperture, which has many other names and then lists about twenty other titles for the dimension. This place 'takes on whatever form would be the most acceptable to the observer.' I wonder what that means."

Jade jabbed Anti's ribs, which made her snap the book shut and spin around. Other people, and creatures, stepped through different doors in the hallway. Some walked past Jade and Anti, and some headed down the hall. Everyone was bustling along with determination except for Jade and Anti. They remained still and pressed against the wall.

The people and creatures in the hall varied. Some of them resembled humans, but with unique clothing: lavish dresses, pants made of leaves, headdresses flowing to the ground, and some wore no clothes at all. There was a myriad of skin colors represented, including: pale white, translucent, brown, black, orange, green, and red. Some of them were non-humanoid creatures: anthropomorphic animals, minotaur and other hybrid beasts, and ghostly, hazy beings who appeared to be made of clouds.

Jade recognized the man who had entered the glass dome ahead of her, the one with the banded leather hat and words of encouragement. He walked farther down the hall and turned the corner.

"We should follow him," Jade pointed. "Unless you think you can feel Harriet."

Anti paused, then said, "She's here, but she's hard to feel. A lot is going on."

So, they followed the man with the Agria hat and the encouraging words. Out of curiosity, Jade had to read the labels on some doors as they passed.

She read what seemed to be the names of exotic locations, such as "*Hamlet of Loregag: World of Frator*," and "*Qwarag: Warning: Timeless*," and "*Lumix: A Cyber Dimension*."

"There might be a door home here," Jade said.

"Why not?" Anti shrugged. "There seems to be a door to everywhere else."

The clean but long hallways led to an open atrium, accessible by one of two grand staircases. The atrium was open and airy, the ceiling seemed to be made of light purple glass. The floor of the atrium had a half dozen long desks, each operated by a handful of people and creatures. A few of the desks were labled "Information." The man wearing the Agria hat disappeared among the masses of people flooding in and out of the Atrium.

"Should we try to find Harriet? Or should we check out an information desk?" Anti asked. "This place looks much more modern than the other worlds we've been to. Maybe they can just look her up on a computer or have the authorities find her."

Jade agreed, and they sidled up to the Information Desk that had the most human-looking attendants.

A remarkably tall woman with a head of downy, green hair, leaned over the Information Desk. She had "Grackon" on her name tag.

"Hello," she said crisply. "How can I help you?"

"We are from Earth," Anti said, and then added, "Grackon," because she believed in using people's names, even if they were alien beings from another dimension.

"Hold on," Grackon said. She used her fingers to manipulate a computing device embedded in the information desk's surface.

"Which Earth?"

"Earth One," Anti guessed. "I'm not sure."

"Earth One is classified as an unattached dimension. How did you get here?"

"We came through Flurcross," Anti said.

Grackon tapped at her computer. "But you must have used a dimensional bridge to get there?" Grackon's voice had taken on a strange tone, and Jade was unsure how to react. "Did you make it yourself?"

"Yes." Anti backed away from the desk, preparing to run.

"Congratulations!" Grackon squealed and clapped. "Welcome to the multiverse, Earthlings!"

A bright, loud song played, and a light flashed on in the floor below Jade and Anti, illuminating the women. Half the individuals in the atrium turned to Jade and Anti and cheered; the other half trudged along as if it was business as usual. When the song stopped, the light below them faded. All the beings in the atrium carried on with whatever they'd been doing before.

"I've never gotten to do that before," Grackon said breathlessly after the song had finished. "Wait right here, and your Aperture liaison will be around."

Jade and Anti looked around uneasily as they waited for their liaison. Part of their uneasiness was because of Grackon, who stared at them with unabashed awe.

"Can I get you anything?" Grackon asked. "I'm not sure what an Earthling eats or drinks. Do you eat or drink? The Tagus get their subsistence through osmosis."

"Sure, just pour me a glass of Pinot Grigio, and I'll roll around in it," Anti smirked.

Grackon reached for her console as if she were about to order up some wine for rolling, but Jade stopped her.

"She's joking. We eat and drink through our mouths." Jade pointed to her mouth, then pinched her fingers to her forehead. "But we don't need anything to eat or drink, thank you."

Their liaison was a head shorter than Jade and looked vaguely like a troll, with thick, leathery skin, a bulbous nose, and a few scraggly hairs on the top of his lumpy head. His name was Adellum, and he vigorously shook both Jade and Anti's hands.

"Wassup dudes! We were not expecting Earthlings to drop in for at least another century," he beamed. "Far out!"

Adellum raised his chunky, troll hand up, so it was a few feet from Jade's face. She looked at Anti nervously.

"Don't leave me hanging, bro," he said.

Anti nodded encouragingly at Jade, who reluctantly raised her hand and slowly tapped Adellum's palm, giving the multiverse's worst-ever high five.

"Sweet!" he said and beckoned for them to follow.

Adellum led Jade and Anti through the crowd in the atrium and brought them to another hall of doors, but these doors had unique titles on them. Jade read a few, including, "*Ambassador to the Midnight Shores*," and "*Ringmaster of the Circus Berserk*."

Adellum's office had vast windows overlooking a shining, modern city. With its skyscrapers and sidewalks full of bustling people, it might have been New York City, if it were not so clean and if the sky was not a distinct shade of light lavender. The vehicles on the streets were windowless, rolling, polished chrome spheres.

After he let Jade and Anti take in the city's view, Adellum motioned for Jade and Anti to sit on a bench that lined the far wall of his office.

"We're setting up a welcome bash for you, cool cats. You will be our ambassadors from Earth," he said.

"A party!" Anti said with excitement.

"We're actually fairly busy," Jade said, "but, thank you for the offer."

"Later, you can choose anyone from Earth to be ambassadors, but we have to start with you because you are the first."

"Well, we might not be the first. We're following someone who came in just before us."

"You are the first. We have the most advanced particle detection in all the multiverse. If anyone else from your neck of the woods came through here, we'd know."

Jade and Anti exchanged glances.

"I don't mean to give you bad vibes about showing up here, but you aren't supposed to be here for a least a hundred years." Adellum went on, "Either our analysis of Earth's capabilities is straight-up whacked, or someone has been messing with your world's dimensional technology. In any case, what's been done can't be undone, so let's party."

"I'm sure another person from Earth came here," Anti said. "We watched her step through the gate in Flurcross."

"That's not possible. You went right up to an info desk and checked in, but even if you didn't, we would have picked you up in a few shakes of a puppy dog's tail. Our sensors would detect anyone from an unattached dimension," Adellum said. "But I can help you find your friend, no matter where she's from. What does she look like?"

"She's about five feet ten inches and has brown hair she puts up in a gravity-defying bun," Anti said.

"Sorry, bro," Adellum said. "Our translations system didn't catch that."

Anti turned to Jade. "Jade show him."

Initially, Jade was unsure of what Anti meant, and then she realized. She shifted into Harriet and then stood up so that Adellum could see what Harriet was wearing.

"I did not know you folks on Earth could do that." Adellum looked alarmed. He shuffled through a file folder on his desk, looking for a missing piece of information.

"No, Jade's the only one."

"Stay like that. I gotta record your image to see if Harriet is in our database."

Adellum held up a tablet-like device and used it to scan Jade's version of Harriet. "Say cheese," he said and then sat down to use the computer inset in his desktop. "You can change back."

Jade shifted back and watched as Adellum's face grew more and more grave.

"Well, I figured out how you ladies got here a century early. Harriet is not from Earth. She is a criminal, and she was a prisoner of Earth, banished there because of high crimes perpetrated against the multiverse, including creating illicit gates."

"You have the wrong Harriet," Anti snickered.

"Why would you use Earth as a prison?" Jade asked.

Adellum's countenance changed as if someone had flipped a switch. He sighed. "We have a lot of ground to cover. Let me take you to the architecture room."

Adellum led Jade and Anti back through the atrium and stood in front of a door, one that didn't seem to lead to another hallway. Instead, it led to a massive room with a white tiled floor and white walls. There were dozens of glass cases and domes holding incomprehensible artifacts, shifting pieces of reality, and ancient books.

"Oh, I love museums. I like the kinds that let you touch the exhibits," Anti exclaimed. Anti reached for a floating cube.

"No!" Adellum and Jade shouted in unison.

Two imposing, seven-foot, reptilian figures standing on either side of the museum's two doors took a step toward Anti. They did not suggest they'd entertain any exhibit touching either.

"Fine," Anti grumbled.

Adellum guided Jade and Anti to a digital, mural-sized map of the multiverse, with Aperture at the center. It took up an entire wall of the museum.

"Behold." Adellum manipulated the map with his hands while he spoke, bringing circular representations of the dimensions in and out of focus. "This is us here, in Aperture," Adellum explained. "Like other dimensions, there are millions of shifting, similar dimensions attached to us." Adellum illustrated this by overlaying dozens of identical circles over the first Aperture circle. "These realities are constantly moving in and out of existence. The folks living in the dimension may not even notice when they have left one and entered another, and this is because the foundational dimension does not change."

"Like a person changing clothes," Jade said. "They are slightly different, but they are still the same person underneath what they're wearing."

"Right on," Adellum continued. "Then, there are other dimensions, like the one you came through to get here. If alternate realities are clothes for a person, then other dimensions are another person entirely, one who also wears a bunch of different clothing. In these new dimensions, you would not notice shifts, unless you were attuned to these changes or had a machine that could detect them. Are you following?"

"Yes." Jade nodded, but Anti shook her head no. They ignored her. Jade said, "We have encountered these reality shifts in our own dimension. We noticed them because we were involved in a dimensional wormhole mishap."

Adellum acknowledged her by looking even more concerned. "Gnarly," he said. "Now, on to the history of Aperture. Thousands of years ago, we discovered a way to connect to a nearby dimension."

He pulled on the Aperture circle, and a line appeared, leading to a second circle that looked very different from Aperture, "This is a dimension called Kopes, it's where our receptionist Grackon is from. The people of Kopes were advanced, and they were on the verge of creating their own multidimensional transport system, which is likely how their dimension ended up next to ours. We buddied up and worked with the citizens of Kopes to create advanced technology. Eventually, we connected to more and more dimensions."

Adellum pulled at the edges of the Aperture circle, and dozens of lines leading to their own circles sprung off it. "Some in the multiverse calls us the World of All Gates. We connect to even more worlds beyond the ones linked to ours, by moving through adjacent worlds." Adellum laid his chubby palm flat on the mural, and hundreds of other lines and circles sprung from the ones connected to Aperture. What had once been a small, solitary circle was now the pulsating hub to thousands of colorful discs.

"We can see into almost any dimension," Adellum continued. "But we limit our travel to and from worlds that have already discovered multidimensional travel. We don't connect to worlds like your own."

"I'm not sure why your sensors didn't pick up on our technology. It's been in use for a least a year and in development for much longer," Jade said.

"I have an idea, hang on, it will be a trippy ride." Adellum made another circle on the mural. "This is your Earth."

The circle that represented Earth was filled with images of people and art from a multitude of cultures interspersed with photographs of animals and lots of pictures of water. The Earth circle did not connect to any of the other rings by any lines. It wasn't even near any other loops.

"Your Earth is alone and unreachable. It takes a great deal of time and energy to get a person to Earth, and once they are there, they are not coming back. Therefore, we use your dimension as a prison, and we are sorry about that. Criminal beings can be hard to confine in the multiverse. It's easier to contain them in a place where the harm they can do is limited to a single dimension."

"Are you saying that Harriet is a multidimensional criminal mastermind so dangerous you had to isolate her from all other worlds?" Anti scoffed. "I don't believe it. Harriet can't even do her hair like it's from this millennium. She communicates through a weird thumbs-up. She talks like a mean robot." Anti paused, thinking. "Actually, yeah, I can see Harriet as a being from another dimension. And her journal pointed to some nefariousness."

"Journal?" Adellum raised a bushy eyebrow. "What did her journal say, and how did you get it? I'm listening. Lay it on me."

Anti relayed the story of the Orion Center accident, explained the threat of being carried farther and farther away from their home dimension, and with scientific support from Jade, she narrated Harriet's story as told by her notebook.

"Well, a lot of what you read about Harriet is true—it just didn't happen to her on Earth. Harriet was part of an organization dedicated to preserving dying alternate realities because she was one of those rare individuals who could perceive when they shift from reality to reality. She became ensnared in a loop of alternate realities where she kept gaining and losing her family members. Harriet didn't realize the Harriet she was when she didn't have a family never had a family. She was longing for something she never actually lost. The opposite was true as well; the Harriet she was when she had a family should have had no idea what it was like to lose them. She became obsessed with becoming and staying a version of Harriet who had a family. But, that's not possible... we all move through alternate realities constantly. Her attempts to stabilize herself in a single reality was causing all the other connected realities to destabilize."

"We talked to a scientist in our dimension who said that Harriet's presence was causing our set of realities to fall apart," Jade said.

"Was he using his own data or data provided by Harriet?" Adellum asked.

"Harriet's data," Jade gave a curt nod. "He also wasn't the greatest scientist."

"You leave Gustavo alone," Anti interjected.

"I suspect Harriet was using manipulated data to get the two of you to follow her here. There is another, more serious potentiality. Harriet may have purposely destabilized your world," Adellum said.

"Why would she do something like that?" Anti asked.

"Let's hope she didn't," Adellum dismissed. "Anyway, this kind of problem with Harriet happens, rarely, but it happens often enough that we have a protocol to help contain individuals like her. We first tried to separate her from the malfunctioning equipment causing her to remember her alternate selves, but too many versions of Harriet had contact with the machine, so that failed. Next, we attempted to clear her mind of any memories of her other lives, but she kept finding out. So, as a last resort, we imprisoned her in a dimension cut off from all others."

"Harriet developed Earth technology to create a door here so she can head back to her home dimension. That all makes sense," Jade thought out loud, "but there's one thing that doesn't make sense... why did she bring us here?"

"I think the reason is obvious," Anti said, and then paused for effect. "Because we're awesome."

"I couldn't think of a more inappropriate time and place for a joke," Jade said.

To their surprise, Adellum began laughing. "I like the cut of your jib," he said to Anti.

"At least someone does," Anti smiled.

"But," Adellum's brow furrowed again, "finding Harriet is crucial. The good news is she couldn't have left this building. The same technology that would have sensed you if you tried to leave would stop her and bar her from entering the rest of Aperture. The bad news is that almost the entire multiverse is inside this building."

"What a terrible system," Anti said.

"I like the cut of your jib less now," Adellum replied.

"Could I sense where Harriet is? I have before," Anti offered.

"We can try to use our sensors alongside your abilities to locate and extract Harriet."

"How?" Jade asked, but she already had an inkling, and she didn't like the direction Adellum's talk was taking.

"Our system may give inaccurate information concerning the whereabouts of Harriet because her multidimensional nature confuses our sensors. But if Antigone's extra-dimensional sentience can help locate her, Jade can disguise herself so that Harriet won't suspect that you are closing in on her. Are you up for that?"

"We really don't have a choice," Jade said.

"There's always a choice. For example, you could choose not to help us locate Harriet and doom yourself to eternity as interdimensional flotsam." Adellum paused and tried to read the women's expressions. "Questions?"

"Why do your interdimensional gates appear as doors? When Anti sees them with her sentience, they look like colored mists. Everyone else that we've encountered can't see bridges at all unless they're stabilized inside a specialized environment, like our Quark Collider or the glass dome in Flurcross."

"I'm not sure what doors are," Adellum smiled. "Similar to the translation software in your device, Aperture's translation software doesn't make just language comprehensible to everybody in the multiverse. It makes the physical reality of Aperture understandable to anyone in the multiverse. I assume, on Earth, you use doors to move from one area to the next, so Aperture sensors made dimensional passageways into doors for you."

Adellum paused for a moment. "Similarly, I don't look or sound the way you see and hear me. Neither does this room or the map on this wall. Our system uses an amalgamation of information from your homeworld along with data stored in your sensory cortex to create a version of Aperture that makes sense to you. Would you like to see what Aperture looks like without reality filters?"

"Yes," Anti said, ignoring Jade vigorously shaking her head no.

Without further warning, the museum room they were in dissolved around them. Jade felt weightless. Instead of a mural and Adellum in front of them, all Jade could see were pools of color floating in luminous swirls, as if she was looking, or living, inside of a gasoline puddle.

She looked down at her own body and saw it had dissolved into an orange-colored pool. When she tried to reach forward, little bits of her orange pool were sucked into the swirl around here, and the swirl turned a little more orange.

Not only did Jade feel weightless, but her mind was free of every hang-up. All anxiety and every bit of restlessness floated away. She realized her definition of self had been much too narrow, and she was not only part of the universe but made of the world, and therefore a part of everything. She felt simultaneously huge and very tiny. *Maybe*, she thought, *this dimension is so small, it could fit on the tip of a well-sharpened pencil, and so big that it never ends, and neither do I. I am this dimension, and I go on and on forever.*

Time was nearly meaningless in Aperture's pools of color, but Jade sensed the passage of time, only slightly. She was mostly careless, but she remembered she had something to do. She felt, in the most nebulous definition of the concept of feeling, a tug at her side, and she saw a turquoise color pool moving through the swirl toward her own pool. It moved by contributing bits of its turquoise to the surrounding swirl. The floating, turquoise pool landed next to Jade, and, with a jolt, she was back in her own body, in the Aperture museum, standing next to Anti and looking at Adellum the troll and his marvelous mural.

"That was an eye-opening experience," Jade said. "Thank you."

"Yeah, that was freaky. Never do it again," Anti said. "How do we find Harriet?"

"Yes, well first, we must formally welcome you to the multiverse," Adellum said. "It's time to party on."

CHAPTER 23
LIGHT IT UP

"We've recreated some of what we know about Earth to aid in the festivities. Including customs, food, and general celebrations."

Adellum opened a pair of wide, white, double doors with a flourish. Inside, it looked like the residents of Aperture had recreated a high school prom. The room was a replica of a school gym with gauzy streamers, balloons, and a white banner hung over a stage at the far end, reading: "Welcome to the Multiverse, Earthlings."

"We collected a database of your media and have provided a set of features most connected with celebrations." Adellum beamed, and his troll face almost looked handsome.

Members of the delegation from Aperture, including Grackon, were dressed in puffy prom dresses and ill-fitting suits, regardless of the apparent gender of the wearer. There was also a smattering of wedding dresses and tuxedos. A table in the corner held a giant wedding cake.

Waiters circulated the room carrying canape trays, laden not with appetizers, but covered in thick steaks and baked potatoes instead. A few plates had Christmas cookies, and one large table held a full Thanksgiving feast.

"I didn't go to my prom," Anti said as they stepped into the wild ballroom, "but I'm sure it didn't involve steaks and potatoes."

"I didn't go to mine either. My parents bought a dress for me, though. I didn't want to let them down, so I put on the dress, and got on a bus and rode it until the end of the line, then got on another bus and did the same thing, until about the time that the prom would have been over, and then I rode the bus home."

"That's awful. I just stayed home and watched *Carrie*." Not wanting to appear rude to the circulating servers, Anti picked up a baked potato from their tray when offered. "At least it's not hot," she said, holding up the potato and inspecting it. A pat of butter fell from, and it the floor with a splat.

"I technically never said I was going to the prom," Jade clarified. "My parents assumed. The dress was red; my sister said it complimented my skin tone," she lamented.

"I bet you looked fantastic on that bus. Let's get something to drink." Anti headed toward a buffet table, which held not only the towering, tiered wedding cake but also five crystal punch bowls, each with a different colored punch: amber, blood red, bright pink, clear, and dark green.

"I'll try the pink one." After setting her uneaten baked potato down on the white, embroidered tablecloth, Anti used the gaudy, patterned glass ladle to pour the pink drink into an even more opulent crystal goblet.

She took a sip. "It tastes like... bubblegum flavoring," she reported, taking another sip. "It's not the worst thing I've had to drink."

Adellum sidled up to them. He had taken the intervening time to don a simple, satin wedding gown.

"You look lovely, Adellum," Anti smiled.

A noise that sounded almost like music filled the dance hall. There was a drumbeat, some guitar plucking, and, occasionally, a trumpet or tuba would blare.

"Do you ladies want the first dance? As the guests of honor," Adellum said while gesturing to the dance floor, sure he was providing Jade and Anti with some great favor.

The other guests moved, so there was an open area in the middle of the dance floor. The terrible music warbled even louder.

Wide-eyed, Jade shook her head and started looking for an exit.

"This is hilarious," Anti chuckled, she looked Jade in her terrified eyes and said. "Dance with me."

Jade said, "No," but Anti didn't hear her and pulled her toward the circle of formally dressed creatures.

"I said, no!" Jade shouted, wriggled from Anti, and ran around the other side of the buffet table so that no one else could pull, or coerce her onto the dance floor. She remained there for a minute, looking like a wounded animal.

"I was just trying to have fun," Anti called to her. "This is our party." Anti turned to Adellum. "You'll be my dance partner."

"Sure thing, baby," he said as he took her hand, and the two made their way to the dance floor. The "music" changed from what was, perhaps, the ingredients of a rock song, to what was supposed to be pop music. It was similar to the last "song," but the beat was faster, and there was a loud, synthetic vocalization over the whole noise.

Anti moved to the middle of the circle and spun around and waved her arms, not wildly, but more mechanically, as if she were a windup toy that someone had wound one too many times. Adellum tried to copy her, but he looked like he was under attack by aggressive bees and was attempting to wave them all off.

Jade laughed despite herself, and her anger at almost being forced to dance in a room full of people melted away. Anti's next set of dance moves included hip gyrating and shoulder shimmying, and Jade lost herself to gales of laughter.

When the music changed again, to something resembling jazz, Anti left the dance floor and headed back over to Jade, who was sipping on a cup of green punch that tasted like wet grass but not wholly unpleasantly.

"Like my dancing?" Anti grinned.

"That was ridiculous. I am beyond glad I didn't go out there with you," Jade said.

"As ridiculous as riding a bus alone for hours, wearing your prom dress?" Anti asked.

Jade was about to reply, but she took too long, and Adellum whisked away Anti so she could teach her dance moves to the eager team of multidimensional anthropologists. They were the same group who had studied Earth and assembled the prom.

"I wonder if they'll name me prom king," Anti said when she returned from the impromptu dance lesson.

At the end of the party, a group of Aperturians rolled a Christmas tree out onto the dance floor. They decorated it with replicated store receipts, wadded-up newspapers, candy canes, and unlit, full-sized light bulbs.

"They got the candy canes right," Jade said. "Somehow, that's the strangest part."

"And now, to close the party," Adellum announced. "We will have the ceremonial lighting of the Pine Tree." He held a lit torch, which he offered to Anti. The heat from the live fire warmed her already flush face.

Anti turned to Jade. "This one is on you. I danced."

"All right." Jade took the torch from Adellum and approached the tree. She turned to Anti and asked, "What do I do?"

"You heard the man," Anti shouted. "Light it up!"

Jade bent down and used the torch to set the bottom of the tree ablaze in three different spots. She handed the torch back to Adellum. They watched as the fire engulfed the whole tree. The attending Aperturians laughed and clapped until sprinklers popped out of the gym ceiling, and sprayed the entire party, soaking the guests and food, while extinguishing the torch and tree.

"You guys throw a magnificent party," Anti said.

CHAPTER 24
ONCE IMAGINARY, NOW REAL

After the party, Jade and Anti met Adellum in the atrium, where he served them an Aperture drink supposed to taste like coffee, but may have been anything from rainbow tears to juice squeezed from a dying star.

"The hair of the dog," Adellum raised his coffee cup.

"It wouldn't surprise me," Anti quipped.

"Not really dog hair. You're supposed to drink it after a rockin' party," Adellum said defensively. "We found the term 'the hair of the dog' used in reference to a drink after a rockin' party in over 726 of our media samples from your world."

"We know," Jade reassured.

When the "hair of the dog" was over, Adellum guided them up the atrium stairs to a set of doors.

"We could locate Harriet's last known location in Aperture," he explained. "She went through one of these doors." Like the hallways they'd encountered when they first arrived, this one resembled a hotel hall, lined with a dozen white doors with black lettering. "We can't be sure which one."

Anti said, "It will be hard for me to find her after you messed with my head for your 'Real Aperture' trick."

"Most people find the experience transcendental. I'm sorry you didn't catch the vibe." Adellum did not sound sorry.

"I'm not most people."

Anti walked up and down the hallway, reading the doors. "*Stogath: A Dead Dimension,*" "*City of Blador, World: Cravesh,*" "*The Lyric Nebula: Once Imaginary, Now Real.*"

"What does that mean, 'Once Imaginary, Now Real'?" Anti asked.

"I'm not familiar with all the dimensions, but that's a classification. It means the dimension was created in someone's mind and willed into existence," Adellum said. "Do you think Harriet is in there?"

Anti placed her hand on the door and said, "No, but I wish she was. I'd like to walk around in someone's daydream." Anti continued down the hall, reading some doors and touching others. "*Implam: Wilderness, Caution: Regressive,*" "*The Strawberry Islands,*" "*Runnait Empire, World: Joldin.*"

Anti paused and walked back a few doors to the one that read, "*Implam: Wilderness, Caution: Regressive.*"

"I think she's gone in here," Anti declared.

"Bummer," Adellum said. "The classification 'Regressive' means time in this dimension flows opposite to the time here in Aperture. It's wilderness now because it's regressed far past the time when it was a place where its people created multidimensional technology compatible with our own. Implam is dangerous because time will move backward for you while you're in there. Stay in for too long, and time here will regress to where I've never met you, and you'll have to explain yourselves all over again."

"At least we'll get to go to our Welcome Party again," Anti joked.

"Why did Harriet go in there?" Jade asked.

"She might try to wait out the regression on this side and come out when it's before anyone knew what she was up to."

"If we're in there for the right amount of time, won't we just come out and meet ourselves, hanging out with you in the museum or in your office?" Anti wondered.

"No, from the second you walk in there, you'll fade from this dimension, creating an alternate reality where you were only here before the amount of time that regressed. It may have already happened with Harriet, we could have seen her walk into that dimension moments ago, but time regressed here, so that version of reality never existed. Capisce?" Adellum asked.

"No," Anti laughed. "And I won't ever understand. It's best if you just tell us what we need to do next."

"Go in Implam, find Harriet, and be as quick as possible. If you dilly dally, you'll come back out of Implam before you came here. I won't know who you are, and you'll have to describe it all over again."

Anti turned to Jade. "You heard the man. Um... sorry, are you a man?" She asked Adellum.

"Technically, no."

"Okay, noted." Anti turned back to Jade. "Are you ready?"

Jade nodded her head 'yes,' and they plunged through the door and into pure wilderness, waving to Adellum through a door-shaped rectangle that showed a diminishing gate back to Aperture. Anti pulled her device out of her messenger bag. She stabilized the bridge behind them, and the open rectangle turned into a permanent portal that appeared in the form of a natural, knotty, wooden door carved into the trunk of a massive redwood tree.

Once she stabilized the door, Anti pulled the *Almanac of the Abyss* from her messenger bag.

"Tell me about Implam," Anti directed the book.

The book revealed pages of sketches of futuristic cities with explanatory text along the sides.

Anti read, "Implam was one of the multiverse's most advanced societies and is speculated to be one of the first civilizations to discover interdimensional travel, at least, from the perspective of most of the multiverse. Sadly, the culture and its technological advancements were lost to time, due to the regressive nature of the dimension."

"There was a massive city here once." Anti stomped on the ground. "Right where we are standing."

"Or, a massive city will be here someday."

Jade and Anti were near trees, but they were not in a forest, they were instead in a grassy field, scattered with a few humongous trees with uneven, mossy roots at their base. They were not close enough to each other to call the area woodland, it was more like a loose collection of trees.

Colored mushrooms grew at the base of these trees and peeked through the tall, thin grass. It was these mushrooms, especially, that gave the entire area a distinct fairytale feeling. There was no sign of civilization in sight, nor were there any animals, at least at first.

"Harriet," Anti called into the wilderness.

Jade shushed her, "Now, she'll know that we're here."

"She would have known anyway," Anti shrugged. "I can tell that she wants us to find her, but I think she wants to find her in a special place, or in a certain way."

Anti's contemplation was cut short by a pack of large, tan, mountain cats creeping toward them from the left. Both women turned to watch the cats approaching, and for a moment, the sight of the animal's synchronized movements through the grass mesmerized them, but Jade sprang into action.

"Run!" she yelled as she grabbed Anti by the arm and pulled her behind one of the thick trees.

"I don't know that we needed to run, actually," Anti said. "It's not like they were coming at us quickly or looked menacing. I have an idea." Anti grinned suggestively at Jade.

"No," Jade said.

"What's the worst that could happen?"

"Fine." Jade peeked around the tree to get a better look at the pack of pumas, then she transformed herself into an attractive version of one cat near the head of the group. Her ears were a little small, and her whiskers were too long, but otherwise, she made a decent puma.

Jade approached the pack while Anti looked on. The other cats encircled Jade, taking turns sniffing her and laying their ears flat. Eventually, the other pumas all sat in the tall grass. Their relaxed posture signaled that it was okay for Puma Jade to lie with them, which she did for the better part of ten minutes, after which she strolled back to Anti, who was still hiding behind a tree, and transformed back into human form.

"Did you have a lovely bask in the sunlight?" Anti asked.

"Well, I know you don't mean it, but I did," Jade replied. "I enjoyed being a puma. I think it's my favorite animal I've been so far."

"So, are they calm? Can we walk past them and keep looking for Harriet?" Anti asked.

"Oh, I talked to them. Pumas can talk, and I can understand them when in my puma form," Jade said. "I told them about you, and they promised not to hurt you."

"Did they now? Can I have that in writing?"

"Stop it. The pumas also said they saw Harriet by a creek."

Anti exaggerated looking around. "I don't see any creeks around here, do you? Maybe your slick recent friends can lead us to where they saw Harriet."

"That's an outstanding idea; I'll ask them." Jade slipped back into her puma form and sauntered over to the puma pack. She flopped down in the grass beside them. All seven pumas sniffed the air around each other for a minute.

The entire pack, Jade the Puma included, stood up and strode over Anti.

"Should I follow you guys?" Anti asked.

Jade, who was the puma at the back of the pack, offered a slight nod, and the entire group moved forward in loose formation. Fanning out and then wandering back in, some kept their noses to the ground while others kept their eyes fixed ahead, their heads and thick necks steady.

"I'm blaming you if any of your buddies try to gnaw on me," Anti grumbled. "I'm not sure what a puma promise is worth."

Puma Jade turned and offered Anti a slow, serious gaze before continuing with the rest of the pack. Anti tagged along.

As Anti followed the pack of elegant, tan mountain lions through the thickening, emerald wilderness, she felt like an Amazonian goddess—commanding a herd of powerful, ethereal creatures. The effect became even more pronounced when they entered a dense forest. Dark green moss grew up the tree trunks and spread over dead and fallen timber. Anti had to walk more carefully than before because there were roots and rocks hidden in the soft leaves of the forest floor.

Everything was silent. Anti didn't notice the stillness at first because she was just getting a handle on this new dimension, but there was almost no noise. The strolling of the pumas made no sound, and the first hint of noise came from Anti's soft footfalls on the leafy ground in the thicker part of the forest. Anti heard herself breathe, and it was almost quiet enough that she could listen to her heart beating or her blood pumping through her veins.

The soft babble of creek overtook the silence, and Anti heard it minutes before they came upon it. Anti and the pumas followed the stream until they came to an area where an enormous, mossy tree had fallen across the water. The fallen tree was not impeding the creek's flow, however, because the fallen tree's root system was so tall that it propped the tree up, high enough for a person to walk under it without ducking.

And there was Harriet, under the toppled tree, looking as though she'd had a rough few days. Her tall hair was tousled and tumbling, and she was covered in minor scratches and bruises.

The puma pack turned and left, gracefully picking their way back through the forest. Jade, the Puma, not ready to be human again, sat on her haunches next to Anti as they both froze in place, staring at Harriet, who looked back at them with open curiosity.

"I'll say something to her," Anti said.

Jade seemed to agree.

"What should I say? 'You're under arrest, by order of The Multiverse!'"

Jade, the Puma, liked that.

"No, you know what? I'll hear Harriet out first. Maybe she can explain herself."

Jade flattened her ears and snarled.

"Are you good?" Anti called out to Harriet. "Are you a good person, Harriet? Because I think you are."

Jade looked at Anti as if she were insane, as best as she could with her puma face. Harriet matched Jade's astonishment.

"You chased me across three universes to ask me if I'm a good person?" Harriet, who had been leaning on the felled tree trunk, uncrossed her arms and stood up straight.

"No, but…" Anti searched for the right words, "I wanted to know if you would come with us, without a big fuss, because a good person would, even if they'd made some terrible choices before. Because good people choose what's better for everyone over what's better for themselves."

"How about what's best for me, and what's neutral for almost everyone else?" Harriet seemed intrigued with Anti's question. "Because what I'm doing is the equivalent of my making a ham sandwich as far as the rest of the multiverse is concerned. No one else noticed the shift to alternate realities, and, by the time we get back from here, the people in Aperture will no longer know you existed, and they'll think I'm still trapped on your Earth."

"We're not planning on staying here long enough for that to happen. Come with us back to the bridge to Aperture."

Harriet opened her arms and looked defiant. "No," she said.

"Jade here will rip you to shreds," Anti suggested, though she was unsure about that.

Jade paced back and forth in front of Anti.

"I don't think she will. You two don't have the constitutions for violence, and, second, you need me alive to put me back where I belong so that your home dimension stabilizes. No Harriet, no Earth for you to come home to."

"Why us, Harriet?" Anti asked. "Why drag us all the way from the Orion Center to here?"

"I witnessed thirty-seven Orion Center press day accidents in alternate dimensions, but the mishap that befell you was the one I'd been waiting for," Harriet said.

"Not cool, Harriet," Anti said.

"What would you do if you were me?" Harriet pleaded. "I assume someone from Aperture filled you in on what was true and what was deceit in my journal. Put yourself in my place, just for a second... what would you do if you lost your entire family?"

"You haven't lost your family," Jade reasoned as she transformed back into her human self. "They are absolutely fine in thousands of alternate realities, just not always in the one you're in."

"All I want is to get into a world where my family exists and stay there; no more shifts to other realities," Harriet said. "I'm not hurting anyone. There is no collateral."

"We are. Anti and I are the collateral. There are consequences for us as you move through dimensions. What you're doing is permanent to Anti and me," Jade reasoned.

"Is that so bad? You've just said more to me in the last two minutes than you've said out loud in your entire life. And with you two attached at the hip, Antigone here will never have to think for herself again. I have given you both a gift."

"Aperture's people wouldn't have imprisoned you on Earth if your crime was victimless," Jade said. "Your crusade to find and stay with your family has a cost, even if most other people don't realize when they pay it. You are wiping out whole words, entire lives, whole—"

"Families?" Harriet finished.

The three women fell silent, contemplating the weight of Harriet's loss.

Then, Harriet said, "It's my birthday."

"What?"

"In almost all realities I've been in, today's my birthday," Harriet said. "It's been my birthday for even longer because of the time flowing backward here. If I go back and forth long enough, it will be my birthday forever."

"Is that supposed to make us want to help you, Harriet? Saying today is your birthday?" Jade asked.

"No," Harriet shook her head. "It just is."

"Happy Birthday," Anti said. She shoved Jade lightly when she didn't say it as well.

"I'm not saying 'Happy Birthday' to her," Jade hissed. "She's tricking us."

"To what end? To dupe us into eating cake?" Anti said. "No cake Harriet, we've already had party potatoes."

Harriet watched the two women snipe at each other with smug satisfaction.

"Can we go somewhere where Harriet can't hear us and talk this through?" Jade suggested.

"Fine," Anti said. "Whatever we do, we had better decide fast. Time is running out."

Jade and Anti walked back through the forest at a quick pace. They had to get farther from Harriet than they would have in a different environment, because of the virtually soundless nature of the dimension.

When Anti guessed that they were a sufficient distance from Harriet, she said, "I think we should help her."

"Why?" Jade rolled her eyes. "Because it's her birthday?"

"No, not because it's her birthday. Because if we take her to Aperture and give her to Adellum, they'll throw her in some other prison. If we help her, we can put her back in her home dimension."

"Why do we have to get involved? Let Adellum sort it out."

"We're already involved, and she's a person, and she's suffering... and we could help her," Anti implored.

"You really fell for the 'it's my birthday' stunt. We didn't go through all of this to get Harriet just to let her off the hook."

"She was only causing issues because she was searching for a reality that had her family in it, but Harriet wouldn't have to search or cause problems if she had our help."

While the women were talking, the sky above them had taken on an odd, yellow color, which they hadn't noticed until it grew extreme. Along with the color, the atmosphere darkened, and the once emerald forest took on an ominous, murky, green hue.

"I think it's going to storm." Jade held her hand up, but no raindrops fell onto her palm. "We should get her back to Aperture before we revert to a time where we never existed in that dimension. We can decide if we want to help her there, with time flowing around us, normally."

Figuring she may have made some headway in changing Jade's mind, Anti agreed to walk toward Harriet. On the way, the women decided to tell Harriet they'd help her, just to get her back to Aperture, and, once there, they'd determine their actual course of action.

THIS CHAPTER DIDN'T HAPPEN

"You'll have to come back to Aperture with us," Anti said. "No one paid attention to Jade and me until we went up to the information desk, so I'm guessing they'll ignore us so as long as we don't make a fuss. From the halls of Aperture, we should be able to sneak you back into your homeworld where I can search for your alternate reality."

Harriet took a deep breath, and her high hairdo bobbled on her head. "Okay," she said. "I will trust you... but just once. If you lie to me, there will be no next time."

"Like you haven't lied to us before." Anti turned and walked back through the woods toward the Implam door. "Let's go."

"We should run back to the Aperture bridge," Harriet suggested.

"Why?" Jade asked.

"Because it's about to rain here and the rain is toxic to hominids who are not native to this dimension. A little exposure could knock you out. Long-term exposure will kill you."

There was a low, deep rumble in the Implam sky. Harriet took off and ran right past Jade and Anti, who hesitated for just a moment before pursuing her. Jade transformed back to her puma form, while running, and she overcame both Harriet and Anti, who found her standing at the tree trunk Aperture door.

"Show off," Anti said breathlessly.

Harriet agreed. "Remarkable, Jade."

A few thin droplets of rain fell on them as they neared the door.

"I feel a little woozy," Anti said.

"Me too," Jade admitted.

"Let's go!" Harriet insisted.

All three of them piled through the wooden door carved in the tree trunk. In the next instant, the women stood alone in the Aperture hallway.

"Well, we're in the clear. Adellum isn't waiting for us."

"We may have regressed in time to a point where we haven't come to Aperture yet. At least we won't have to distract anyone to get Harriet back to her homeworld."

"Look at you with a devious plan," Anti feigned shock.

"We don't have time for this," Jade deflected. "Harriet, what is the name of your homeworld?"

Anti read some doors in the hallway. The nearest one was simply labeled, "*The Forty-Fourth Dimension: Quarantined.*"

"That's the thing," Harriet said. "My homeworld is Earth, just not your Earth."

Before she could explain herself further, Adellum rounded the corner, and his little troll face looked delighted to see all three women. "Wonderful," he said. "Thank you for bringing Harriet to us." Adellum advanced on the women.

"Apparently, we have not regressed," Anti pointed out.

Harriet looked stunned, but only momentarily. Acting quickly, she opened the door closest to Anti, shoved her in and followed behind.

Jade exclaimed, "Hey," and turned to Adellum.

"I wouldn't," he warned.

It only took Jade a moment to decide—she followed Anti and Harriet though the door marked "Forty-Fourth Dimension." Once she was on the other side, Jade spun around to catch the door before it closed, but she was too late. She saw Harriet closing what looked like a piece of the dimension itself behind her. Once she shut it, the door disappeared, blending seamlessly into the surroundings.

Jade stood in a foot of snow, and the surrounding air was cold and heavy. All around here were piles of muddy snow and patches of wet dirt.

"Anti," Jade called. "Can you stabilize the bridge here? I don't see a door."

Anti was looking straight up, distracted by the sky in the Forty-Fourth Dimension. "Sky" wasn't entirely correct. Instead, it was the lack of sky that captivated Anti.

Instead of an atmosphere, a hunk of earth hung above them, identical to the snow and mud they currently stood upon but crawling with human-sized insectoid creatures.

The upside-down world was near to the ground, about the height of a medium-sized skyscraper. The lizard people scurried around their buildings, which were many shapes from squat domes to tall towers, but all of it seemed made of mud.

"Where's the light coming from?" Anti muttered. "How can we see it?"

Jade shouted, "Antigone! I can't see the bridge. Stabilize the door we came through."

Anti snapped out of it, swung around, pulled her stabilizer from her hoodie pocket, and ran it up and down the space where the Aperture door should have been.

"Do you see a bridge there?" Jade asked. "It was strange. It looked like Harriet was closing some of the dimension behind us."

"I can see the bridge," Anti said. "But it's not right; it's faint and weird. Let's try to get back through it. Harriet thinks we've betrayed her, so she's disappeared into this dimension."

"We might fix it if we get back fast enough," Jade offered.

There was a massive thud as one of the lizard creatures jumped down from the inhabited side of the dimension and landed about twenty yards in front of Jade and Anti. Another half dozen of the beasts quickly followed it.

Close up, Jade saw the creatures walking on four legs with an additional two hands, making six appendages in total. Their smooth bodies were a variety of colors, including red, burnt orange, lavender, and sky blue, and they looked more arachnid than insectoid upon further inspection.

Each creature had four eyes, two sets below the first. Though they had flat, snake-like noses, their eyes betrayed intelligence, possibly wisdom. They held their heads high on long necks, and, combined with their bright, upturned eyes, this gave the effect of making them look haughty. They clothed their considerable bodies in a paste made of mud and ice, but their dress didn't look primitive because they had created intricate patterns with the materials.

The arachnid beasts spoke with each other through quick hand gestures and curt nods, and, after conversing this way for a minute, a few of them turned toward Jade and Anti and gestured at them.

"Well, the translator is useless here," Anti lamented.

As soon as Anti spoke, the creatures looked startled and pained. They flailed their hands around and moved toward the women.

"What did we do?" Anti asked. The creatures startled again.

"Stop talking!" Jade hissed.

One creature, a blue one at the front of the group, raised his hand, and a thick, white beam shot out of it. Anti, whether it was reflexes or her extra-dimensional sentience, grabbed Jade and pulled her out of the way just in time. A massive chunk of ice stood in her previous location.

"It tried to freeze ray you!" Anti yelled.

"We've got to get back through the door!" Jade ran but was stopped when another creature, the dark orange one, held up its hands, releasing a spray of colored red crystals that enveloped Jade and Anti and held them up off the ground.

"Get off us!" Anti shouted as she struggled in the red crystal cloud. The volume of Anti's voice was enough to pain the creatures to distraction, and the cluster of crystals fell to the ground, along with Jade and Anti.

Laying sideways on the ground, Anti saw a bright blue glow emanating from the horizon.

"That's where the light is coming from," Anti said with interest, despite herself.

"Look," Jade sat up and pointed. Some of the creatures were shrinking as their skin became smoother and lighter.

Anti cocked her head to one side. "They're changing into... us. They're shifters, like you."

The creatures screamed again when Anti spoke, though their screeches sounded much more human than before. The entire group of monsters, about half a dozen now, advanced on Jade and Anti, all in terrifying stages of transformation from creature to human.

Jade grabbed the antimatter cannon from her pocket, pointed it, and shot. Nothing happened. She hadn't turned off the device's safety switch. Anti screamed something indecipherable and grabbed for the cannon. Jade turned off the safety and shot. The gun ripped a hole in one monster, and it crumpled to the ground. The other creatures stopped advancing and rushed to the fallen beast.

Jade and Anti stood to run, though neither was sure where to run to on the open plane. As they got to their feet, Adellum came from behind them. He waved his troll hands at the monsters, who gesticulated back at him before using their sturdy hind legs to jump back to the sky of the dimension. The last creature to jump leaped up, clutching his injured companion.

Adellum made a *shushing* gesture with his finger on his lips and led Jade and Anti to the open door, which, from their side, looked like a rectangle cut out the fabric of the dimension, filled with a hotel hallway. As fast as they could, Jade and Anti hustled out of Forty-Fourth Dimension and into the Aperture hallway.

"What the actual fuck were you doing in there?" Adellum lost his composure for the first time since they had met him. "I understand exploration, but you have to investigate these worlds before you just run into them. The Forty-Fourth Dimension is under strict quarantine. There is a vast array of rules, laws, and dangers. Keep this up, and I'll be known as the commander who killed our first Earth ambassadors."

"You knew we were in there," Anti said when Adellum stopped to breathe. "You watched Harriet push us in five minutes ago."

"I saw nothing of the sort," Adellum insisted. "If I didn't come around the corner and notice the door to the Forty-Fourth Dimension disturbed, they would have killed you."

"Does time their flow backward?" Jade asked, hoping for an explanation of why Adellum didn't remember events that happened moments ago.

"Time there flows wildly, it's impossible to tell. Everything in there happens according to what Dirt Wizards want. They can alter dimensional space, and they are not nice."

"Jade shot one," Anti said as if tattling on an elementary school classmate.

Jade gave her a scathing look.

"Well, you're lucky we confine them to the Forty-Fourth dimension. The only thing keeping Wizards in there is their inability to tolerate the noise from other dimensions. They see it as a contagion. You escaped death. From now on, let's refrain from going into unfamiliar dimensions and shooting the inhabitants."

"We just told you, Harriet shoved me in there."

Adellum looked confused.

"Harriet must have escaped to Implam, and she's reversing time," Jade reasoned. "So, to him, it didn't happen. Soon, none of this will have happened, and no one will have any recollection of it, but Harriet."

"Sound reasoning," Adellum said. "The last time you were in Implam, you didn't run into yourselves, did you?"

"No," Anti said.

"Well, I'd send you in there to counteract the effects of the time-reversal, but an earlier version of you is already in there, and since you didn't see yourselves before, that means that something will prevent you from getting in there in time."

"If none of this is happening," Anti asked, "why are we here?"

"We're just in a little pocket of an alternate reality, a remnant of the no-longer-existing time this all happened in. No one will remember this, aside from, well, the creatures from the Forty-Fourth Dimension. We can't study time effects there. The Dirt Wizards from the Forty-Fourth Dimension have killed and eaten seven Aperture researchers, to date."

"Maybe they're just upset you didn't throw them a 'Welcome to the Multiverse' party," Anti joked. "Hey!"

The air grew thinner, and the colors of the hall and their clothes faded as if they had been left in the sun for a week.. Anti felt stretched, and Jade felt itchy. Their reality seemed old and thin.

"Well, that's all folks," Apellum announced. "This reality bubble is about to burst."

CHAPTER 25
SUCH A DRAG

With Jade still in mountain lion form and Anti making as quiet strides as possible, they picked their way through the luxuriously green Implam forest. When they came upon Harriet, it surprised them to see her wearing a full-length, hooded black poncho, the sort that often came in emergency safety packs. She was also wearing elbow-length black rubber gloves. She tried to put on a face mask, but between the gloves and the hood, she was having some difficulty.

"I am sorry about this," Harriet said.

"What are you sorry about? Your outfit?" Anti laughed, but no one else joined in.

Jade shifted out of her puma form just in time to frown at Anti.

"As I've said, I've gone back and forth between this universe and Aperture several times, gaining more time and then spending it," Harriet explained. "Also, it's my birthday today."

"Happy birthday," Anti said and nudged Jade in the ribs, encouraging her to acknowledge the day.

"I'm not saying 'Happy Birthday,'" Jade said. "It's a trick."

"You always think it's a trick," Harriet said. "It's not a deception. However, it has been my birthday for so long, I daresay it hardly counts as my birthday anymore. Again, I apologize. I found out about the rain the hard way. I would only do this if you wouldn't help me, and it seems like you will not help me."

Harriet pulled her mask down over her face and, in that same second, torrential rain poured down from the yellow and gray sky, and the previous near silence was washed away in the sudden cacophony of rushing water.

"We could have used your umbrella," Jade held her palm up to the downpour.

"I gave it to Adellum for his museum," Anti said. "Do you feel strange? I feel weird like I might be high or something."

"I don't know. I've never been high before." Jade's voice sounded dreamy and distant, not only to Anti but to herself as well.

Jade felt increasingly heavy, at first, it was as if she could not raise her arms, then it seemed as if her spine could not support the upright nature of her body.

"I think she put drugs in the rain." Anti slurred her words. "Harriet drugged the rain."

That statement was the last thing that Jade heard before everything went black.

Once she was certain the rain took effect, Harriet crept over to the women and stood over Jade and Antigone's prone bodies. She took a moment to adjust her mask and cap to ensure no rain trickled in and incapacitated her. She considered the women and decided Jade was the heavier of the two, and so she should carry her first.

Harriet hoisted Jade up, intending to sling her over her shoulder, but realized she didn't have the strength. Instead, Harriet stood Jade up, wrapped Jade's arm around her shoulders, and fixed her hand on her waist. Harriet carried Jade along through the wilderness of Implam, looking like a benevolent friend helping a drunk buddy home from the pub. All the while, she hummed "Happy Birthday" to herself.

Harriet had no trouble locating the Implam gate to Aperture. Even with the pouring rain, she recognized the door carved into the ancient tree trunk as a familiar friend. Without her hands free, Harriet had to kick in the door, which caused her to stumble into Aperture's hallway. She winced at the ruckus she had made but was surprised to find the hall empty. This was disconcerting. In her dozens of times through, Harriet had never seen the building empty before. She had just begun to wonder where everyone had gotten to when a sudden alarm startled her. A voice that spoke in every known language at once but was still comprehensible accompanied the alarm.

"Quarantine has been breached. Return to your home dimension. Quarantine has been breached. Return to your home dimension."

"No need to shout," Harriet harrumphed. "I'm going there anyway."

Using the route she'd memorized, Harriet shuffled through Aperture's maze of halls, going slower every minute as she struggled under Jade's weight. As she neared her home portal, Harriet heard shouting and a sudden clamor indicating a struggle.

Harriet paused. The noise came from the hall she needed to travel through to get to her door.

"Figures," Harriet mumbled.

The fracas tumbled into Harriet and Jade's vicinity, causing her to press against the wall. A handful of Aperture's reptilian armored guards clashed with massive mud-covered arachnids. The Aperture guards attempted to hold the arachnids at bay with electrified harpoons that simultaneously looked both antique and futuristic.

One of the Aperture guards focused on Harriet and her captive. He sized them up and assumed Jade had been injured in the fray.

"Get her to the medical bay," the guard garbled through his helmet. "Dirt Wizard injuries are dimensionally destabilizing." He gestured down the hallway towards the medical bay.

Harriet straightened up and prepared to lug Jade to her door at top speed, but the day's activities caught up with Harriet's middle-aged body. Her back tweaked, and a shot of pain ran down her spine and leg. Instead of hustling, Harriet limped and meandered through the battle between the Dirt Wizard's and the Aperturian guards, which was in full fervor. Both sides ignored her as she shuffled past.

With her last ounce of energy, Harriet wrenched open the plain, white door marked *"Earth Two"*. She stumbled into a laboratory furnished with wood and warped glass. She laid Jade down on a pile of puffy blankets and stood over her, not so much to admire her handy work but to hunch and catch her breath. Holding herself up straight hurt horribly.

With her hands cradling her lower back, Harriet slunk through a nearby portal which, in this dimension, resembled a weathered door of cobbled together wood and rusted tin. Harriet tottered into the Aperture hallway. The Aperturian skirmish had moved on to another area of the dimension, leaving Harriet free to pick her way back to the Implam door.

Twenty agonizing minutes later, Harriet, covered in protective gear, stood over Anti, who was sleeping peacefully in a misty glade in the silent forests of Implam. After considering for a few moments, Harriet grabbed Anti by the ankles and dragged her through the damp woodland. Harriet did her best to avoid rocks and roots, but Anti's hair and back were covered in thick mud and moss that trailed behind them once they were out of the Implam forest as Harriet dragged Anti back through Aperture's halls.

"Well, this will lead them right to us. I hope it won't matter by then," Harriet said through a clenched jaw. She almost made it all the way back to her door when she saw a familiar figure turn the corner and freeze.

"I know you," Adellum said to Harriet, "You're from another timeline. Wait while I access it." The troll stood still, wrapped in thought.

Harriet was not going to wait for Adellum to access his Harriet memories. She made a lunge for her door, as best she could with Anti in tow.

"What's wrong with that Earthling?" Adellum's concentration broke. "Is she wounded?"

Harriet slammed the dimensional door behind her, dropped Anti beside Jade on the pile of blankets. She grabbed a device made of a glass bulb filled with two metal prongs, mounted on a wooden handle. Harriet flipped a switch, activating the device, and the prongs rotated so fast they turned into a blur. Harriet touched the bulb to the rusted door she used to travel from Aperture, and the door vanished.

She looked from the absent door to the heap of sleeping women on the floor and then collapsed against her desk in a blend of relief and back pain.

CHAPTER 26
HARRIET'S EARTHS

Jade awoke to pleasant warmth and a soft humming sound. In the brief moments before she became cognizant, she felt like she was asleep in her own bed, but a jolt of sudden awareness woke her as abruptly as if an electric shock had hit her. Jade sat upright and surveyed her surroundings. She had been asleep on a thin mattress stuffed with soft material, probably organic, possibly feathers. The blanket lay on the ground, a natural wood floor, polished to shine. Someone had placed a thick blanket over her, and it was almost as heavy and stuffed as the mattress.

Anti lay on a matching mattress on the floor next to Jade, she was still asleep and snored softly. Anti looked filthy with muddy clothes, and her red hair tangled with leaves. Jade patted her own hair and body and was relieved to find she was not in the same ruined state.

They were in a room the size of an elementary school classroom. Tables made from the same light-colored, shiny wood as the floor were pushed against the walls. Many of the tables held half-built contraptions, made of more wood, glass, and tin. A few sturdy chairs were scattered about, and, sitting in one of them, was Harriet, looking pleased with herself.

"We're just going to wait for Antigone to wake up," Harriet said. "I don't want to explain myself twice."

"We were in the forest," Jade said. "Time was moving backward."

"Yes, the rain in Implam is a toxic analgesic. It renders most humanoids unconscious. You might have a terrible headache." Harriet stood up and walked over to a sink in the room's corner that Jade hadn't noticed before. She handed Jade a polished wood cup filled with water before sitting back down in her chair.

"Where are we, and how did you get us here?" Jade asked after she'd gulped down the entire cup.

"Wait for Antigone." Harriet folded her hands in front of her.

Jade reached down and gave Anti's shoulder a vigorous shake. She did not rouse from her deep slumber.

"I imagine it may be hard for you to cope without your mouthpiece, but she should wake shortly, don't worry," Harriet said.

"Unnecessary." Jade stood up and took a few, shaky steps from the floor mattress. "I can cope without Antigone."

"Forgive me," Harriet said. "I've been through an ordeal getting you here."

"Where is here?" Anti asked. She sat up on her mattress and blinked. "What did you do to us, Harriet?"

"I didn't do much. The nature of the dimension Implam did most of the work for me. I knew I would need to find a place with regressive time, so I could stay in the dimension until it erased me from the memory of Aperture, and I could start over if I made a mistake. The paralyzing effect of the rain in Implam was a happy accident. It knocked me out during one of my brief trips. When the rain was over, and I had awakened, I knew how to use it to my advantage. After I gathered protective supplies, I stayed in Aperture until the rain in Implam reset. Then, I waited for you to find me. When the rain rendered you unconscious, I carried you, one at a time, through Implam, then through Aperture, to the portal to my dimension. It was quite an ordeal, and I'm suffering from lower back pain." Harriet rubbed her back and winced. "And it's my birthday."

"Happy birthday," Anti grumbled.

"How did you carry us through Aperture with no one noticing?" Jade asked.

"I didn't. I tried to wait until we stayed in Implam long enough for time to regress beyond when you first entered Aperture, but there was a fuss from another dimension. A breached quarantine."

Anti pouted and rubbed the back of her head. "That explains the mud. You didn't have to drag me, Harriet."

"I did. I was too weak after carrying Jade. The Aperturian guards saw us but didn't follow due to the chaos with demons from an invading dimension. But they'll be after us soon enough."

"You seem awfully calm about all of this," Anti observed.

"There's no use getting riled up. I've been through this, or something similar, dozens of times. Plus, this is my home universe, and I'm a brilliant quantum physicist. I have my own failsafe in place for when the Aperture cavalcade arrives."

"You didn't have to knock us out and drag us here, Harriet. We were talking about helping you." Anti was gaining her wits.

"No, you weren't. You were just going to bring me to Aperture under the guise of helping me, then you would turn me into the authorities there." Harriet stood, winced, and placed her hand on the small of her back again. "Do you want to know how I know? Because I believed you and watched you do it, then I escaped back to Implam and waited for time to revert. As I stated before, it has been my birthday for a long time."

There was nothing that Jade could say. How could she justify something she didn't remember doing, something this Jade, in this timeline, didn't do to Harriet?

Anti spoke quietly; she seemed to contemplate the same conundrum as Jade. "Harriet, you brought us to *your* home."

"Yes, but we're not in my home reality. My family isn't here. I need you to help me find them. Strangely enough, this place is also called Earth. It has many similarities to the world that you come from, but the technology is much more advanced. We learned, early in our society, to manipulate matter, they might call it magic on your home dimension, but it's science. Maybe, my Earth and your Earth were once the same, long ago, but a branch of alternate realities broke off and made the places separate."

"Magic!" Anti turned to Jade. "I told you."

"It only looks like magic. You ignored most of what she just said." To Harriet, Jade said, "I'd love to see some of your illusions and hear about the science behind it."

"Having lived on your Earth for so long, I learned many of the stories and myths. I think many of your stories, particularly the older ones with magic and wizards, and gods walking among you, are echoes of alternate realities and dimensions that have split off from your own. That said, get me back to my home, and my family and I will show anything magic you want."

"I have a serious question." Anti had now stood up and was eyeballing the long tables full of ambiguous wooden and glass equipment.

"I doubt it," Jade said.

Anti ignored her. "What if we don't help you? Are we free to just get up and walk out, find a dimension bridge, and start our long trek back home? Or are you going to stop us? Do you have a weapon? Is their more coma rain?"

"No, nothing is stopping you, but I'm the only one who can explain who you are to the angry group of Aperturian guards who are about to plunge into this dimension in search of the hooligans who have been tearing through the multiverse. Time has gone back and forth many times. Who knows how much they remember of you, or if they remember you at all. If you try to go back through there, you'll end up in prison, one not nearly as nice as your Earth."

"If we help you, you'll be gone. You won't be here to explain who we are and why we're here."

"But I can give you something that will explain all of this. My notes and inventions for you to turn over to Aperture."

"I don't believe you." Jade looked into Harriet's eyes, she was quiet and cold.

"You don't have a choice," Harriet returned her chill.

"We do."

Harriet shook her head, she paused and took a deep, ragged breath, her face turned red as she fought back the tears. "If you don't help me, then I give up. Maybe you return home, and nothing happens to you, but you are my last chance. If you do not help me, I will..." Harriet searched for the right words. "I will cease to be."

"Are you going to kill yourself, Harriet?" Anti asked with frank curiosity. "That is some heavy emotional manipulation."

"I have always been as honest with you two as I could," Harriet pleaded. "Almost everything I wrote in my journal was true, even though I meant for you to find it. And, maybe I am manipulating you, but it's out of desperation. My life is not worth living without my children and my husband."

Instinctively, Anti walked over to Harriet and put her hand on the woman's shoulder. A few leaves and clods of dirt tumbled to the floor, and several more transferred to Harriet. "I believe you. You can be both a manipulative monster and a loving mother. You should meet mine."

Anti's soft, filthy touch opened a raw spot inside of Harriet, and she cried. Jade watched the two of them as if she were scrutinizing an alien species.

Harriet said, "I have dreams I can't remember. But when I wake up, I'm calling for them, screaming their names into the night. When I wake up, it's midnight, and I am in yet another strange world. I have been to foreign lands and seen unbelievable wonders, but nothing has been as bizarre to me as having to navigate even a single day in a world where my children don't exist. Please."

"I will," Anti said. She looked at Jade, her own eyes welling with pleading tears. "I will help you."

"Fine," Jade agreed. "But, I want to study some of your advanced technology when we're done."

Anti clapped, and more dirt and leaves fell from her hair. "How do we get started?"

Harriet reached into her beehive hairdo and pulled out a photograph. Jade and Anti looked at her with astonishment. "Storing it in my hair is the only way I could be sure to keep it with me through all the alternate reality shifts and trips through dimensional bridges," she explained.

"Jeeze Harriet, you got anything else in there?" Anti snickered.

Harriet handed the picture to Anti. It was a worn, sepia-toned image of a smiling Harriet with a balding man, and three children; two girls and a boy. They were standing in a field, and there was a large, wooden tower in the distance.

"That's my Frank and the children. I've kept this with me since I started noticing large reality shifts. Anti, can you find a bridge to the world that this picture is from?" Harriet asked, her voice brimming with hope.

"I mean... maybe?" Anti took the picture and examined it. "I found you in multiple dimensions, but it takes time and focus. Even when I can focus, what comes through is sometimes random."

Harriet continued to look at Anti with bleary-eyed anticipation.

"But, I'll try," Anti finished. "Can I take a shower?"

CHAPTER 27
SPOOKY COOKIE

The streets in Harriet's home dimension were coated in thin sheets of metal, which conducted the electricity powering the word's vehicles: rickety contraptions made from slabs of wood, strips of metal, and yellowed glass. The metal streets were not in good repair either, the edges were rusty, with large spots of rust the vehicles had to swerve to avoid, and pedestrians jumped out of the way to keep from being struck by the wooden behemoths.

Anti pulled her *Encyclopedia of the Abyss* from her bag. "Where am I?" She asked the book.

A few drawings of a round, blue planet resembling Earth popped up on the book's pages. *"You are on a planet called Earth in an ancient dimension on the very edge of the known multiverse,"* the text read.

"If you call your dimension 'Earth,' too, how do they tell it apart from ours in Aperture?" Anti asked Harriet.

"Well, in the true Aperture, the one with no translation filters, nothing has names, just feelings, and shapes. This Earth has a different ambiance. Besides, no one talks about your Earth anyway, because it's not attached to the rest of the multiverse. Although, now that Earth can connect, we'll have to figure it out. We'll call my dimension Earth One and your dimension Earth Two," Harriet suggested.

"Since we're helping you out, we get to be Earth One," Anti said.

Anti sidestepped to avoid a swerving vehicle, then stopped on the side of the road. "I have to concentrate on this." She gripped Harriet's family photo in her hand and looked deeply at it.

"Can you see any bridges here?" Harriet asked.

"A few, but they're not the right ones. Also, I've never tried to find a bridge to an alternate reality before, just other dimensions, so I don't know if this will work. I told you to let me concentrate." Anti's voice rose.

Harriet quieted down, and she and Jade tried not to stare at or otherwise disturb Anti while she took deep, meditative breaths and fixated on Harriet's photo. Her coppery red hair slipped from its usual place, tucked behind her ear, and fell in front of her face, brushing onto Harriet's picture.

"I think I have it," Anti said after several minutes. "That way," Anti pointed to the left.

"Are you certain?" Harriet asked.

"I am *not* sure, Harriet," Anti grinned. "But we have to go with what I got."

"That's a rather disturbing part of the city," Harriet said. "We call the area The Great Dark."

"Well, I guess we're going to The Great Dark," Anti shrugged.

The closer they got to The Great Dark, the worse the conditions of the roads grew, until they were mostly dirt, with a few rust patches, and barely any metal. No one could drive on them, but there weren't any vehicles anyway, all the pedestrians were on foot.

Once they were deep in The Great Dark, Jade heard singing and brass instruments. A large group of people rounded the corner in front of them, it looked like a mini street parade. A group of colorfully dressed, masked people danced on the worn roadway, followed by a handful of people playing brass instruments, and, bringing up the rear, was half a dozen pallbearers carrying a coffin.

"The Great Dark is where we celebrate the dead," Harriet explained. "They are bringing the dead to The Cadaverous Ball."

"Fascinating," Jade said, she looked at the procession longingly, as if she wished she could follow.

"In there." Anti pointed to a connected strip of shops across the road from them. The buildings were low bungalows made of polished wood with hand-painted signs, denoting a baker's shop, a tavern, and an incense shop. "In one of those buildings."

"Which one should we try first?" Jade asked.

"The bar," Anti said.

"Are you sure?" Harriet asked.

"No, but when given a choice, always pick the bar," Anti winked.

The tavern's sign read, "The Crucible." The interior was the same wood that seemed to permeate the entire dimension. There was a mix of small round tables and long counters that could seat a dozen people. The serving station ran the width of the back of the room, and a large, wall-mounted glass case took up most of the adjacent wall.

When the women entered, the bartender called out to them, "Hello, Anee." He gave a friendly wave. Anti was the only one who waved back, and the bartender lowered his hand, looking irritated.

"What does he mean by 'Anee'? It sounded a little like my name." Anti asked. Harriet shrugged.

It was early afternoon, so the bar was empty aside from a group of people dressed in rugged adventuring gear, including leather caps and glass goggles. They leaned into mugs of beer and looked morose.

"What's wrong with them?" Anti whispered.

"The king put a ban on multidimensional exploration, ever since…" Harriet paused, "ever since realities destabilized."

"No collateral damage?" Jade raised her eyebrows at Harriet. "It seems likely you caused the destabilization."

Harriet had no response. She just looked sad.

Anti glanced from Jade to Harriet and then said, "We've come this far. Let's put her back in her home reality. We're not responsible for what she did before or what she does after."

Anti walked across the tavern and peered into the glass case that ran the length of the bar. It was a miniature museum of sorts with a dozen different gadgets on display. A banner across the top labeled it as "Artifacts of Adventurous and Hero Accolades."

"I can read these!" Anti exclaimed.

One apparatus was labeled a "Barrier Revitalizer Matrix." It was a glass tube with a handle made of metal and wood. A brief description was written on a piece of paper nailed underneath the Barrier Revitalizer Matrix's plaque. It read, "*Used to hold open the bridge between Earth and Jequia during the exploration of Jequia. Earth citizens secured Jequia, creating a vigorous, interdimensional trade route that functions to this day.*"

"Hey Jade," Anti called, "this looks like it does the same thing as my stabilizer."

Jade walked over to the glass case and scrutinized the shelf's tools.

"I think you're right. This must be how Harriet created the stabilizer and other items for the Orion Center; she was copying the technology from her world."

Harriet slunk over while Jade and Anti were studying the glass case.

"Is the travel ban really your fault?" Anti asked.

"Only partially," Harriet answered. "I was already studying the destabilization, likely caused by our large number of trips through permanent portals, but it accelerated when I started searching for my family." This admission did not deter Harriet. "Are we close to where you sense the alternate dimension in the picture."

"It's not in here," Anti said. "Let's try the bakery next store."

The business next to the tavern was called Anee's Bake Shop. No one was visible when they walked into the bakery, but a little brass bell rang when they stepped through the door. To the women's shock, the baker who greeted them when they walked through the door was identical to Jade in every way, except for her messy apron and flour-covered hands.

"Hello, welcome to Anee's. I'm Anee," she said and then froze when she saw Jade. She studied Jade for a moment then asked, "What kind of sorcery is this? Did my husband send you as a joke?"

Jade and Anti were not sure what sort of sorcery it was.

"It's not funny," Anee pressed.

"It's not sorcery," Jade said tentatively. "It seems to be an odd coincidence."

Jade's doppelganger stepped around the bakery counter and display case and stood in front of Jade, looking her up and down. Jade looked back at her with frank curiosity. "Maybe I have a sister I never knew about," the baker said.

"Unlikely," Anti said. "We're not from around here."

"Where are you from?" she asked.

Harriet gave the baker a significant look, "We're not from *here*."

The doppelganger baker nodded with understanding.

While Harriet smoothed things over, and Jade gaped in disbelief, Anti studied the baked goods in the display case. There were cookies shaped like skulls, bread shaped like coffins, and cakes that looked like tombs.

"Why is your food spooky?" Anti asked.

"We're in The Great Dark, and we serve those who serve the dead." Anee seemed confused for a moment, then said, "I suppose you wouldn't understand if you came from someplace else."

"Is this the right place, Antigone?" Harriet attempted to bring Anti's attention back to the current task.

Anti stood up and looked through the kitchen toward the rear of the bakery. "There's something back there. I think it's what we're looking for." Anti wondered if she should continue to speak in coded messages. Harriet gave no indication.

"I know this is an unusual request, but may we have a tour of the bakery? We just want to go back into the kitchen for a few moments."

"I'm sorry," Anee said. She put her hands up. "This is all too strange for me."

"I understand," Harriet said. "Have a lovely afternoon."

The three women exited the bakery and stood in a small circle outside.

"What was that? Why did that woman look like me?" Jade demanded.

"As I told you," Harriet said, "I believe this dimension was once an alternate reality to your Earth or vice versa. She's likely an alternate version of you."

"I do enjoy baking and cooking," Jade said ponderously.

"Not to pressure you too much, but can we get to the matter at hand?" Harriet urged. "We have to figure out how to get into the back of the bakery. If you're certain the area holds the gate to my true reality, Antigone."

"I'm as sure as I can be." Anti was unconvincing, but they all silently pressed forward, anyway.

"Can we wait for the bakery to close and break-in?" Anti offered after a prolonged silence.

"It will close as soon as the Ball starts, but we can't wait for the streets to empty, and we'd be caught if we did it during the Ball," Harriet said. "Besides, it may only be a matter of time before the Aperture battalion comes in here after us." Harriet wrung her hands. "It could close soon. Alternate reality bridges are notoriously unstable."

"Anti, go into the bakery and stabilize the bridge from the front of the store. We can worry about how to get to the back later." Jade ordered.

"Can do, sir," Anti gave a sarcastic salute. Anti pulled her dimensional stabilizer from her bag and reentered the bakery.

Five minutes later, Anti walked out with a bakery bag full of tombstone and skull-shaped cookies. "I stabilized the bridge to Harriet's reality, so it should be there for a while. Spooky cookie?" She extended the bag to the two other women, who declined.

While Anti was eating, another group of people walked by, all of them wearing jeweled masquerade masks.

"Good Afternoon, Anee," one of the masked men waived at Jade, and she waved back.

"We won't need to break in if we own the place," Harriet said. "But, let's get off the street before more people see us."

In a dim alleyway which there was an abundance of The Great Dark, Harriet asked Jade if she could transform her clothes to match those of Anee, the baker. After a few tries, Jade got the costume almost perfect, aside from the exact color of cream and a dusting of flour.

"There are a few items you won't be able to replicate, though. There is a certain dress requirement for denizens of The Great Dark at night. We will all need to comply." Harriet led them to a Great Dark clothier who fitted them with jeweled masquerade masks and gaudy, floor-length cloaks.

The wizened tailor, with pins clenched in his teeth, asked, "Is this your first time as revelers in The Cadaverous Ball?"

"Perhaps it is," Anti smirked. "Perhaps it isn't. Would you like a spooky cookie" She offered the bakery bag to the tailor who took one, with hesitation.

Harriet watched the whole interaction, shaking her head in terror. Half an hour late, the three women left the clothier bedecked and bejeweled.

"You didn't have to act so cagey in there," Harriet chided Anti. "No one around here cares where you're from as long as you're an active participant in the celebration."

"We've been going to too many parties lately," Jade observed.

"Lucky for you, we'll miss most of it. Anee's bakery will close by early evening," Harriet explained, "because, after sunset, The Dark belongs to the dead and those attending their ball. We'll have to join the Ball for a little, and, I must warn you, it will make you uncomfortable.

"How so?" Jade asked.

"Like going to a funeral for someone you've never met?" Anti suggested.

"In a way." Harriet lowered her mask to signify that the conversation was over. Jade and Anti also dropped their masks and followed Harriet into the heart of The Great Dark.

The citizens had transformed the area after sunset. The streets were full of people, all in masks, dresses, and robes. There were several brass bands accompanied by marching drums, and someone had wheeled a piano out into the street. The music of the groups and the piano warred with each other, but there was an underlying harmony unifying the sound and making it more pleasant.

True to what Harriet had said, all the businesses were closed, aside from the handful of taverns. Masked patrons strode in and out of these taverns carrying thick glasses of assorted drinks.

Three coffins held prominent positions in the street, each of them held chest high by wooden platforms. Masked people danced around the coffin, moving in uncoordinated circles.

"This is way more fun than my great Aunt Christie's funeral," Anti whispered from underneath her sparkling gold and mask. It was patterned after the face of an owl with broad black feathers that hung from the eyebrows.

"This isn't a funeral," Harriet said.

"Can you elaborate?" Jade asked. "Because I can't imagine what else it could be."

Harriet gestured for her to watch the street dancers. The top of one of the nearest coffins opened, from the inside. The corpse of a youthful woman sat up, looked around, and climbed out. One of the masked dancers placed a mask on the body, and another wrapped her in a robe so that the deceased woman looked just like every other masquerade dancer. The same process happened with the other two coffins until they adorned all three corpses in finery and standing in the street. The people dancing expanded their circles to include both the caskets and the risen dead.

Wide-eyed, Jade said, "Oh, you were right. I don't like this."

"So, in your dimension, you have zombie dance parties?" Anti asked. "I have to say, this is creepy."

"The Cadaverous Ball is an archaic custom, and most don't subscribe to it anymore," Harriet said.

"You said that there were things in your dimension that looked like magic but were actually science. How is *this* not magical?" Anti asked. "It's necromancy, at least."

"Our deal was that I would explain all of this after you returned me to my home reality," Harriet said. She was on the verge of snapping. "We're so close. Please just bring me there."

For the second time that day, the three women entered The Crucible, but this time, Jade marched right up the bartender and spoke her well-rehearsed lines. "Hello, it's Anee from the bakery next door. I got about halfway home when I realized I locked my keys in my bakery. Do you have keys for the other shops in this block, or should I contact the landlord?"

"Yikes. Jade sounds like someone who's being forced against their will to perform at a community theater," Anti whispered to Harriet.

By some miracle, Jade returned to them, holding a set of master keys.

"He said he *is* the landlord, then asked if I was drunk. I said yes," Jade panted. "He just gave me these keys, anyway."

The street revelry was dying down as they left The Crucible. The corpses were crawling back into their coffins, still dressed in their Cadaverous Ball finery, the band played a little softer, and the dancers were less vigorous.

A fresh group of revelers rounded the corner. At first glance, they seemed to wear complicated, lizard costumes, but Anti realized they were not costumed carousers. They were the guards from Aperture, and it took them only moments form them to focus in on Harriet and advanced toward the three women.

"Into the store, chop, chop." Anti tried to hustle them into the bakery, drawing no further attention.

She didn't have to worry yet, one conductor of the Cadaverous Ball, a tall man dressed as a sparkling, spotted hyena, approached the four guards.

"The Ball is over for tonight, fellas. We have another set of dances in a few days, though," he offered.

The guard in front of the pack grunted an acknowledgment. The conductor's intrusion was enough to distract the guards while the women slipped into the bakery, but Anti knew their luck wouldn't last long.

Jade, Anti, and Harriet hustled to the back of Anee's Baked Goods, where, according to Anti, the bridge to Harriet's home reality was held open by the stabilizer.

"It's right there, Harriet." Anti gestured to what looked like a freezer door. "You just have to step through with intent."

"And you're following behind me?" Harriet asked.

Jade and Anti exchanged looks. There was a rapid, unspoken conversation between the two.

"We're tired, Harriet. I think we're just going to go back to Aperture and find our way home," Jade said.

"Maybe one of those nice-looking lizard soldiers will help us," Anti quipped.

"You'd forfeit my part of the agreement to demonstrate the science of my dimension?" Harriet looked concerned.

"I don't think I'd be able to understand it anyway, my mind is so overworked by everything we've been through," Jade said.

Harriet reached her arms outward and beckoned to them.

"What's happening? What are you doing?" Jade furrowed her brow.

"She's hugging us," Anti explained as she accepted Harriet's embrace. Harriet kept one are outstretched until Jade shambled into Harriet's grasp. Anti handed Harriet's family picture back to her, and Harriet stuffed it back into her stiff hair.

"Thank you," Harriet whispered. She gave two thumbs up, then she turned to face the freezer door, opened it, and walked through.

Jade and Anti stood in silence and waited for something else to happen. When nothing did, Anti asked, "Is it over?"

Jade nodded. "I think I will have a spooky cookie. I'm starving."

CHAPTER 28
BETRAYED, FOR SCIENCE

Jade locked the bakery door and returned the keys to the bartender of the Crucible, while Anti stood in the street, watching as the processions carried the coffins away, preceded by dancers and followed by marching bands.

"Where are the Aperture guards?" Jade wondered.

Anti shrugged. "No Harriet, no guards."

"I'm not sure that's how it works."

"What's the point of your being so smart then? Half the time, you say you don't know."

"Intelligence is in knowing what you don't know. Can you focus on a bridge back to Aperture? I just want to go home."

"I can. There's one right around here. It almost feels like that zombie dance party opened up a ton of bridges," Anti said.

She led Jade one street over, stabilized a bridge, and pulled Jade through it. They walked through an Aperture door that read, "The Great Dark Vale: A Former Earth."

"I knew that was Earth Two," Anti said as she read the door.

"No, you didn't. You just couldn't handle coming in second place," Jade said. "Let's find Adellum and figure out if we've ever existed here in this timeline."

To their relief, Grackon, the seven-foot-tall, green, receptionist recognized them, though she met them with less enthusiasm and more concern. Grackon grilled Jade and Anti on their recent whereabouts and ushered them into Adellum's office.

Anti offered a redacted version of their adventures to Adellum. She left out that she and Jade helped Harriet escape to her home dimension and instead said that they could never find Harriet in Implam. He didn't seem to notice they'd changed into the garish costumes of the Cadaverous Ball. Perhaps to Adellum, all human clothes looked like a costume.

Adellum offered to throw them a "Welcome Back to the Multiverse: We're Glad You're Safe" party, but they pleaded exhaustion and took a raincheck.

"We'll cook up a door for you here," Apellum told them. "It will bring you close to the original source of the dimensional bridges."

"That would be near the Orion Center," Jade said.

"Yes, but we won't be able to construct a permanent bridge to the Orion Center until you bring our Aperture engineers through to your side," Apellum explained.

"It's on our to-do list," Anti smiled.

Aperture's temporary bridge deposited Jade and Anti in the lobby bathroom of a spa located several blocks from the Orion Center. The Nourish Spa and Resort staff were beyond surprised to see two women dressed in jeweled, velvet cloaks emerge from their restrooms. Outside of the spa, Jade and Anti parted ways, with promises to meet again in a few days to discuss and debrief.

When she returned home, Jade was bone tired, dirty, depleted, and wanted nothing but a long shower followed by ten hours of sleep. When she opened the door to her parent's house, Jade was surprised to see her entire family sitting at the kitchen table, with her father hunched over a computer screen. The moment she stepped through the door, her mother rushed over and embraced her. In the ensuing chaos, she realized she would see Anti much sooner than she thought.

"Thank God!" Jade's mother screamed and rushed toward her.

"What are you wearing?" Amber screamed louder.

Her mother was followed by her father, and then sister, all hugging her and talking at once.

"We didn't know where you were," her father said.

Her sister Amber, almost shaking, said, "We thought you were gone."

Her mother just sobbed and clutched onto Jade for far longer than Jade's range of comfort.

"I told you," Jade shook her head, confused. "I spent the night at my friend's house. We were on assignment; it took a little longer than I thought."

"Darling," Jade's mother said, "you've been gone for almost a week. It's all right now that you're home, but please don't lie to us."

Jade did some quick mental math. She thought she'd been gone just one extra night; the night they'd spent with Zofia, but with movement between dimensions, reversed time, and flowing time, it seemed she and Anti were away for much longer.

"We know what happened... well, not exactly what happened, but we know you were in another dimension," Jade's mother said.

"You and Antigone ought to sue the Orion Center," her father said. "I can get a lawyer lined up."

Jade felt the unique sensation of disparate worlds colliding. Her parents speaking the names 'Orion Center' and 'Antigone' was so foreign to her she felt like she was still in an unfamiliar world.

"What do you know?" Jade asked. "How?"

Without answering, Jade's father walked over to the kitchen table and turned the computer he'd been watching when she first walked in.

"Doctor Osborne," her father said, "and thank the Lord for him."

Jade watched the video on the computer screen. It was a typical Doctor Osborne online video, the aging professor with his salt-and-pepper facial hair, talking in front of a whiteboard which he occasionally turned to or drew on. The only thing out of the ordinary was what he drew on the whiteboard; it was an illustration of the Einstein-Rosen Bridge, with schematics pulled from Harriet's journal.

Dr. Osborne's interspersed his lecture with several replays of the same five-second clip of Jade and Anti disappearing into a dimensional bridge in the lot outside of the warehouse. The video featured a shaking camera and Dr. Osborne's nail-biting rescue of Eliot as the dog tried to follow Jade into the next world.

"We believe that Jade and Antigone may have moved beyond an adjacent dimension and may be trapped in a world far removed from ours," Dr. Osborne said. "I will be back tomorrow with an update with the potential progress of the two women."

The view count on the video was close to half a million. Jade looked from her parents to the video and attempted to tamp down a volatile mix of sadness for her parents' worry and rage at Dr. Osborne's betrayal.

"Well, I'm safe, and I wasn't trapped anywhere," Jade said and then realized that wasn't true. "... that I couldn't get out of," she added.

"What does that mean?" Her mother asked.

"I'll explain later. I need some time to process all of this." Jade walked up the stairs to her bedroom, calling "I'm sorry," down to her family.

Jade rushed into her bedroom, sat on the edge of her bed, and called Anti. "Doctor Osborne sold us out to go viral."

"I know," Anti said to Jade. "We're famous."

"He's got to tell everyone that we're home and safe," Jade said. "My family was frantic."

"Gustavo has been working with my family. They're ecstatic that I'm involved in some actual science. Doctor Osborne wants to meet with us to do a follow up for his show."

"As long as he doesn't record us," Jade said. "And I'm not meeting him soon. I could sleep for a week."

Anti agreed and told Jade she would arrange a dinner meeting with Doctor Osborne in a few nights. "I'll set it up at an exclusive restaurant, and he can pay," Anti added. "I'm sure he's made a *ton* of money from our story."

Jade took a shower she'd been craving, crawled into bed, and fell into a deep and dreamless sleep.

CHAPTER 29
OMISSION

The Savor was one of the most expensive eateries in the city and was, by far, the fanciest restaurant Jade had ever been to, though she didn't dine out often. Anti seemed right at home among the thick, white tablecloths, and the three distinct drinking glasses arranged at each place. The reasoning behind the vast number of glasses and cutlery was incomprehensible to Jade.

To add to Jade's apprehension surrounding the excess of cups, Dr. Osborne was late, so Jade and Anti sat alone at The Savor's table. While they waited, Jade and Anti commiserated about their sudden fame, at least among a subset of people interested in quantum metaphysics and the Dr. Osborne vlog.

While Jade had slept, Anti could not rest for more than a few hours, so she'd watched all of Dr. Osborne's broadcasts about Jade and herself, so she filled Jade in while they waited for the Doctor to arrive.

Dr. Osborne began the web series by discussing the Orion Center experiment that had started the adventure. Then he explained how Jade and Antigone had come to him to consult about anomalies they'd experienced, and how they'd disappeared afterward. The remaining blogs were in-depth lectures on Einstein-Rosen Bridges and other information on interdimensional physics, most of which he lifted straight from Harriet's journal, which he still had in his possession. And the entire series was full of repeated clips of the women's miraculous disappearance into the next dimension.

There was no mention in the series of Jade and Anti's new powers or Harriet's role in degrading Earth's alternate realities. Dr. Osborne, apparently, had an ounce of discretion.

The last of Dr. Osborne's videos, recorded just that morning, reported Jade and Anti home safe and resting with their families. He had, however, promised an update on their experiences in other dimensions.

When he entered the restaurant, nearly twenty minutes late, the Doctor was wearing a fedora and looking like the cat who got the cream.

"Greetings!" Dr. Osborne said as he sat down. "How was your incredible journey?"

"You shouldn't wear your hat to eat at a place like this," Anti pointed out.

"I was just taking it off." Dr. Osborne. He removed his hat and placed it on the remaining, empty seat.

When he sat down, Jade and Anti bombarded him with questions.

"Why did you make our story public?"

"What did you tell our families?"

"Were you presenting the schematics from Harriet's journal as your own?"

"I understand how this looks, it looks like I'm attempting to gain fame and profit from your situation," he said.

Anti nodded for him to go on while Jade sat with her arms folded. He could not continue, however, because an enthusiastic server interrupted them to rattle off the daily specials, which were rosemary crusted quail and peppered crab. Jade faltered when it was her turn to order. She'd never bought food of this quality or complexity, so Anti ordered her trout with lime glaze and couscous, with a promise that Jade would love it.

Once they ordered, Dr. Osborne continued his apologetic explanation, "You two were official missing persons. According to phone records and witnesses who placed Eliot and me at Antigone's flat, I was the last person to see you. I had two options: I could attempt to cover up what I knew about your disappearance, which was quite a lot, or I could tell the truth. I did something in the middle of the two options," he finished.

"But, did you have to do it to everyone?" Jade asked. "You could have just told our parents and the authorities. I can't see a reason to go public with our story."

"At first, I did only tell your parents and the police, but word traveled, and people wanted to understand the science behind what was happening to you. I figured my vlog was the best way to disseminate the information to everyone simultaneously."

"While still increasing your fame and potential sponsors," Jade pointed out.

Dr. Osborne leaned forward and lowered his voice as if he were letting them in on an important secret. "Hey, this is good for you two. There will be a line out of the door to interview you. They will pay you handsomely to write articles and books. Think of it as my handing you a blank check."

Possibilities floated through Jade's mind. Money had always been an elusive resource for her and her family. But she realized Dr. Osborne was not handing her a blank check, but the possibility of unconventional work for another type of money.

"I can write my own checks," Anti said. "But I'm not as bothered by all of this as Jade is. She's not a fan of attention."

"Yes, the cat is out of the bag, and there is no way to put it back in," Doctor Osborne said. "However, I was careful to keep some vital pieces of information secret for you."

"Are you threatening to reveal my shifting and Anti's extra-dimensional sentience? Because no one would take you seriously. How many people believe you, even now? You're a sideshow, one step up from the guys who hunt for Bigfoot." Jade's face flushed with anger during her tirade.

"Oh, bravo, Jade," Anti clapped. Then she turned to Dr. Osborne, "Sorry, Gustavo, it's just she rarely speaks up for herself."

"It wasn't a threat. I'm trying to tell you I'm innocent in all of this," Dr. Osborne protested to Jade, then added, "mostly innocent."

Their food arrived, and they shared a noiseless meal. Dr. Osborne broke the silence to ask if either of the women would mind discussing their other extra-dimensional experiences.

Anti was about to respond, but Jade shut her down with a simple "No."

After the meal, the women met at Anti's house to debrief and discuss their next actions, if there were any more actions to take. Both of their cellphones rang endlessly in their own vehicles on their way to Anti's, but neither woman answered because they were both responsible drivers.

The calls, many of which originated from The Orion Center, were the first order of business once they hustled into Anti's apartment.

"What do you think they want? They didn't leave a voicemail," Jade asked.

"Of course, you listen to voicemails." Anti raised her eyebrow. "If people waited for me to listen to my voicemail, I'd be a missing person forever."

"That's why Orion is calling," Jade exclaimed. "We've gone back to our home dimension, which means Harriet is missing. They're wondering where she is and if we have anything to do with her disappearance."

"But, if she *is* a 'missing person' like we were, the police would have already contacted us," Anti pointed out. "My guess is the Center wants to know why their name is all over Doctor Osborne's weird videos and what we have to do with it.

Anti picked up her cell phone and began to make a call, but Jade grabbed her hand.

"What are you doing?" Jade asked.

"Calling the Orion Center," Anti said. "To see which one of us is right."

"Wait, what do we tell them? We still have the devices they gave us. Do we give them back?"

Anti sat down on her sofa, removed her dimensional stabilizer from her back pocket, and set it down on her coffee table.

"If we tell them everything, then we'll have to return this. This stabilizer is our link to other worlds, if we need to, or want to, go to another dimension again. What if going back to the Center resets everything? Would we know what happened without the stabilizer? We could drift into other realities without knowing. We'd be like reverse Harriets," Anti said, "losing people without realizing it."

"Look, we'll go to The Orion Center tomorrow and tell them everything they need to learn to connect with Aperture. We can exchange our knowledge for exclusive rights to publish the stories," Jade decided. "I guess we don't have to tell them about the stabilizer, for now. We can figure it all out later. But, that's it, no more lies, by omission or otherwise. It's too stressful for me."

Anti brightened. "Okay, we'll go to Orion in the morning. Do you want to stay in the guest room again tonight? I've been craving your breakfast burritos."

"No, I have to stay at home. My parents have been so upset over my disappearance. I don't blame them."

The women arrived at the Orion Center at 8:45 the next morning, planning to go in right when the center opened at nine. Jade promised to bring homemade breakfast burritos.

"I'll bring coffee," Anti said.

"I thought you weren't drinking it because it made you anxious."

Anti laughed. "I'm living on the edge."

The next morning, both women arrived ten minutes early, so they sat in the Orion Center parking lot, in Anti's hybrid because Jade didn't want anyone to eat breakfast burritos in her car.

"I say we don't put it all out at once," Anti said as a pepper fell from her burrito, where it sat on the car floor, ignored. "We don't know what they don't know. We shouldn't lie, but there's no reason to tell them everything."

"Technically, that's a lie by omission. I can handle that," Jade said.

At nine o'clock, Jade and Anti stood at the reception desk and asked to speak to someone from the research department. The receptionist shuffled them off to the multi-purpose room they were intimately familiar with by that point.

While Anti was busy eyeing the coffee pot, Jade gasped as Harriet's familiar face, and oversized beehive hair entered the room. She reached out to shake hands with them.

"Harriet!" Anti shrieked. Coffee sloshed over the side of her Styrofoam cup. "What happened? Did they catch you and stick you back here? Was that not your right world?"

A shadow of thought flickered across Harriet's brow, but a moment later, her countenance smoothed back over.

"You two have been through quite a bit. Why don't you have some doughnuts? You can catch us up on what happened." Harriet gestured to the box of doughnuts that may very well have been the same one that sat there the last time they were in the break room over a week ago.

"The rain in Implam. Spooky cookies," Anti said, and she searched Harriet's face for any signs of recognition. She saw none.

"Pardon?" Harriet asked, "Are you all right?"

"Can you leave us for a few minutes?" Jade asked. "Anti's having some kind of breakdown."

Anti nodded vigorously.

Harriet narrowed her eyes and said, "Of course," before leaving the room.

"I almost threw up my breakfast burrito," Anti said. "What is she?"

"That's not our Harriet, at least, not the one we left in the bakery in The Great Dark. Remember what Adellum said? He said it was impossible to shift Harriet back to her home reality because she always drifted away from the world with her family. That 'always' might mean the people in Aperture tried several times to lock up Harriet. They imprisoned multiple versions of Harriet here on Earth, in different realities."

"So, we'll just sneak this Harriet back to her world." Anti shrugged.

"What happens when the next Harriet shows up? How many times are we going to put Harriet back?" Jade paced back and forth in front of the break room door.

"Well, I will tell her, at least." Anti sat down on one of the room's uncomfortable, resin chairs. "She should know we tried, we helped her, we got her home, once."

"Yeah, but we didn't get this Harriet home, so we're of no help to her. We know her, even though she doesn't know we know her. She'll do whatever she has to until she gets herself back to her version of her world. She would start again and drag us along with her on a repeat of the journey we just took. I could live for the rest of my life and never re-encounter Zofia."

There was a polite, uniform knock on the break room door. "How's Antigone's breakdown going? Can I come in?" Harriet asked through the closed door.

"No!" Anti shouted.

"What are our options here," Jade paced faster. "We have to think this through immediately. If we tell her the entire story, she'll realize she can't be returned home."

"At least telling Harriet will keep *us* out of trouble, she'll figure out we're on to her. If we don't tell her, well, she'll keep trying to use her schemes on us," Anti mused.

"There's a third option," Jade stopped pacing, "and it may solve some of our problems too. I hate to suggest it."

CHAPTER 30
THE DOCTOR GUSTAVO OSBORNE SHOW

Dr. Gustavo Osborne had been a minor Internet celebrity before the business with Jade and Antigone. But, his sound science, lifted from Harriet's journals, and his titillating speculation on the whereabouts of the missing women had boosted his regular view count from just under 50,000 to half a million.

He expected the end of his gravy train, however, when the woman returned home safely, especially when they were miffed at his apparent exploitation of their multidimensional adventures. He was honest when he told Jade and Anti he was only looking for a way to explain the science behind their disappearance to multiple people at once; however, his surprise at the popularity of the videos was disingenuous.

Anti's phone call two days after their disastrous dinner was a surprise but not unwelcome. He agreed to meet with the women in Anti's apartment, without Eliot. During the meeting, the woman regaled him with wondrous tales of their adventures through the multiverse, and they told him about the reoccurring thorn in their sides, Harriet. Jade also suggested Dr. Osborne help them with their Harriet problem in a way to benefit all involved.

"But she has to agree to it," Anti stipulated. "None of your sneakiness, or we'll refute all of your claims regarding us, and you'll look like a con man."

Dr. Osborne agreed, and a few days later, he was sitting in his office, preparing to record a video with Harriet, who was, allegedly, from another dimension. He used his laptop to record his science videos, but he was often on his own, so he had to work to position the computer to record both himself and Harriet. Jade and Anti oversaw the proceedings from the other side of the room, well away from his laptop camera.

Once he'd situated the camera, Dr. Osborne gestured for Harriet to sit down in the extra chair he'd placed at his desk. "Are you ready?" he asked Harriet.

"Last chance, because there's no way that he will not upload it once he has you recorded," Anti called from across the room.

Harriet nodded.

Dr. Osborne turned on his laptop camera and began talking. "I have a guest today, and she is very unusual." Dr. Osborne paused. "This is Harriet. She had her entire life ripped away from her, her whole family lost. When she tried, desperately, to get them back, they imprisoned her. You may see Harriet, here, and say she doesn't look like a prisoner. That's because, and this is very shocking, Earth is her prison. You see, Harriet is not from our world."

"He sounds like a cut-rate Rod Serling," Anti whispered, and Jade glared at her hard enough to make her settle down.

"Harriet is a being from another world," Doctor Osborn continued. "She has been put on Earth because, until recently, we had minimal contact with other worlds. So, Earth was a way of keeping her from communicating with or entering other dimensions. Let's put aside our feelings about Earth being a dumping ground for multidimensional criminals, we can explore that aspect of this whole thing later. Today, I want to speak just with Harriet," Dr. Osborne turned to face Harriet. "Why were you imprisoned on Earth?"

"I'm not a criminal," Harriet said in her cold, clinical voice. "I'm doing what I think any other rational person in my place would do—I'm trying to get my family back."

"And, where did your family go, or should I say, how did you lose them?" Dr. Osborne asked with sympathetic interest.

Just then, Jade heard a light tap on Dr. Osborne's office door. She looked through the semi-frosted glass and saw the squat, trolly figure of Adellum, looking cross. Jade tugged at Anti's sleeve, and they walked through the door together and closed it gently so they wouldn't disturb the ongoing interview.

"That was fast. Gustavo hasn't even broadcasted anything yet," Anti said.

"You already broadcasted it in several alternate realities. One of you ladies listened to your voicemail when the Orion Center first called, so you realized Harriet was a permanent fixture a day earlier. You've caused quite a mess."

"That's why you shouldn't listen to voicemail, Jade," Anti laughed.

Jade took a deep breath and started talking, "You Adellum, personally, have always been kind and fair to us, but the people of Aperture made some mistakes—with us, with Earth, and with Harriet. You can't just force your criminals on us without our knowledge, for one. And secondly, you must come up with a better solution for Harriet. She has done little wrong… at least, not enough to live the rest of her life in torment."

"There are plenty of people who haven't done anything wrong who have to live a tormented life. I'm not sure what guilt or innocence has to do with it. However, we have figured out we can do nothing about Harriet. No prison can hold her, and no law can stop her."

"No," Anti yelled, her voice echoing in the empty hallway, "don't kill Harriet!"

Adellum looked at Anti like she may have lost her mind, "I will not kill her. We're not barbarians."

"What are you going to do with her then?" Anti clutched her chest and feigned a heart attack.

"It will be simpler to just show you. We've tested this in several of your Earth's realities, and it has worked so far. I'll be back in a jiffy." Adellum disappeared with a sudden blip.

"That was cool, I didn't know that he could do that," Anti said.

Jade replied, "Think about it, the people from Aperture have access to every kind of technology in thousands of dimensions. It's not a tremendous surprise that he can teleport."

"Don't act like you weren't surprised," Anti snipped.

Adellum blipped back, and this time three children accompanied him, aged around seven to thirteen, and a middle-aged man. They all looked stunned.

"Frank!" Anti yelled so loud that she startled everyone. "I stared at your picture so long in Harriet's world, I'd know you anywhere."

"Your solution was to bring Harriet's family to her," Jade said. "But won't that cause problems for the alternate versions of Harriet who don't have their families."

"Don't question the man… troll," Anti grumbled. "He knows better than us."

"I will have to bust my hump and do this a few thousand times. I need to reach all the alternate realities where Harriet has lost her family and is attempting to escape. The more times I do this, the less of those realities there will be as Harriet's escape attempts stop and the number of alternate realities she creates shrink."

"Will that stabilize our dimension?" Jade asked.

"Mostly," Adellum said. "No dimension is completely stable, there will always be a few alternate realities that the world drifts in and out of, but this should put an end to the wild, noticeable, swings in reality."

Jade and Anti exchanged meaningful glances.

"How are you, Frank?" Anti asked. "Are you ready to meet Harriet again?" Anti opened the door and led the family back into Dr. Osborne's office.

Jade hung back. "Where are you getting these Franks and their children? All of our Harriets lost their families because they shifted into realities where their families never existed, so they wouldn't exist either, or they wouldn't know her."

"There are several realities where Harriet disappeared, and her family remembered and missed her. They just didn't shift around and spawn a ton of new alternate realities because there was no Harriet there to use disruptive technology," Adellum explained.

"But once you came in and started removing Frank and the kids, it created enough alternate realities to supply all the versions of Harriet that are out there, at least, the one who is stuck on Earth."

"Something like that."

Inside Dr. Osborne's office, Harriet had spied her family and jumped up to greet them, upsetting the contents of Dr. Osborne's desk and interrupting his interview.

"How?" Her voice shook as she cupped her children's faces in her hands and then hugged her husband. Then she saw Adellum, hanging back, in the door frame.

Dr. Osborne got up, grabbed his laptop, and pointed it around, attempting to capture all the people, including Adellum—the troll being from another dimension—and the happenings around his office.

"You!" Harriet pointed at Adellum. "I suppose you're the delegation from Aperture," she snarled, her expression softened as she realized the entire situation. "You brought them here; you gave them back to me."

Adellum nodded.

It took Harriet several more seconds to process. Then she asked, "Why?"

"Harriet, you are one of the most tenacious beings in the entire multiverse. We have never encountered someone as determined as you are. When we realized you would never stop, we hid you away in a weak, unreachable, underdeveloped world."

"Hey, that's our weak, underdeveloped dimension you're talking about," Anti interjected, sounding wounded.

"But you didn't stop, Harriet," Adellum said. "In this wasteland—"

"Again, *our* wasteland."

"You still got back to them, so our only option is breaking our own laws to bring your family to you, for good. Your reunion is contingent upon you and your family cooling your heels here, in this version of reality, for the rest of your lives."

Harriet turned to her husband, "You agreed to this?"

Frank nodded and smiled, "You were gone, and we were lost. At least now, we'll be lost together."

Forgotten in the corner, Dr. Osborne—who was holding his laptop facing outward and positioned so he could catch as much of the scene as possible—said, "This heartwarming and unexpected reunion of interdimensional beings is the first of its kind ever recorded."

"Who is this man?" Frank asked while Harriet ignored everything to coddle and kiss her children.

"He's part scientist, part leech," Jade said. "Although today he's leaning toward leech."

"I'll edit that out. Would it be possible to include you all in a group interview?" Dr. Osborne asked now that he had the floor. "We could do it right now or wait until we settle everything."

"I don't want to be included in his interview," Jade whispered to Anti.

"Okay."

Jade and Anti slipped out of the door, almost unnoticed because of the commotion that Dr. Osborne's request had caused. Harriet saw them leave, however, and she gave them a quick, discreet, double thumbs-up on the way out.

In the university parking lot, the women were headed toward their respective vehicles when Anti stopped Jade and asked, "Do you want to come over to my house for dinner? You don't have to cook it if you don't want to. Or, I mean, you can cook it if you want to."

Jade laughed, "Do you like Thai?" she asked.

"I love it! Let's order in."

CHAPTER 31
NO PLAN FOR MADNESS

That evening, Jade and Anti ate honey chicken and lo mein while they watched Dr. Osborne's vlog of the day's events. It was poorly edited and confusing, as he was in a rush to upload the extraordinary facts. The video had made its intended impact, though, and the Doctor's video view count was just under one million.

"Don't you think it's strange, and unethical, that Adellum is farming alternate universes so he can harvest families for Harriet?"

Jade thought about it before answering. "I believe once you use technology to change one minor thing on even the tiniest quantum level, you open up the possibility of drastic change or destruction down the road. But I could say the same in life. You never know—you can guess, but not know which choice will lead to which consequence. So, Harriet's fate was sealed, and so was ours, the moment she created the invention that disrupted her reality on her home planet. Adellum's 'farm universes' are the same thing; they might wreck the multiverse, or they might do nothing at all."

"I'm glad that Harriet made her doodad in her scary, zombie home dimension because none of this would have happened otherwise," Anti noted.

Dr. Osborne's video led to a disappointing development for the women. He had caught both Jade and Anti on video in the room with the multidimensional chaos. Previously, Dr. Osborne had discussed them in the abstract, neither offering their last names nor providing images of the women aside from the shaky video of them vanishing. Their identities could be gleaned by someone willing to do the legwork, but now their faces were closely tied to the debacle.

"We're even more internet famous," Anti said through a mouth full of noodles. She held up her phone, so Jade could see yet another article about the pair.

"Yay," Jade said sarcastically, "just what I've always wanted." She picked up her phone, which had been buzzing nonstop all evening, declined another call, and set it back down.

"Is your sister back to um… normal?" Anti asked.

"Well, she ate four bites of dinner last night, asked if I want to use her agent, and suggested we do a vlog together because we're both public figures. So, I'd say so."

"She sounds nice," Anti said, unironically. "I guess we can give the bridge stabilizer back to The Orion Center." Anti pulled the device out of her pocket and turned it around in her hands. "Adellum said there wouldn't be any more noticeable shifts in reality since Harriet got her family back."

Anti looked at Jade longingly.

"I've been thinking," Jade drawled, "what if we kept all of it?"

Anti's face brightened, and she waited for Jade to continue.

"We never know when things with Harriet might go south, or the dimensions could become unstable again, or we might want to take a trip to Paris, and the translation function may come in handy."

"Aw, you said *we* might go to Paris," Anti beamed. "Because you like me. It's getting late, Jade. Do you want to stay in the guest room?"

"I already sent a text to my mom, telling her I won't be home tonight." Jade smiled and held up her phone, which buzzed as another call came through.

"I figured you were planning on staying here tonight. I meant, do you want to stay longer? Like, it won't be a guest room anymore. It'll be Jade's room."

Jade mused for a moment, "Let's see what the fortune cookie says." She grabbed one of the three cookies that sat on the edge of Anti's coffee table, amid the remnants of takeout.

Jade cracked open the cookie and read, "*There's no plan for madness.*"

"That sounds terrifying," Anti said.

"No," Jade shook her head, "I like it because everything is madness, and you have to just go with it. Chaos theory."

"Does that mean you're moving in?" Anti asked hopefully.

"Yes."

And that's the story of how Jade and Antigone became roommates.

NOTE FROM THE AUTHOR

Word-of-mouth is crucial for any author to succeed. If you enjoyed *Tripping the Multiverse*, please leave a review online—anywhere you are able. Even if it's just a sentence or two. It would make all the difference and would be very much appreciated.

Thanks!
Alison

ABOUT THE AUTHOR

Alison Lyke is an English professor and the author of three science fiction and fantasy novels, including the award-winning cyberpunk *Forever People* (2019), the modern mythology *Honey* (2013), and *Tripping the Multiverse* (2021), a mind-bending journey to other dimensions. She manages a popular blog on sci-fi, fantasy, and speculative writing. Lyke lives in Rochester, NY with her partner, two sons, and two cats.

Thank you so much for reading one of
Alison Lyke's novels.
If you enjoyed the experience, please check out
our recommended title for your next great read!

Forever People by Alison Lyke

"High concept, thought-inducing sci-fi."

– *TaleFlick*, April 2019 Top Pick

View other Black Rose Writing titles at
<u>www.blackrosewriting.com/books</u> and use promo code
PRINT to receive a **20% discount** when purchasing.

CPSIA information can be obtained
at www.ICGtesting.com
Printed in the USA
FSHW010625190321
79638FS